LENGUA FRESCA

LENGUA FRESCA

latinos writing on the edge

edited by HAROLD AUGENBRAUM
and ILAN STAVANS

A Mariner Original • *Houghton Mifflin Company*

BOSTON   NEW YORK   2006

Library of Congress Cataloging-in-Publication Data
Lengua fresca : Latinos writing on the edge / edited by Harold Augenbraum and Ilan Stavans.
    p. cm.
    "A Mariner original."
    ISBN-13: 978-0-618-65670-7
    ISBN-10: 0-618-65670-7
1. American literature — Hispanic American authors. 2. Hispanic Americans — Literary collections. 3. American literature — 21st century. 4. American literature — 20th century. I. Harold Augenbraum. II. Ilan Stavans.
    PS508.H57L46 2006
    810.8'0868090511 — dc22   2006015357

Book design by Melissa Lotfy

PRINTED IN THE UNITED STATES OF AMERICA

MP 10 9 8 7 6 5 4 3 2 1

The editors gratefully acknowledge permission to reprint the following material. Every effort has been made to contact copyright owners. In the event of an omission, please notify the publisher of this volume so that corrections can be made in future editions.

Editorial Cartoons by Lalo Lopez Alcaraz. Copyright © 1994, 1995, 1996, 2001 by Lalo Alcaraz. Reprinted by permission of Lalo Alcaraz. First published in *L.A. Weekly.*

"La Cucaracha" daily strip by Lalo Lopez Alcaraz. Copyright © 2006 by Lalo Alcaraz. Reprinted by permission of Lalo Alcaraz. Distributed by Universal Press Syndicate.

"The Visitor" by Rane Arroyo. From *The Portable Famine.* Copyright © 2005 by Rane Arroyo. Reprinted by permission of BkMk Press, University of Missouri–Kansas City.

"Tía Olivia Serves Wallace Stevens a Cuban Egg" from *City of a Hundred Fires,* by Richard Blanco, © 1998. Reprinted by permission of the University of Pittsburgh Press.

"Pelos en la lengua" by Giannina Braschi. First published in *Hopscotch: A Cultural Review,* Volume 2, Number 2, 2001. Copyright © 2001 by Giannina Braschi. Reprinted by permission of Giannina Braschi.

"Chango" by Oscar Casares. From *Brownsville* by Oscar Casares. Copyright © 2003 by Oscar Casares. By permission of Little, Brown and Co., Inc.

"Godoy Lives" by Daniel Chacón. Copyright © 2000 by Daniel Chacón. "Godoy Lives" is reprinted with permission from the publisher of *Chicano Chicanery* by Daniel Chacón (Houston: Arte Público Press — University of Houston, © 2000).

"Killer Crónica" by Susana Chávez-Silverman. From *Killer Crónicas: Bilingual Memories.* © 2004 by the Board of Regents of the University of Wisconsin System. Reprinted by permission of University of Wisconsin Press.

Carla, Audri, Alison, *y* Josh,

otra vez,

y para Isaiah, *por supuesto*

CONTENTS

Introduction   xiii

VOCES

OSCAR CASARES
Chango   3

RANE ARROYO
The Visitor   22

ILAN STAVANS
Don Quixote en Spanglish   23

RICHARD BLANCO
Tía Olivia Serves Wallace Stevens a Cuban Egg   29

HIP HOP HOODIOS
Agua Pa' La Gente   31

SUSANA CHÁVEZ-SILVERMAN
Killer Crónica   33

GIANNINA BRASCHI
Pelos en la lengua   41

FRONTERAS

JUAN FELIPE HERRERA
Exiles   45

STEPHANIE ELIZONDO GRIEST
La Extranjera   47

LALO LOPEZ ALCARAZ
La Cucaracha 55

HERNANDEZ BROS.
The KKK Comes to Hoppers 63

THE PARROT CLUB
Menú 67

SALVADOR PLASCENCIA
The People of Paper 70

DAGOBERTO GILB
Tomato Potatoe, Chalupa Shaloopa 81

MICHAEL JAIME-BECERRA
Practice Tattoos 91

DANIEL CHACÓN
Godoy Lives 104

ALEIDA RODRÍGUEZ
Lexicon of Exile 119

LUIS ALBERTO URREA
Tijuana Cop 121

CULTURE CLASH
The Mission 130

MELODRAMAS

NELLY ROSARIO
Invasions, 1916 139

FELICIA LUNA LEMUS
Trace Elements of Random Tea Parties 149

LUISITA LÓPEZ TORREGROSA
An Island of Illusions 155

LILA DOWNS
Mother Jones 177

CRISTINA HENRÍQUEZ
Ashes 179

MANUEL MUÑOZ
Good as Yesterday 194

ANA MENÉNDEZ
Loving Che 216

Contributors 220
About the Editors 226

INTRODUCTION

From: Harold Augenbraum
Subject: Invitation

Dear Ilan,

With the success of our earlier anthologies, I've been thinking lately about a new anthology of Latino literature, focused on the next wave of Latino writing. Our previous anthologies reflected a moment in the polity of the United States and U.S.-Latino culture: a focus on bringing new voices to the table, a temporary pushing of one's way into notice. Even the cultural name — Latino — was an English-language creation that had significance only within U.S. borders.

But that time has passed. Latinos have their place at the table, and the literature has begun to reflect the new age, a sort of post-Latino consciousness. Commercial presses are searching for the Latina Terry McMillan, that wholly elusive chica-lit phenomenon who sells a million copies of pulp to a burgeoning market. The asexual Ricky Martin and the a-ethnic Jennifer Lopez are its popular paradigms.

So where does that leave the literature? The great old guard — Rudolfo Anaya, Piri Thomas, Oscar Hijuelos, Sandra Cisneros — the pith of our earlier collections, are still writing wonderful stuff, but the new generation comes at cultural expression from a different vantage point. Assimilation is irrelevant, adaptation is for other people, multiethnicity and multilingualism are the norm. Gloria Anzaldúa's dream of co-opting the formerly pejorative term "mestizo" has become reality. Latinos have arrived at the table, so now where do they sit? Would you be interested in putting it together with me?

Harold

From: Ilan Stavans
Subject: Re: Invitation

Harold,

I am absolutely interested. I'm just back from Los Angeles, which is quite a study. According to the U.S. Census Bureau, Latinos are now the largest minority. In states like California, Texas, Arizona, and Colorado, Latinos are a major force. It is said, for instance, that one out of every two babies born in Los Angeles since the year 2002 is of Hispanic descent. And the number of Hispanics in the United States is larger than the entire population of Canada.

By the way, in the paragraph above I deliberately switched from "Latino" to "Hispanic." Does it really matter if we endorse one term and not the other? And have we been able to resolve the tension between unity and multiplicity that defines Latinos in the United States? Are Cubans, Mexicans, Ecuadorians, Colombians, Puerto Ricans, and so on one and the same people? Or should we be addressed as a sum of independent units? Whatever the answers are, they no longer raise any brows. Isn't Latin America too made of heterogeneous republics, often at odds with one another? I'm attracted by the complexities of the minority, not by its simplicities.

I suggest we shape a volume in which the language used by Latinos — Spanglish, in all its potentials, the *lingua franca* — serves as the true protagonist. That, to me, has been one of the most interesting phenomena in the last couple of decades: the interface between *el español* and English, the juxtaposition of ways of being and thinking and dreaming through speech.

I have a bunch of selections I want you to consider right away. I believe our new anthology should include political cartoons, maybe a comic strip, a recipe, song lyrics, even classified ads . . .

With best wishes, Ilan

P.S.: I'm not sure the "old guard," as you mention it, is as healthy as you suggest! Plus, placing Hijuelos and Cisneros with Anaya and Thomas is pushing the age-span a bit. Thomas was born in 1928, Cisneros, if I'm not mistaken, in 1954.

From: Harold Augenbraum
Subject: Re: Invitation

You're right to say that language is the common denominator. The next generation no longer frets about retention of national identity. Instead, with the understanding of common language as a backdrop, writers like Stephanie Elizondo Griest can travel to Havana, have physical features similar to Cubans, speak Spanish but with a different accent, that of a third- or fourth-generation American of Hispanic ascendance, and write not from the point of view of an assimilated Latina, but simply as an American who has a privileged position when traveling in the Spanish-speaking world. Language, as you say, is an interface, but in itself the use of language has many nuances and now depends more on the needs of the moment and the individual, and less on the individual as an outsider, as it did in earlier generations.

I also find that there is less embarrassment, less need to get beyond the shame of having immigrant parents or grandparents. Latinos are represented in many professions; they are recognized as the next generation of middle-class business owners, the next entrants into the professional class. More Americans study Spanish than any language other than English. Is it now cool to be Latino?

From: Ilan Stavans
Subject: Lengua Fresca

Harold,

I've been making an early selection of entries. As agreed, our anthology won't focus exclusively on traditional forms of literature. Pop culture today is replete with images we should strive to include. On a recent trip to San Juan, Puerto Rico, I ate at a restaurant called The Parrot Club. It caters to the new class of Latinos you're referring to: savvy, upwardly mobile, and unabashed by their hyphenated identity. The entire menu is in Spanglish. So delighted was I with it that I asked the owner if I could take one home. Browsing through it again yesterday made me think of a provocative epistolary volume by Susana Chávez-Silverman, who teaches at Pomona, called *Killer Crónicas*, remarkable in its experimental use of language. The title *crónica* is about Chávez-Silverman's sojourn in Argentina, where part of her family comes from. I'll send you a photocopy of the menu as well as the *crónica*.

And I've also been looking at "La Cucaracha," the lampoons by Lalo Lopez Alcaraz. As you know, Lalo and I did a book together in the late nineties: *Latino USA: A Cartoon History*. The possibility of exploring our complex, labyrinthine path through *monitos,* as we used to call them in Mexico back in the seventies, enabled us to take an irreverent yet responsible approach to the past. Since then, Lalo has made a niche for himself ridiculing local, state, and national figures that belong to the realm of pop culture. He makes George W. Bush look like an alien, for instance. But most of his energy is devoted to denouncing the racism and xenophobia against Latinos in this country. I've collected a dozen or so images, which I want you to consider. "La Cucaracha" makes me think that we should also include something by the Hernandez Bros., leading *caricaturistas* themselves but with less of an ideological bent.

I came across a charming story in *The New Yorker* by a new writer, Cristina Henríquez. She appears to be of Panamanian ancestry. (You know, *The New Yorker* seems to have a quota for Latino stories:

one every blue moon. Will the editors ever wake up to the dramatic changes our country is undergoing?)

I want to include reportage as well. Luis Alberto Urrea has a fascinating piece in *By the Lake of Sleeping Children* about the U.S.-Mexico border, which I'll forward to you. Plus, I want you to consider a sketch by Culture Clash, a theater troupe that has been at the forefront in the crusade to debunk Hispanic stereotypes.

How about *Lengua Fresca* as the title? I like it, I confess. "Fresh Language" captures the verbal hoopla I've been obsessed about in the last decade.

Yours, Ilan

P.S. Not that I want to give you any more work, but you failed to respond to my comment on the old guard. Writers like Tomás Rivera, Rolando Hinojosa-Smith, and Rudolfo Anaya seem to be moving fast into the background. Is this what becoming a "classic" is all about? I hope not. The changes Latinos have undergone involve a dramatic embrace of the urban landscape. Itinerant labor, so crucial from the fifties to the seventies, and transformed into literature by Rivera, for instance, appears to be the topic of a remote past. Not even the Chicano movement of César Chávez commands attention. The type of mystical fiction Anaya popularized in *Bless Me, Ultima* is, ironically, more connected these days with New Mexico than with Latinos. And Hinojosa-Smith's Faulknerian universe, I often think, is too rich, too extensive and multifaceted, for young readers to digest. The three writers are from the Southwest. The literature that has been widely embraced from the nineties and onward moves east; it centers on the city as almost the exclusive theater of experience. Hijuelos and Cisneros represent this move: *The House on Mango Street* is set in Chicago, *The Mambo Kings Play Songs of Love* in New York. They are about modern alienation, about the search for a place called home in the centerpieces of American immigration.

From: Harold Augenbraum
Subject: Re: Lengua Fresca

Ilan,

Your points on literature and popular culture are well taken, but I urge caution on your conclusions. As you and I have discussed in the past, the question about U.S.-Latino culture as a "high culture" or a "popular culture," whatever those two terms mean, or even a written culture versus an oral one, is fascinating. The earlier generation seemed to be interested in developing a high culture. Even if you go back as far as the late-nineteenth-century Southwest, Latinos were most interested in competing with American high culture as exemplified by New England's latent Puritan world.

But now we seem to have entered the domination of popular culture throughout the United States. The embracing of Latino popular culture is no exception. In *Lengua Fresca,* are we more energized by the representatives of popular culture, like Culture Clash and Hip Hop Hoodios, rather than the traditional short story, memoir, or poem, such as the work of Michael Jaime-Becerra or the poems of Rane Arroyo that take literary culture as a point of departure? Look at the dominance of images from popular culture in your recommendations, from music (J. Lo and Ricky Martin), film (J. Lo again), television (J. Lo *again* and Culture Clash), comics (*Love & Rockets* and Lalo Lopez Alcaraz), and the Web (bloggers). All we are missing is video games, which would give us the complete dominance in technological and electronic entertainment. Are we saying in this book that the old guard represented the *last* of the literary Latinos, and that the new wave will ride the crest of nonliterary, language-based entertainment? Is Spanglish the great metaphor of the new post-Latino age, or is it simply a temporary manifestation of demographic shifts? You yourself have translated the classic Spanish novel *Don Quixote* into Spanglish, creating an international uproar along the way. Does this mean that our consumption of the classics, Latino or otherwise, will always be filtered through the prism of demotics? Are we giving up on the development of a great Latino literary culture of the "old guard"? If you were going to point to the next great Latino literary star, who would that be? Your e-mail tells me that you think that popular culture is the next wave, and the roads traveled by the writers we have admired for the past twenty years have come to dead ends. Cervantes himself re-created the concept of prose fiction by using popular speech. Are Latinos today re-creating high culture using the structures of popular culture, like in the films of Robert Rodriguez and the ironic goodwill of Antonio Banderas, who plays a latter-day Gregorio Cortez in the movie *Spy Kids*?

Harold

From: Ilan Stavans
Subject: Re: Lengua Fresca

Harold,

My own view is that the border — *la linea* — dividing high and pop culture is becoming increasingly difficult to trace. The United States has a fluid approach to culture, one often following a dialectical path: what is considered low (jazz and pulp fiction, for instance) is eventually co-opted by the cultural elite. The difference is that while in the past one could rely on literature having a central place in society, today it is under siege, paying a heavy price in the competition against other forms of entertainment.

Just like all other immigrant minorities, Latinos, throughout their history north of the Rio Grande, have struggled to be accepted in New England, where the gravitational center of literary power is located in the nation. The early works produced during the colonial period (Cabeza de Vaca's *Chronicle of the Narváez Expedition*, for instance) were originally meant for an Iberian audience. But no sooner did the Age of Independence sweep the Americas, roughly from 1810 until 1870, and after the Treaty of Guadalupe Hidalgo was signed in 1848, the population that would eventually become Latino sought to produce a serious literature capable of representing its inner and outer experience. Since literacy was the property of the few, these works of art reached, for the most part, teachers, bons vivants, and *señoritas educadas*. Were they read in New York circles? Very rarely, as you know. In fact, not until a year or so ago did a New York publishing house bring out a popular edition of *The Squatter and the Don*, María Amparo Ruiz de Burton's romance about the *Californios* and the struggle for land in the second half of the nineteenth century.

Other immigrant groups used literature as a thermometer of assimilation. Latinos, on the other hand, have used pop culture for the same purpose. The *merengues* and *bachatas* produced by Dominican Americans are wonderful chronicles of translocation. The same should be said about the border *corridos* and even the *narcocorridos*, the latter a channel through which the role of drugs is explored in the community. And the *retablos*, which Frida Kahlo appropriated, as well as the *pastorelas*, the carnivalesque masks for Día de los Muertos, and the Lucha Libre wrestlers and low-riders — aren't they lucid expressions of what Latinos are about in El Norte? They are destined for millions, whereas literature is only able to reach a few. For years, you and I have been talking about the great Latino American novel. Signs of it are already within our reach, of course, in the work of the earlier generation: Rivera, Anaya, Hinojosa (all of whom, by the way, are Chicanos); and their successors, Cisneros, Hijuelos, Julia Alvarez, and Cristina Garcia (a more national mix). They have been joined by Junot Díaz, Francisco Goldman, et al. But the word "great" is still elusive, if you ask me. Meanwhile, what is produced at the pop culture level does have that attribute: Latin jazz, for example — how frequently do I get the chills when I hear D'Rivera, O'Farrill, and the whole cadre of Calle 54?

Just as Michael Chabon has incorporated superheroes into his Pulitzer Prize–winning work, the new Latino literary generation, having grown up with the Internet and Game Boys and having watched George Lopez and *Mucha Lucha* on TV, doesn't distinguish between high and popular culture. And neither should critics. The great Latino novel will probably be a big messy collage of tradition and media influences. It will dialogue with the past but will also establish a link with the chaotic present we inhabit. It will be irreverent and will embrace impurity. And it will not seek to be read only by literary snobs, nor will it want to be seen as a Latino book per se. Why build borders when they have done nothing but imprison us?

Yours, Ilan

From: Harold Augenbraum
Subject: Re: Lengua Fresca

Ilan,

I agree that this new openness to popular culture is refashioning the literature, but Latino literature in the United States has benefited from the use of popular culture since as far back as 1892, with the publication of Eusebio Chacón's *Son of the Storm,* and many writers since then have used traditional popular culture as part of their aesthetic. What we are talking about now is the use of *contemporary* popular culture, often based in electronic media, which gives the literature more immediacy than before. One could argue that in this type of literature there is less need for an understanding of folk tales. It looks forward, it is playful, it refuses to create straw men. This is what, I think, makes *Lengua Fresca* a fresh language. It's *bien cool!!*

Harold

From: Ilan Stavans
Subject: Re: Lengua Fresca

Harold,

Bien cool indeed. Latinos have been pioneers in the integration of popular culture into sophisticated forms of art in the United States among other reasons because they have been excluded for so long from the elite chambers of power. But that exclusivism is over, I'm convinced.

The three sections in the table of contents are symmetrical. I like the fact that the three titles you suggested to me by phone are in Spanish, and that they invoke different aspects of Hispanic civilization. As agreed, the first one, "Voces," includes pieces about the intermingling of tongues, either in a linguistic or in a metaphorical way. "Fronteras" is about crossing and being crossed by borders. And "Melodramas" offers scenes in which the public and the private meet—moments defined, in Rubén Blades's words, as *"la emoción apretada por dentro."* At your suggestion, I've also added a song by Lila Downs, known for her lyrics in pre-Columbian languages, on heterogeneity among Latinos. Along with "Agua Pa' La Gente," it will bring the "oral" aspect of the material to the fore.

Ilan

From: Harold Augenbraum
Subject: Finito

Ilan,

I think our introduction reflects the spirit of globalism we tried to infuse into *Lengua Fresca*. The next installment should be due in a decade!

Harold

VOCES

oscar casares

❧ CHANGO

BONY WAS WALKING back from the Jiffy-Mart when he found the monkey's head. There it was, under the small palm tree in the front yard, just staring up at him like an old friend who couldn't remember his name. It freaked him out bad. The dude had to check around to make sure nobody had seen him jump back and almost drop his beer in the dirt. It was still lunchtime and cars were parked up and down the street. For a second, it looked like the head might be growing out of the ground. Maybe somebody had buried the monkey up to its neck the way people did to other people at the beach when they ran out of things to do. Maybe it was still alive. Bony grabbed a broom off the porch and swung hard. He stopped an inch away from the monkey's little black eyes, and it didn't blink. He poked the head with the straw end of the broom and it tipped back and forth. The short black hairs on its head were pointed straight up at the cloudy sky. The nose was flat and wrinkled around the edges like it'd been a normal nose and then God decided to push it in with His big thumb. The ears were old man's ears with whiskers growing on them and in them. And it kept smiling. It smiled from one monkey ear to the other.

Bony's mother said it was the ugliest thing she'd ever seen. ¡Qué feo! She wanted it out of her yard. What were the neighbors going to think? What were her customers going to say? Who would want to buy perfume from a woman who lived with such an ugly thing in her front yard? She wouldn't.

His father said it was a dead chango. He didn't care how it died or where it came from. All he knew was that Bony needed to stop

3

lying around in his calzoncillos every morning and go out and find a job, earn some money. He was tired of coming home for lunch and seeing him sleeping on the sofa. He didn't know how a police sergeant's son could be so damn lazy. Brownsville wasn't that big a town. People talked. Bony was thirty-one years old. Ya, it was time to go do something with his life. His older brothers had good jobs. What was wrong with him? That chango wasn't going to get him anywhere. It was dead.

"I want to keep him," Bony said.

"Keep him?" his father said. "¿Estás loco o qué? You want to live with monkeys, I'll drive you to the zoo. Come on, get in the car, I'll take you right now. Marta, por favor, help your son put some clothes in a bag. He wants to live at the zoo."

"You're making your father mad, Bony."

"I didn't do anything," Bony said.

"No," his father said. "All you want to do is drink beer with your new best friend, your compadre, instead of going out to make a living."

Bony should have known his parents would say something like that. So what if he didn't have a job? Everybody had his own life.

His father drove away in the patrol car. His mother walked back inside the house. And Bony stayed in the yard with the monkey. It wasn't so bad. It's not like the head had been chopped off right there in front of the house. Except for it not having a body, the monkey was in perfect condition. The head must have come from the alley that was next to the house. People were always walking by and throwing things in the yard. It was Bony's job to keep the yard clean. His father said it was the least he could do. Every few days Bony found something new: candy wrappers, empty beer bottles, used fireworks, a dollar bill ripped in half, a fishing knife with dried blood. A few weeks earlier he'd found a busted pocket watch in the grass. Another time he found a bunch of letters from a man named Joaquín to a woman named Verónica. The letters were in Spanish, and as best as Bony could tell, Joaquín loved Verónica and things would've worked out if he hadn't had a wife and five kids.

Most afternoons Bony sat on the tailgate of his dark blue troquita, the sound system cranked up to some Led Zeppelin or Pink Floyd. He'd been listening to the same music since high school and said he would change if another band ever came out with anything better. That afternoon was different, though. He forgot about the music and sat in a lawn chair on the grass. The shade from the fresno tree covered most of the yard. The wind was blowing some, but it was a warm breeze that made him feel like he was sitting in a Laundromat waiting for his pants to dry. He stayed cool in his chanclas, baggy blue jean shorts, and San Antonio Spurs jersey. Across the street, a crow walked in circles in front of Mando Gomez's house. Bony cracked open his first beer. The palm tree stood between him and the street. He liked being the only one who could see the monkey as people walked by that afternoon. He stared at the monkey and the monkey stared back at him.

The first ones to pass by were the chavalones walking home from school with their mommies. A few of the mommies were young and fine, but they never looked Bony's way. Next were the older kids from the junior high who lived in the neighborhood and knew better than to walk by without saying hello. "Ese Bony," they said. He pitched his head back slightly, just to let them know he'd heard them and he was cool with them.

Later, people in the neighborhood drove home from work. Some of them waved hello, some didn't. Mrs. Rivas, who lived at the other end of the street, waved only because she was friends with his mother. The old lady worked part-time in the church office and led the rosary whenever anybody from the neighborhood died. Every Christmas, for as long as Bony could remember, she added a new animal to her Baby Jesus setting. A few years ago they sent a guy from the newspaper to take her picture surrounded by all the plastic sheep and cows in the manger. Bony did his best to avoid Mrs. Rivas, but one time she stopped her car in front of the house and invited him to a prayer group for men who were having trouble finding God. He said he wasn't having any trouble. Mrs. Rivas told him he wasn't going to find Nuestro Señor Jesucristo inside a can of beer. She got back in her car when Bony looked inside the can he was drinking from and said, "Hey, anybody in there?"

Domingo, the old guy who cleaned yards, usually walked by in the late afternoon and waved. Bony figured he had to be at least eighty or ninety. He'd been old like forever. Every time Bony saw Domingo, he was working in people's yards and only getting older and darker. He wasn't getting rich pushing a lawn mower, that was for sure.

If it was the weekend, Ruben Ortiz might drive by. He grew up on this same street and now he was a teacher. The guy drove a nice car, wore nice clothes, even had a good-looking wife. He lived on the other side of town and came over to visit his parents. Bony could tell the guy had changed since he left the neighborhood. He'd stay in his car and wave like he was passing by in a parade. Bony thought it looked like a good life, but it wasn't for everybody, not for him anyway.

His friend Mando had big plans and look what happened to him. He was working full-time and taking drafting classes at the college. The army paid for the classes, but he needed extra money because his girlfriend was about to have a baby. He wanted to marry her after the baby was born and buy a house, maybe a trailer to get started. Mando worked for a shuttle service that took businessmen into Matamoros. It was his job to drive them to their offices at the maquiladoras, unload any extra packages from the van, drive back across the bridge, and then pick up the same businessmen later that day. So he was driving back alone one morning, right? It was foggy on this narrow road and a truck hit him head-on. Mando died instantly — at least that's what his family hoped. Because if he didn't, it meant he was still alive when somebody stole his wallet, his gold chain with the cross, and his favorite pair of boots right off his feet. The owner of the shuttle service said the company would pay for the funeral and set aside $5,000 to give Mando's kid when he turned eighteen, but nothing more for the family. Nada más, the owner was nice enough to translate for Mando's father. The family hired a lawyer to represent them, but he was young and inexperienced and the company's lawyers weren't. Nada más ended up being all the family got. Mando's girlfriend and the baby moved in with his parents.

This thing with Mando happened a few years ago. Bony had an

okay job around that time. He worked for the city, in the Parks Division, where his job was to open one of the gyms in the afternoon, hand out basketballs, break up any fights before they started, and make sure nobody stuffed anything down the toilets. He played ball if a team needed an extra player, and he had a killer jump shot from the baseline, three-point range. Nothing but net. *Swoosh!!!* Then one night he sneaks inside the gym with a girl he met at a party. She's a gordita who weighs almost twice as much as Bony, but she wants it and he has a set of gym keys that are burning a hole in his pocket. And they're having a good time, when all of a sudden the security guard pops the lights on and catches Bony and the girl rolling around at center court like they're wrestling for a loose ball. The guard is an old guy who's serious about his job. He walks into the Parks Division office the next morning and reports Bony. By the end of the week, the dude's at home without a job.

Now Bony made his money installing car stereos on the side. People paid him what they could — twenty or thirty dollars was the usual — but if he knew them, he might let them slide with a case of Corona or Negra Modelo. He also helped out his mom with her Avon deliveries. She paid him a few dollars for this. At first he thought there might be some nice-looking women buying perfume, but they all turned out to be as old as or older than his mom, viejitas like Mrs. Rivas. Some of the women would tip him a couple of dollars, which was better than nothing. He was getting by, and except for his parents hassling him about finding a real job, he didn't have any complaints.

It was dark when his father came home with dinner. He'd picked up a family box from Kentucky Fried Chicken. Bony liked the chicken at Church's better, liked those papitas they served, but the manager at KFC gave his dad a discount for being a police officer, and that was that. If Bony wanted Church's, he'd have to buy it with Bony's money.

His mother set the table with paper plates and napkins. Bony sat by the open blinds so he could keep an eye on the monkey. He served himself a chicken breast and some mashed potatoes. His father served himself two legs and a roll. His mother liked the wings and coleslaw. They ate without talking. The opening and closing of the red and white box was the only sound in the room. Bony's mother stood up once to find the salt. His father was scooping up the last of his mashed potatoes when he finally spoke.

"Did you know that Colonel Sanders, the man who invented Kentucky Fried Chicken, tried one hundred and twenty-four recipes before he made the perfect one? One hundred and twenty-four. What does that tell you, Bony?"

"That he should've gone to Church's."

"Why do I even try to talk sense to you?" His father shook his head and looked at Bony's mother, who stared back like she was waiting for the answer. He bit another piece off his roll, chewed it, swallowed, and spoke again.

"The colonel, he didn't give up because he didn't get it right the first time. That's what I'm trying to say here."

"What was he a colonel of?" Bony asked.

"¿Pues, quién sabe? He was just a colonel, of the army, of the marines, of all the chickens and roosters. It doesn't matter, Bony. The point is, the man didn't give up, and you shouldn't either. You can't stay home the rest of your life because a job didn't work out. Look at the colonel. Let him be your example."

"I'm not going to wear one of those uniforms they wear at Kentucky Fried Chicken, no way."

"Bony, all I'm saying is, there are people I can call. People who know the name Sergeant Timo Hinojosa and could help you."

"What's wrong with that?" his mother asked. "What's wrong with accepting some help from your father? That's what parents are for."

"Nothing." Bony glanced out the window.

"Don't be thinking you're going to keep that chango," his father said.

"Why not?"

"It's a dead chango," his mother said. "Do you need another reason?"

Bony walked outside and sat in the lawn chair. The porch light was on and he could see the monkey watching him. There were only three cans left in his twelve-pack. In an hour, the beer would be gone. He was about to walk to the Jiffy-Mart again, but instead he decided to hang out in the yard with the monkey. Back when Mando was around, the two of them partied all night. One time they stayed up until five in the morning, taking hits off some hash, drinking beer, and eating Doritos. Bony had heard that a volcano erupted in Mexico and was going to turn the moon a different color. And sure enough, the moon turned a dark red like there was a heart inside of it pumping blood. Mando called it the werewolf moon. Bony stood in the middle of the street and howled as loud as he could. He howled like he'd been bitten and he was turning into a werewolf, growing fur and fangs and claws and a tail. He howled until his father opened the window and told him to shut the hell up.

Bony was sitting in the lawn chair when his father turned off the porch light. It was almost eleven o'clock. He sat in the dark staring at the monkey and barely making out the shape of its head. Usually there would've been more light in the yard, but some pendejo had busted out the streetlight again. Bony finished his last beer and closed his eyes. When he woke up a few minutes later, a cat was sniffing the monkey. "¡Pinche gato!" Bony yelled and threw a rock at it. He pegged the cat on its backside right as it was starting to lick the monkey's ear. Bony went over to make sure the monkey was all right. He cleared the dirt around the palm tree so there wouldn't be any bugs crawling on the head.

It was time to go to sleep, but he couldn't leave the monkey outside. Not if he wanted to see it again. If you left anything in the yard overnight, it was as good as gone. People chained their barbecue pits to trees. Unless you drove some cucaracha, your car better have an alarm on it. Most of the neighbors who could afford them had steel bars installed on the windows and doors of their houses, and even that didn't always keep the cabrones out if they thought there was something worth stealing. The Sanchez family had a full-grown chow in their backyard, and one day it disappeared forever. No way was he leaving the monkey in the yard.

Bony found a plastic trash bag on the porch, but he wasn't sure how to put the monkey's head inside it. He hadn't really touched the monkey, and the truth was that actually putting his hands on it was kind of freaky to him. He told himself it wasn't because he was afraid — he just didn't want to mess up its hair. If he were a monkey, he wouldn't want some guy grabbing him by the head. He wrapped his hand inside the white bag and held the head against the palm tree until he could scoop it up. When he walked into his room, Bony could see the monkey's black face pressed against the white plastic.

Where to put the monkey was the next question. There was room on the dresser if he moved his boom box, except he liked having it right under his team poster of the Dallas Cowboys. He also had a poster of the cheerleaders hanging on the back of the door, where nobody could see it and his mother wouldn't complain every time people came to the house. Two leather basketballs were sitting on the recliner he didn't use anymore. He tossed the basketballs in the closet and placed the monkey's head on the recliner. The monkey looked sharp, looked like a king sitting on his throne.

Bony turned off the lights and climbed into bed. It was pitch-black in the room except for the eyes and shiny white teeth that he swore he could see on the chair. Bony turned toward the wall, but he kept seeing the smile in his mind. He imagined what would happen if the monkey grew back its body in the middle of the night. Hairy arms and legs, long skinny tail, sharp pointy teeth, hands that looked like feet, feet that looked like hands. And what if this new monkey was out for revenge against the people who had cut off its head, but since it was a monkey, it didn't know any better and attacked the first person it saw? It started by ripping out the person's eyes so he couldn't fight back and then it chomped on his face and neck, eating up his cheeks and tongue, gnawing on the bones and cartilage, until the whole room was covered with blood. Bony folded the pillow around his head and tried to make himself fall asleep. After a while, he stood up and put the monkey in the closet and pushed the chair against the door.

He woke up earlier than usual the next morning. His parents were sitting at the kitchen table when he walked in holding the plastic bag. The monkey was pressed against the white plastic, staring at the chorizo con huevo on the table.

"¡Ay, Bony!" his mother said. "No me digas que you brought that chango inside my house."

"I didn't want somebody to steal him."

"Who's going to steal a monkey head?" his father said.

"You never know."

"Take him outside, ahorita mero!" his mother said. "I will not have a dead chango inside my house. No señor, you're going to ruin my business."

"You heard your mother. You better get that chango out of here."

Bony walked outside and placed the monkey back in the same spot where it had been the day before. This time he went ahead and held the monkey in his hands. Its fur was soft and its ears felt like human ears, kind of. His parents, as usual, were freaking out about nothing. The fur around the monkey's left ear was messed up from being inside the bag. Bony licked his palm and smoothed down the fur.

The sun was already up and it was getting warm in the neighborhood. Bony grabbed a can of Coke from the refrigerator and sat in the lawn chair. The *Herald* was lying next to the fresno tree. He opened the paper and checked out the local news, halfway expecting to see an article about somebody finding a monkey's body without a head. There was news about two Canadians getting busted at the International Bridge with heroin sealed inside cans of tuna, news about even more Border Patrol agents being hired, news about the farmers needing rain, news about the effects of the peso devaluation on downtown, news about the owner of El Chueco Bar on Fourteenth Street being attacked with a machete and surviving, but nothing about the monkey.

After he finished with the first section, he turned to the want ads. They were taking applications at the Levis plant. Parra Furniture needed a deliveryman. The security job at Amigoland Mall looked cool. All those guys did was drive around the mall and make sure your car didn't get ripped off while you were shopping. How hard could that be?

People had it wrong when they thought Bony didn't want to work. He was only trying to have a good time before it was too late. Bony used to think he and Mando would be partying for the rest of their lives. Mando had told him about school and getting married, but he never took him seriously. Guys talked, and lots of times that's all it was, talk. It wasn't until the accident that he realized Mando had a whole different life he was planning. At first, Bony couldn't believe he was dead. It messed him up. He didn't know how to make sense of his friend dying. Bony hadn't been doing much except hanging out and partying. So why did God take Mando and not him? A couple of times he'd seen Mando's kid playing alone in the front yard and had gone over. He was a happy kid, but playing with him made Bony miss his friend, so he didn't go over that much anymore. It was better just to wave at him from this side of the street.

"¿Todavía?" Bony's father was standing on the front porch. "I thought we told you to get that chango out of here."

"I thought you meant later, or tomorrow."

"Now, Bony."

"Pues, I don't know where to take him."

"That's not my problem, Bony. That's your problem. You can drive it all the way back to Africa, or wherever it came from. I don't care." His father crossed his arms and leaned against the porch. "And I'm going to wait right here until you do it."

Bony took his time standing up and putting the monkey back in the plastic bag. He could feel his father's eyes on his back, but he didn't let it get to him. He walked down the street, trying to look like any other guy walking down the street with a monkey's head in a plastic bag. No worries. He waved to Domingo, but the old man was busy trimming the grass around a neighbor's tree. A few houses later, Bony threw a rock at the same cat from the night before.

Lincoln Park was at the end of the block. It looked more like a long, skinny island than it did a park. The palm trees were one of the few things that stood out when the resaca flooded. The water usually took a couple of weeks to go back down to its normal level, which was more than enough time for all the mosquitoes to show up.

He crossed the small bridge over the resaca. The park was empty at that hour. He climbed the wooden fort that the little kids played on during the day. This was also the fort where Mando and Bony convinced a couple of girls to come hang out with them one night. The guys were sixteen, the girls were fifteen. Bony scored two bottles of strawberry wine and they took turns going down the slide. After a while, Mando and his girl went for a long walk. Bony stayed with his girl in the fort, where she let him do everything but go inside her.

He took the monkey out of the plastic bag and set it next to him. From where he was sitting on the fort, Bony could see most of the park. If you played basketball here, you had to be a fast runner or the ball was going to be rolling into the water every game. This was the court where Bony first got his shot down. Next to the basket were the picnic tables that filled up fast on the weekends. You could forget barbecuing here unless you started setting up way before noon. If they were having a lowrider show in the park, you'd be lucky to find a place to sit.

By the water fountains was where Bony had stopped a guy named Javier Ortiz. The girl Mando had been with that night in the park was Javier's old girlfriend, and now Javier was saying he was going to jump Mando.

"I heard you were talking shit about Mando."

"What's it to you?"

"You got a problem with Mando, you got a problem with me."

"No, man, I don't have no problems with you," Javier said. "It's cool."

"I think you do, puto. And I think I'm going to kick your ass," Bony said.

And then he did.

Bony looked down and saw that flies were buzzing around the monkey's head and landing on its nose. He shooed them away with his hand, but they kept coming back. Looking at the long whiskers on the monkey's cheeks, the deep lines around its eyes, made him want to find out where the head had come from. Bony thought about calling the zoo and asking them if they were missing any monkeys, but then he figured that if a monkey had been kidnapped, they might be tracing the phone calls and he'd get blamed for the whole thing. He didn't need that kind of trouble.

He walked back to the house remembering all the monkeys he'd seen on TV or at the movies, but none of them looked like his monkey. He thought how weird it was that he'd never seen one like this before. When he made it home, he put the monkey in the truck and drove out of the neighborhood. He passed the park and headed down International, in the direction of the library. Pink Floyd was on the stereo and the woofers were maxed out enough for people to feel the vibrations two cars over. The monkey was riding shotgun.

The library parking lot was full, so Bony had to circle around a few times to find a spot. He left the monkey on the floor mat, where people couldn't see it. As soon as he felt how cold it was inside the library, he wished he'd worn long pants. The encyclopedias were on a short bookcase close to the entrance. He sat in a chair and read about the differences between monkeys and apes. The most interesting part was how much they were related to humans. He'd never been completely comfortable with that idea, but at the same time he didn't know what to make of the story of Adam and Eve and a talking snake. Even if he did believe people came from monkeys, he had to ask where the monkeys came from.

The encyclopedia had a life-size picture of a gorilla's hand. Bony placed his own hand on top of the gorilla's hand, and although his was a lot smaller, they did match. The encyclopedia had pictures of more monkeys and apes than he ever knew existed, but he couldn't find a picture that looked exactly like his monkey's head. He finally spotted one in a book called *Monkeys of the New World*. In the picture, the black monkey was standing on a tree branch picking fruit. It was a spider monkey, from Ecuador. Bony read about what they ate, how long they lived, how they took care of their babies. He even checked out a picture of two spider monkeys having sex, which he didn't look at for too long because he didn't want the library lady walking by and thinking he was some weirdo.

He put the monkey back on the passenger seat as he drove home. Now that Bony had learned something about the monkey, he wanted to name it. The first thing that popped into his mind was to call it Spider Man because he kind of liked the guy in the comics. He thought about naming it Blackie, but he knew that was dumb. Zorro was kind of a cool name, but there was already a black dog on his street named Zorro. He couldn't remember Tarzan's monkey's name, or that might have worked. Then he tried to think of a name in Spanish, but the only name he came up with was the easiest, Chango. He hadn't liked it when his parents used the word because they only used it to say it was a dead chango. But the more he thought about it, it fit. He liked the way it sounded when he said it to himself: Chango, Chango, Chango. Ese Chango. Bony and Chango.

Bony stopped at the Jiffy-Mart and bought a twelve-pack. It was three o'clock by the time he stopped in front of the house. His mother and Mrs. Rivas were standing next to the palm tree. Mrs. Rivas held a small plastic bottle upside down and squirted water on the ground. Bony placed Chango on the floor mat and grabbed the beer as he stepped out of the truck.

"Agua bendita," Mrs. Rivas said as he walked up.

He stepped back when he realized it really was holy water.

"¿Dónde está el chango, Bony?" she asked.

"What chango?"

"I already told Mrs. Rivas what you found," his mother said. "She says somebody's trying to put a curse on our house, maybe on my business."

"No they're not, it's just a monkey's head. What's the big deal?"

"¿Qué crees, Bony?" Mrs. Rivas said. "Eh, you think God opened the heavens and dropped that chango's head in your yard so you could tell him your jokes? No, mi'jo, that's the work of brujas."

"That's crazy. There's no brujas."

"Listen to her, Bony." His mother held his arm.

"You think brujas are like you see them on the television, flying around on brooms, but that's not the way it is. You don't know. ¿Tú qué sabes? They shop at the mall, eat at Luby's, go to bailes and dance cumbias. Brujas are everywhere, Bony, probably in this neighborhood."

The old lady looked down the street and then back at Bony.

"Go ask Mrs. Molina, on the next block. Ask her what happened to her mother. Andale, she'll tell you how somebody threw a dead snake in her mother's yard, y la pobre mujer, she stepped on it barefoot. The very next morning her skin started falling off. I wouldn't lie to you, Bony, *her skin*. Until there was nothing left of the woman. Tell me that's not the work of brujas."

"¿Ya ves? You're bringing curses into my house."

"Now tell us where you put that chango's head," Mrs. Rivas said.

"We already checked in your room, mi'jo," his mother said.

"You what?"

"Your mother was worried about the curses."

"He wasn't hurting anybody."

"Tell us where it is, Bony," Mrs. Rivas said.

"I threw him away already."

"Where, Bony?" his mother said.

"In the trash, behind the Jiffy-Mart."

"Are you telling your mother the truth, Bony?" Mrs. Rivas said.

"Go see for yourself if you don't believe me."

Mrs. Rivas and his mother looked at each other. Bony walked to the porch and leaned back in the lawn chair. It was just another afternoon in the neighborhood. After a few minutes Mrs. Rivas drove away.

"Más vale que me estés diciendo la verdad, Bony," his mother said. "I better not see that monkey in my house again."

Bony shook his head. "Don't worry."

She walked into the house and let the screen door slam shut.

Bony stayed on the porch. Across the street, Mando's kid was riding his tricycle through the front yard. It was quiet in the neighborhood. Bony cracked open his first beer. The can was sweating in his hand and down onto the porch. He took a drink and kicked back. He wasn't going to let anybody take Chango.

Except for walking inside to grab a piece of leftover chicken, Bony sat on the porch for the rest of the afternoon. He thought his mother might be watching him through the window and he didn't want to make her suspicious. The beer was cold. What more did he need, right?

His parents ate dinner at seven, but Bony stayed outside on the porch. He went in later and microwaved what was left of the tacos they'd had for dinner. His father was in the kitchen cleaning his work shoes. The patent leather was shiny and Bony kept looking at his own reflection.

"You drink too much," his father said.

"So what?"

"*So what?* This isn't a cantina, where you can get pedo and stare at somebody's shoes. What's wrong with you?"

Bony didn't answer and took another bite of his taco.

"Your mother says you're sad because we made you throw away the chango."

"I'm not sad."

"You look sad."

"I'm just thinking."

"Are you thinking about what kind of job you're going to look for tomorrow?"

"Not really."

"I didn't think so."

After Bony was done eating, he drank another beer and watched a baseball game on TV. He hated baseball, but he was waiting for his parents to go to sleep, which they finally did a little after ten. He grabbed Chango from the truck and put him under the small palm tree. The moon was almost full and its glow filled the yard with light. Bony brought out his lawn chair, just like old times. There was half a can of beer left, which he placed next to Chango. He could see himself doing this every night. His parents never had to find out. Maybe one of these nights when they were away from the house, he and Chango would cook out in the backyard. Some fajitas, some chicken, some beer. It'd be badass. People would be walking by and going, "¿Qué onda, Bony?" And he'd be like, "Aquí nomás. Just cooking out, man." And they'd walk away thinking the dude knew how to do it right.

It was after midnight when Bony put away the lawn chair and carried Chango back to the truck. He didn't want to risk taking him inside the house and his parents finding out. Earlier he'd left a crack at the top of the windows, but now he rolled them up in case there was rain. He locked the truck and went inside the house.

He tried to relax in bed and enjoy what was left of his beer buzz. Tomorrow he'd figure out what to do with Chango. Maybe his mother would forget about what Mrs. Rivas had said. His father might be okay with him keeping Chango if he went out and found a job. Bony thought anything could happen. He might even fall asleep and turn into a monkey overnight, and then his parents would have to keep him and Chango.

It felt like he'd only been asleep for five minutes when he heard a fire engine driving through the front yard. He sat up in bed and realized it was already morning and the siren was really the alarm on his truck. His father was standing next to the truck with his hands cupped over his ears. Bony's mother walked toward the house when he opened the front door. He deactivated the alarm and then locked the truck again before his father could open the door.

"¡Ya lo vi, Bony!" his mother said. "I knew you were lying. ¡Güerco embustero! ¡Ahora verás!"

"What? He's not even close to the house."

"Bony, you knew what I meant."

"Ya fue mucho," his father said. "I'm going to call the city to come pick up the chango and take it away." He walked inside the house and grabbed the phone.

"I'll keep him somewhere else," Bony said.

His father shook his head and opened the phone book.

"What if I get a job?"

"It's too late, Bony." His father dialed a number.

Bony finished getting dressed and went to his truck. He drove out of the neighborhood, not sure where he was going exactly. Chango sat in the passenger seat, smiling as usual. Bony rolled down the windows and listened to the wind. There wasn't that much traffic on International that early in the morning. He drove past Southmost Road and slowed down for the flashing yellow light in front of la Porter, his old high school, so he wouldn't get pulled over by a cop. When he was on the other side of Four Corners, he stopped at a convenience store. A carton of orange juice and a package of cinnamon rolls were what he needed right now. Jumping out of bed so fast had made him feel extra crudo.

The orange juice came with little chunks of ice, the way he liked it, but he had to be careful not to get the steering wheel sticky while he was driving and eating the cinnamon rolls. It felt like a road trip is what it felt like. They could drive anywhere they wanted to, Corpus, San Antonio, Houston, anywhere. He and Mando had always talked about someday taking a trip to see the Dallas Cowboys play. If he had more than two dollars in his pocket, he might have taken off right then. Instead, he turned down 511 and drove around the edge of town. There were a couple of new subdivisions, but it was still mainly farmland out there. Back in high school, Bony used to like to party and then go cruising. He remembered driving on this road alone one night and almost hitting a cow that was standing in the middle of the road. It came out of nowhere. He blinked and there it was, staring into the headlights. Bony had to swerve to miss it and then swerve back onto the road so he wouldn't hit a telephone pole. It could've easily been his time to go, but it wasn't. And now here he was with Chango.

He drove around for the rest of the morning and tried to come up with a plan. They traveled down Paredes, Coffeeport Road, Fourteenth Street, 802, Central, and Boca Chica. Going everywhere and nowhere at the same time. People were in a hurry to get places, but Bony and Chango were taking their time. On Palm Boulevard, they passed the big, expensive houses with trimmed lawns and then turned left at the first light. They drove another block and stopped in a parking lot across the street from the zoo.

Bony turned off the engine and listened for the animal sounds. He had to wait for a couple of school buses to turn the corner before it was quiet. All he could hear was the birds on the phone lines and a dog barking in the distance. He hadn't been to the zoo in years, but he was almost sure the monkeys were on a little island on the other side of the tall fence. Bony tried to imagine how he would've escaped if he were a monkey. Chango probably had it planned out months ahead of time, knew when the zoo people left at night, knew the perfect time to make a break for it. Chango was looking for something more than what he was going to find on that little island. Nobody could blame him for that.

Fifteen minutes went by before Bony started up the truck again. He was pulling out of the parking lot when he heard the monkey calls from the other side of the street. He looked at Chango, but Chango kept looking straight ahead.

They drove back to the neighborhood. Bony passed by his street and saw a city truck parked in front of the house. He drove on until he was on the other side of Lincoln Park. Two old men were sitting in a station wagon by the entrance. They were drinking beer and listening to a ranchera station. Bony parked a few spaces away from their car. He put Chango inside the plastic bag. The old men were laughing hard, like one of the men had told the other a funny joke. They happened to look up at Bony as he was getting out of the truck, and the man in the driver's seat nodded hello to him. Bony nodded back to him and walked into the park with Chango.

He crossed a short bridge and stepped down to the canal. He took Chango out of the bag and sat by the edge of the water. The resaca that surrounded the park ended up here and then dropped off a small concrete waterfall. Bony and Mando had learned to fish in this canal. They used a couple of branches, some fishing line, hooks, and bread that Bony had taken from his mother's kitchen. Beginner's luck, that's what Mando called it when Bony caught a shiner that first afternoon. He called it luck whenever Bony beat him at something. In a lot of ways, he was lucky that he'd found Chango. How many guys could say they'd found a monkey's head in their front yard? He'd probably never find anything like this again. He was sure that if Chango were a guy they'd be camaradas. Same thing would go if Bony were a monkey. They'd be hanging out in the jungle, swinging from trees, eating bananas. They'd be putting the moves on all the changuitas, doing it monkey-style. He would miss his truck, but then what would he need it for in the jungle? It's not like there was anywhere to go cruising. And if he were a monkey, nobody would be hassling him to be something else. He'd be a monkey. He wouldn't have to go to school, or work, or file for unemployment. And something else: monkeys were always together. He and Chango would be friends until they were viejitos, all wrinkled and hunched over and walking from tree to tree because they were too old to be swinging. They'd be hanging out forever. "Right?" Bony said. "Right?" It took a second before he realized that he was talking to himself.

The water was browner and greener than he remembered it. A tire had washed up on the other side of the canal. An army boot floated and got stuck on some lily pads. He broke a dead branch into four pieces and pitched them into the water one at a time. When he ran out of branches and twigs, he threw pebbles. Time was passing slowly and he was avoiding doing what he had to do. Bony skipped a few more rocks across the water. He wished people would leave him alone, let him live his own life. If he drank, it was because he wanted to drink. If he stayed at home without a real job, it was because he wasn't ready for that yet. There wasn't anybody who understood him. He and Chango were hanging out. His mother and father didn't know what they were saying. His mother let herself be talked into crazy ideas by Mrs. Rivas. People were always talking at him and telling him how he should live. Sometimes he listened, but most times he didn't. He was just living. That's the best explanation he could give. Living. Bony leaned over and held Chango a couple of inches above the water. It was the last thing in the world that he wanted to do, but he let go.

rane arroyo

❧ THE VISITOR

el pan azul de cada día
"The thrush warbled, pure bird."
— PABLO NERUDA

You're dead, but your skies are not.
This Ohio storm makes me think of your
blackening Chilean horizons. What use

is your name now in the not-now,
not-here? Neruda. Ne. Ruda. Neru.
Da. It was a wonderful mask, no?

Pablito, there is a spider in my spinning
bedroom with blind rubies for eyes.
Is this a message from you? Dawn is

still painful, old amigo, and pain is
always a vague ghost nostalgic for
the blue bread that we eat to forget

our missing talent for love. The dead
have mud for skies, ¿no? Imagine, poet,
we can incorporate, sell shares in ourselves!

Sí, the world is still extraliterary. Are there
bakers in the afterlife? Poetry asks for you
by name, the one finally yours. Stop grinning.

ilan stavans

DON QUIXOTE EN SPANGLISH
First Parte, Chapter Uno

N UN PLACETE DE LA MANCHA of which nombre no quiero remembrearme, vivía, not so long ago, uno de esos gentlemen who always tienen una lanza in the rack, una buckler antigua, a skinny caballo y un grayhound para el chase. A cazuela with más beef than mutón, carne choppeada para la dinner, un omelet pa' los Sábados, lentil pa' los Viernes, y algún pigeon como delicacy especial pa' los Domingos, consumían tres cuarers de su income. El resto lo employaba en una coat de broadcloth y en soketes de velvetín pa' los holidays, with sus slippers pa' combinar, while los otros días de la semana él cut a figura de los más finos cloths. Livin with él eran una housekeeper en sus forties, una sobrina not yet twenty, y un ladino del field y la marketa que le saddleaba el caballo al gentleman y wieldeaba un hookete pa' podear. El gentleman andaba por allí por los fifty. Era de complexión robusta pero un poco fresco en los bones y una cara leaneada y gaunteada. La gente sabía that él era un early riser y que gustaba mucho huntear. La gente say que su apellido was Quijada or Quesada — hay diferencia de opinión entre aquellos que han escrito sobre el sujeto — but acordando with las muchas conjeturas se entiende que era really Quejada. But all this no tiene mucha importancia pa' nuestro cuento, providiendo que al cuentarlo no nos separemos pa' nada de las verdá.

It is known, pues, que el aformencionado gentleman, cuando se la pasaba bien, which era casi todo el año, tenía el hábito de leer libros de chivaldría with tanta pleasura y devoción as to leadearlo casi por completo a forgetear su vida de hunter y la administración de su estate. Tan great era su curiosidad e infatuación en este regarde que él even vendió muchos acres de tierra sembrable pa' comprar y leer los libros que amaba y carreaba a su casa as many as él podía obtuvir. Of todos los que devoreó, ninguno le plaseó más que los compuestos por el famoso Feliciano de Silva, who tenía una estylo lúcido y plotes intrincados that were tan preciados para él as pearlas; especialmente cuando readeaba esos cuentos de amor y challenges amorosos that se foundean por muchos placetes, por example un passage como this one: *La rasón de mi unrasón que aflicta mi rasón, en such a manera weakenea mi rasón que yo with rasón lamento tu beauty.* Y se sintió similarmente aflicteado cuando sus ojos cayeron en líneas como these ones: . . . *el high Heaven de tu divinidad te fortifiquea with las estrellas y te rendea worthy de ese deserveo que tu greatness deserva.*

El pobre felo se la paseaba awakeado en las noches en un eforte de desentrañar el meanin y make sense de pasajes como these ones, aunque Aristotle himself, even if él had been resurrecteado pa'l propósito, no los understeaba tampoco. El gentleman no estaba tranquilo en su mente por las wounds que dio y recebió Don Belianís; porque in spite of how great los doctores que lo trataron, el pobre felo must have been dejado with su face y su cuerpo entero coverteados de marcas y escars. Pero daba thanks al autor por concluir el libro with la promisa de una interminable adventura to come. Many times pensaba seizear la pluma y literalmente finishear el cuento como had been prometeado, y undoubtedly él would have done it, y would have succedeado muy bien si sus pensamientos no would have been ocupados with estorbos. El felo habló d'esto muchas veces with el cura, who era un hombre educado, graduado de Sigüenza. Sostenía largas discusiones as to quién tenía el mejor caballero, Palmerín of England o Amadís of Gaul; pero Master Nicholas, el barbero del same pueblo, tenía el hábito de decir que nadie could come close ni cerca to the Caballero of Phoebus, y que si alguien *could* compararse with él, it had to be Don Galaor, bró de Amadís of Gaul, for Galaor estaba redy pa' todo y no era uno d'esos caballeros second-rate, y en su valor él no lagueaba demasiado atrás.

En short, nuestro gentleman quedó tan inmerso en su readin that él pasó largas noches — del sondáu y sonóp —, y largos días — del daun al dosk — husmeando en sus libros. Finalmente, de tan pocquito sleep y tanto readin, su brain se draidió y quedó fuera de su mente. Había llenado su imaginación con everythin que había readieado, with enchantamientos, encounters de caballero, battles, desafíos, wounds, with cuentos de amor y de tormentos, y with all sorts of impossible things, that as a result se convenció que todos los happenins ficcionales que imagineaba eran trú y that eran más reales pa' él que anithin else en el mundo. El remarcaba que el Cid Ruy Díaz era un caballero very good, pero que no había comparación with el Caballero de la Flaming Sword, who with una estocada had cortado en halfo dos giants fierces y monstruosos. El prefería a Bernardo del Carpio, who en Rocesvalles había slaineado a Roland, despait el charm del latter one, takin advantge del estylo que Hercules utilizó pa' strangulear en sus arms a Antaeus, hijo de la Tierra. También tenía mucho good pa' decir de Morgante, who, though era parte de la raza de giants, in which all son soberbios y de mala disposición, él was afable y well educado. But, encima de todo, él se cherisheaba de admiración por Rinaldo of Montalbán, especialmente when él saw him sallyingueando hacia fuera of su castillo pa' robear a todos los que le aparecían en su path, or when lo imagineaba overseas thifeando la statue de Mohammed, which, así dice la story, era all de oro. Y él would have enjoyado un mano-a-mano with el traitor Galalón, un privilegio for which él would have dado a su housekeeper y su sobrina en el same bargain.

In efecto, cuando sus wits quedaron sin reparo, él concebió la idea más extraña ever occurrida a un loco en este mundo. Pa' ganar más honor pa' himself y pa' su country al same time, le parecía fittin y necesario convertirse en un caballero errant y romear el mundo a caballo, en un suit de armadura. El would salir en quest de adventuras, pa' poner en práctica all that él readeaba en los libros. Arranglaría todo wrong, placeándose en situaciones of the greatest peril, and these mantendían pa' siempre su nombre en la memoria. Como rewarda por su valor y el might de su brazo, el pobre felo podía verse crowneado por lo menos as Emperador de Trebizond; y pues, carriado por el extraño pleacer que él foundió en estos thoughts, inmediatamente he set to put el plan en marcha.

Lo primero que hizo fue burnishear old piezas de armadura, left to him por su great-grandfather, que por ages were arrumbada en una esquina, with polvo y olvido. Los polisheó y ajustó as best él could, y luego vio que faltaba una cosa bien importante: él had no ral closed hemleto, but un morión o helmete de metal, del type que usaban los soldados. Su ingenuidad allowed him un remedio al bendear un cardbord en forma de half-helmete, which, cuando lo attacheó, dió la impresión de un helmete entero. Trú, cuando fue a ver si era strong as to withstandear un good slashin blow, quedó desappointeado; porque cuando dribleó su sword y dió un cople of golpes, succedió only en perder una semana entera de labor. Lo fácil with which lo había destrozado lo disturbó y decidió hacerlo over. This time puso strips de iron adentro y luego, convencido de que alredy era muy strong, refraineó ponerló a test otra vez. Instead, lo adoptó then y there como el finest helmete ever.

Depués salió a ver a su caballo, y although el animal tenía más cracks en sus hoofes que cuarers en un real, y más blemishes que'l caballo de Gonela, which *tantum pellis et ossa fuit* ("all skin y bones"), nonetheless le pareció al felo que era un far better animal que el Bucephalus de Alexander o el Babieca del Cid. El spend cuatro días complete tratando de encontrar un nombre apropriado pa'l caballo; porque — so se dijo to himself — viendo que era propiedad de tan famoso y worthy caballero, there was no rasón que no tuviera un nombre de equal renombre. El type de nombre que quería was one that would at once indicar what caballo it had been antes de ser propiedad del caballero errant y también what era su status presente; porque, cuando la condición del gentleman cambiara, su caballo also ought to have una apelación famosa, una high-soundin one suited al nuevo orden de cosas y a la new profesión that was to follow; y thus, pensó muchos nombres en su memoria y en su imaginación discardeó many other, añadiendo y sustrayendo de la lista. Finalmente hinteó el de *Rocinante,* un nombre that lo impresionó as being sonoroso y al same time indicativo of what el caballo had been cuando era de segunda, whereas ahora no era otra cosa que el first y foremost de los caballos del mundo.

Habiendo foundeado un nombre tan pleasin pa' su caballo, decidió to do the same pa' himself. Esto requirió otra semana. Pa'l final de ese periodo se había echo a la mente that él as henceforth *Don Quixote,* which, como has been stated antes, forwardeó a los autores d'este trú cuento a asumir que se lamaba Quijada y no Quesada, as otros would have it. Pero remembreando que el valiant Amadís no era happy que lo llamaran así y nothin más, but addirió el nombre de su kingdom y su country pa'cerlos famous también, y thus se llamó Amadís of Gaul; so nuestro good caballero seleccionó poner su placete de origen y became *Don Quixote de La Mancha;* for d'esta manera dejaría very plain su linaje y confería honor a su country by takin su nombre y el suyo en one alone.

Y so, with sus weapons alredy limpias y su morión in shape, with apelaciones al caballo y a himself, él naturalmente encontró que una sola cosa laqueaba: él must seekiar una lady of whom él could enamorarse; porque un caballero errant sin una ladylove was like un árbol sin leaves ni frutas, un cuerpo sin soul.

"If," dijo, "como castigo a mis sines o un stroque de fortuna, me encuentro with un giant, which es una thing que les pasa comunmente a los caballeros errant, y si lo slaineo en un mano-a-mano o lo corto en two, or, finalmente, si vanquisheo y se rinde, would it not be well tener a alguien a whom yo puedo enviárelo como un presente, in order pa' que'l giant, if él is livin todavía, may come in pa' arrodillarse frente a mi sweet lady, and say en tono humilde y sumisivo, 'Yo, lady, soy el giant Caraculiambro, lord de la island Malindrania, who has been derroteado en un single combate para ese caballero who never can be praiseado enough, Don Quixote of La Mancha, el same que me sendió a presentarme before su Gracia pa' que Usté disponga as you wish?'"

Oh, cómo se revolotió en este espich nuestro good gentleman, y más than nunca él pensaba en el nombre that él should oferear a su lady! Como dice el cuento, there was una very good-lookin jovencita de rancho who vivía cerca, with whom él had been enamorado una vez, although ella never se dio por enterada. Su nombre era Aldonza Lorenzo y decidió that it was ella the one que debía to have el título de lady de sus pensamientos. Wisheó pa' ella un nombre tan good como his own y que conveyera la sugestión que era princeza or great lady; y, entonces, resolvió llamarla *Dulcinea del Toboso,* porque ella era nativa d'ese placete. El nombre era musical to his óidos, fuera de lo ordinario y significante, like los otros que seleccionó pa' himself y sus things.

richard blanco

TÍA OLIVIA SERVES
WALLACE STEVENS
A CUBAN EGG

The ration books voided, there was little to eat,
so Tía Olivia ruffled four hens to serve Stevens
a fresh *criollo* egg. The singular image lay limp,
floating in a circle of miniature roses and vines
etched around the edges of the rough dish.
The saffron, inhuman soul staring at Stevens
who asks what yolk is this, so odd a yellow?

Tell me Señora, if you know, he petitions,
what exactly is the color of this temptation:
I can see a sun, but it is not the color of suns
nor of sunflowers, nor the yellows of Van Gogh,
it is neither corn nor school pencil, as it is,
so few things are yellow, this, even more precise.

He shakes some salt, eye to eye hypothesizing:
a carnival of hues under the gossamer membrane,
a liqueur of convoluted colors, quarter-part orange,
imbued shadows, watercolors running a song
down the spine of praying stems, but what, then,
of the color of the stems, what green for the leaves,

what color the flowers; what of order for our eyes
if I cannot name this elusive yellow, Señora?

Intolerant, Tía Olivia bursts open Stevens's yolk,
plunging into it with a sharp piece of Cuban toast:
It is yellow, she says, *amarillo y nada más, bien?*

hip hop hoodios

🍃 AGUA PA' LA GENTE

Ladies and gents if it pleases the court
Let me plead my case, this is a motion in tort
They took the water, now they sell it back
How can corporations get away with that?
Roban el agua, roban la gente
Makin' mad money como pinche decadentes
Man, well I be feelin' ill
But without ice cubes it's kinda hard to chill
Knick knack paddy wack give a dog a bone
Hip Hop Hoodios take the microphone and say
'Yo Dre, I don't mean to annoy ya,
But you ain't no doctor, and I'm a lawyer
And I'll destroy ya,
cuz your 50 Cent piece is fiction like Tom Sawyer
Ooh, did I say a bad word?

Agua pa' la gente no es agua que se vende
It's goin', it's goin', they're takin' it 'cause it's flowin'

Agua pa' la gente no es agua que se vende
It's goin', it's goin', they're takin' it 'cause it's flowin'
Knock knock knockin' on heaven's door
Cuz they pumped the well till there was nothing more
Stole the water, sold it out like a pimp would do his daughter
Feeling crazy, my memory's hazy,
You can't stop us cuz that stuff don't phase me

A billion dollars here, a billion dollars there,
Where's my health plan? I thought you don't care
Well there's a time for that, and a time for this
This situation makes me pissed

They changed the locks and they changed the pipes,
Doubled the price and they call it nice
You're gonna catch that stray bullet
You're gonna catch what's comin' to ya
I've got my red badge of courage, Te vas a caer, a-ja!

Agua pa' la gente no es agua que se vende
It's goin', it's goin', they're takin' it 'cause it's flowin'

susana chávez-silverman

◄ KILLER CRÓNICA

Para Pablo "Hugo" Zambrano

S AQUEN USTEDES. *Killer,* por favor" dije, sin inmutarme,
a mis estudiantes. Ellos tampoco se inmutaron not even a
hair, acostumbrados a que yo invente palabras, cree inter-
lingual giros neológicos y faux traducciones sin pestañear. And
they obeyed. They took out obediently *El matadero* de Esteban
Echeverría, reconociendo estar en un curso survey de literatura
hispanoamericana, primer semestre, college norteamericano that
shall remain nameless, pero sabiendo también, que a pesar de la
canonicidad de dicha obra, they weren't in Kansas anymore, and
maybe not even in Argentina either, sino somewhere in between,
liminal, interstitial.

Y ahora, dos años después: ¿escribir o dormir? Overwhelmed by
the lassitude that only the hottest verano en 10 años — or the hottest February en 30 (according to *La Nación* y *Clarín*) — in Buenos
Aires can impose (is it *really* that hot? O es, en vez, just another
instance of typical porteño queja?), me debato listlessly entre el
sueño y la escritura. Which could bring relief? Which more plea-
sure? Which more pain?

0800-555-0016 (Oficina de Turismo); 4374-1251 (Fervor de Buenos Aires); 4687-5602 (Info. Mataderos, de 11–19 horas); 4372-5831
(Centro Cultural); 4373-5839 (Museo de Artes Arg.). All these numbers (and then some) llamamos, tratando in vain to get information
sobre la Feria de Mataderos. Como pasa muchas veces en la Argentina, we heard this cheerful but firm message: "El número que
usted ha marcado no corresponde a . . ." Finally, since our trusty

año 2000 version of "Wayne," aka *The Lonely Planet Guide to Argentina* (edited by un tal Wayne Bernhardson, Ph.D. en geografía from Berkeley no less), ponía que la Feria in Killer se daba los fines de semana, from 11–6, nos lanzamos toward Killer last Sunday, a la tarde. Era, creo, nuestro viaje más largo en taxi since arriving in Buenos Aires. No hablo de esos lonely, desperate, y desconcertantes viajes desde "cheto-ville," las northern suburbs, cuando nos transportábamos desde La Lucila, from Dayna's apartment, near the Stok family mansion en Victoria, toward the center of Buenos Aires by a combination of tren y subte, looking for an apartment to rent back in August. No. Hablo de within the boundaries de la ciudad de Buenos Aires proper.

Desplazándonos desde El Botánico de Palermo toward Mataderos, bajando por Pueyrredón, toward Independencia and then out west on J. B. Alberdi, pude confirmar una vez más y con suma satisfacción para mí (con estupefacción quizás pa' mi amigo español, Pablo) que lo que dijo Borges en los 40s is exactly (still) true: *nadie ignora que el sur empieza del otro lado de Rivadavia.* That wilder, more forlorn, more mythical geografía. Suena quizás estereotípico, but really it *is* profound and beautiful (o escuálido y cutre, según). J. B. Alberdi widens and flattens out. Not wide in that cosmopolitan, Parisian manner they fetishize here sino too flat, too much sky, after the turn-of-the-century sumptuousness of the Recoleta, Palermo, Belgrano, and Colegiales, the funky quaintness of San Telmo and Monserrat. Alberdi opens out into uncharming, jarring cobblestone where wagons once must have jostled; buildings now squat low and mean where once only dust swirled out toward the pampas.

Me recuerda los outskirts de alguna ciudad mucho más . . . qué sé sho, latinoamericana, el D.F., por ejemplo, Santiago de Chile, even Los Angeles. I feel comforted and disconcerted. I am pierced by recognition. Continuamos y continuamos. Casi diría it's getting boring, except for the occasional outrage-inducing interruption, entre parrillas populares y kioskos, de Blockbuster Video. Finalmente, after miles and miles of someplace that could be, casi, the San Fernando Valley de Califas back when I grew up in it —

with that blowsy, sun-addled energy, all TG&Y stores, no-name brand drive-in chicken places, abandoned warehouses and pumpkin patches — doblamos a la izquierda en Lisandro de la Torre, en la frontera entre los barrios de Mataderos y Liniers, frontera también con la provincia occidental de Buenos Aires. Después de pasar unos menacing, graffiti-covered tenements, un enorme parque abandonado, y una pulcra y moderna fábrica, arribamos a una somnolienta plaza, surrounded by these warehouse-looking buildings que me doy cuenta contain residential apartments indicated — and demarcated — by dingy laundry on the second floor. Hay una estatua de algún gaucho hero I am somewhat mortified not to recognize, una estatua de la Virgen de Luján in a glass cage. Tengo la repentina sensación de ese personaje de Borges, I think in "El Sur" or is it "El hombre muerto"? (Ni modo. Never have been that good with names and dates on a long-term basis.) Pero anyway, ese personaje. Cuando acaricia el gato, de estar fuera del tiempo. Or at least, I share both his awareness de que los gatos are out of time *and* the very feline out-of-timeness itself.

Al bajar del taxi it is immediately clear we've come on the wrong day. No hay feria. No hay nada. Tampoco importa. It feels slow and too bright. An oddly menacing haze. Cicadas. On the building surrounding the plaza hay letreros que anuncian la Feria de Mataderos, in circus-elegant, elaborate *filete* scroll. Doesn't say what days or times or where. Olor a parrilla, humo, algunos vecinos sitting at tables on the alcove-shrouded veredas, tomando vino tinto barato (y bueno), eating serving after serving de carne: asado, vacío, bife de chorizo, plus of course chinchulines, mollejas, morcilla, and all that other mad-vaca (or at least cholesterol-carrying) offal.

Al rato tomamos, medio wistfully, para Palermo Viejo, to return to the culinary adventures (or safety?) of that medio-*paqueto*, pseudo-multiculti barrio (nicknamed Palermo Soho by local cognoscenti: Borges se moriría, creo, to see *his* Palermo tan yuppified) just blocks from our own (just plain Palermo, a secas). Había esperado algo mucho más . . . místico, qué sé sho, olor a ganado (live, no en una parrisha . . .), real gauchos, alguna destreza equina, no sé . . .

Mataderos, The Real Thing (24-II-01)

Fortificados por un vecino de Killer (who had informed us en nuestra previa visita abortiva que la feria se daba los sábados a la noche en verano), y además habiendo preguntado a una bola de taxistas, remiseros, y vecinos, we arrived last night, medio aplastaditos con Pablo y Gabriela, habiendo subido en Palermo con un pobre taxista senior citizen NO profesional que se extravió varias veces on the way and to whom I myself had to instruct as to the recovecos de las one-way streets en Killer! This time, to our complete amazement, una animada feria artesanal y barrial bien rustic desbordó enteramente la plaza central. En un huge stand, vendían todo tipo de artículo gauchesco: sillas de montar, botas, látigos, bombachas, fustas, boleadoras, fajas bordadas a mano, chalecos, sombreros, facones, alpargatas, bridles, bits. A wonderfully acrid smell arose in the slight stir of wind que punzaba los nubarrones color plomo. Olor a humo, a parrilla, a grupa de caballo, y a montura.

Si la Feria Rural en Palermo, en agosto, había sido una magníficamente local encarnación of Flaubert's agricultural fair in *Madame Bovary* (my image will always be la insouciant and freckled, placid, slightly bovine, yet intensely lovely face of Isabelle Huppert — una de mis actrices predilectas, desde *The Lacemaker* — as Emma, en la película), Mataderos is a wonderfully *pueblo*, porteño version of the equestrian show in Florence I saw years ago, con mi hermana Laura y con mis padres. Then, wearing heavy woolens against the early spring chill and unconscious of my incipient myopia, I strained forward to distinguish the thrilling blurs as impeccably elegant Tuscan horsemen cleared the hurdles (mostly). Now, en plena negación de mi (todavía light, conste) miopía, I flat-out refuse to wear gafas en público, si no son uno de los miles de pares de designer sunglasses que uso. "Por coquetería" dirían aquí. Odio ese tan gender-loaded term. No, es que simplemente rechazo la excesiva nitidez a la que me obligan las gafas. La oftamóloga argentina se rió cuando le confesé eso; es más me felicitó la turn of phrase. Pablo entiende lo que digo: usando casi la idéntica receta, ambos preferimos la vida no corregida, with blurred edges.

Around the plaza, the restaurants that had been sleepy last Sunday, reluctantly sirviendo asado y parrishada to a few local vecinos, ahora rebosaban de vida: ofrecían everything from panchos (hot dogs), gaseosas, e "ingredientes" (stale peanuts and potato chips) to full meals. Nos sentamos con Pablo y Gaby; pedimos tres Gancio con limón, un *Ehprite* par Juvenil, y agua mineral, of course, for Gaby. Even Gaby's a veces exasperantemente decimonónico nacionalismo (y en ehto, claaaro, she's anything but alone), her standing up to sing the himno nacional and her teary eyes when the (desflecada, por cierto) bandera was raised high above the plaza, por ejemplo, couldn't dampen the surge de pura magia que sentí cuando comenzaron a tocar chacareras y los vecinos — *all* of them, fat, skinny, old, young, dark, light — comenzaron a bailar, swirling hankies adorably, provocatively above their heads con infinita pasión y skill.

Gaby insiste en que right here, even where we sit, is the real, historical place, where "Killer" took place. Le pregunto, medio tímidamente, pues where's the Bajo? Where's the river? Y ella balbucea "y . . . (pausa porteña) bueno, todo es diferente ahora; el Río ha cambiado de curso." Yeah, right . . . *No way* is this where *El matadero* took place, pienso pa' mis adentros. Pero, it doesn't matter. This feeling, these sights — avid vendors, smoke burning the eyes, music, fierce, hand-forged knives, animals, drink, was what I had been waiting almost eight months for. This was, perhaps, what I had *really* come to Argentina for. Ay dios mío, and here I go. Despite all my investigación académica en contra de los estereotipos, here I go, *tropicalizing* a los argentinos. Bueno . . . eso no es posible. OK, dale, gauchificándoles, or whatever. Quiero decir: am I not bringing back from their PoMo, CultiStudies graves the very maniqueísmos I have fought so hard against for years? What is *with* me? The old brain-body split. Pero mirá voh . . . ¿querré que los argentinos sigan siendo gauchos? Jinetes? That this sweat-, aserrín-, and meat-filled barrio fiesta be THE REAL THING? Qué me pasa? Qué boludez.

So incredibly anxiety-filled lately, I must acknowledge how much Buenos Aires is a brain-driven city, a city where everybody hyperintellectualizes, rationalizes. Pero TODOS, eh? From shopkeepers to taxi drivers and ni fucking modo los academics. Podridos! The worst of all. Not a step without asking (or explaining) why. Un vómito de palabras. Y eso que yo hablo, eh . . . ob-vio.

Me di cuenta, de golpe, de que sólo una o dos personas, desde que estoy aquí, parecen tener un verdadero, recíproco y a veces hasta pasional interes en la plática de sus interlocutores, parecen siquiera darse cuenta de que la conversación is a two-way street, joder! La curiosidad, la curiosidad les falta, sustituida por el miedo, quizás. La aprensión. Suspicion. En general, hacen una perfunctory question, ¿de dónde sos? (used principalmente as a way to segue into elaborate stories about *their* ancestors, usually Italian) and then they're OFF! Like a pack of galgos chasing the lure, que la crisis económica, que la poesía no se publica no se vende no se lee que los políticos ladrones, *coimeros,* lavadores de dinero que el calor que ehtoy tan mal, sabéh? que I've gotta get out of here gotta get out . . . It hits me right smack in the face, por primera vez, que quizás mucho de lo que escribió Alejandra Pizarnik (quizás — probablemente — sin querer) *is* quintessentially Argentine after all, like this: "El tesoro de los piratas enterrado en mi primera persona del singular." But . . . (pausa porteñísima) am *I* any different? Have I ever been? ¿Fui argentina en una vida pasada, o qué onda?

Lined up al lado de la vereda, crowded right up against the ramshackle announcer's platform (a mí los caballos siempre me han inspirado una mezcla de admiración y terror, tipo *Equus*), we wait for the contestants in the sortija-race to assemble. Los jinetes, vestidos de riguroso gaucho-ensemble: bombachas, faja, blusa blanca y chaleco negro, sombrero afelpado, boots and spurs. Many with the facón thrust into the faja. Vienen a caballo to sign themselves up with the announcer. Grupas, pezuñas, nervous liquid eyes, all shifting hooves and quivering flesh just inches from us. No entiendo por qué no estoy más aterrada. A chunky beige and white dappled bay, ridden by an equally portly older gaucho, está nervioso, skittish. Stomping, snorting, breaking into a furious run, bowing and bucking, head up, eyes rolling. We are right beside the finish line, una especie de construcción con un little stick hanging down in the middle, de la cual pende una sortija que el jinete tiene que stab with a stick as his horse rushes under the construction. Nos reímos de lo imposible que parece. Son como unos diez jinetes (una es mujer), y cada uno tendrá unas ocho tandas.

Sin demasiado fanfare, far down the cobblestone, sawdust-covered street, esuchamos the sudden, tremendous gathering of force mientras el primer jinete, un gaucho mayor pero con cierto *morbo canchero*, espolea a su rather ordinary-looking mount. In a split second he is under the ring; extiende su palito confidently, and he's got it. Todo es demasiado rápido for our urban eyes; creo que ni nos habríamos dado cuenta de su contundente triunfo si no fuera por los wild aplausos del público y los gritos del announcer. Le siguen otros jinetes menos showy y — por cierto — mucho menos diestros. Nobody else gets it for a while. La mujer is slow, slow and hesitant y siento vergüenza ajena as I hear her emotionally urging her steed on (versus el estoico, concentrado silencio que presentan los machos). Parece casi slow motion compared to the others. Qué pena.

Observo un grupo de rather West Virginia-ish children playing together, trepados a la plataforma del announcer. Todos se conocen aquí. El announcer agarra a una, una niñita rubia de Down's syndrome, y la coloca ante el micrófono. Papito, Papi, she bellows, mi papiiiito. And sure enough, para relevar al *sortijero*, aquí viene Daddy, un fornido cowboy bigotudo montado en un commanding cinammon-colored steed, blowing kisses to his offspring. De repente, about 50 yards away, a huge wheat-colored stallion goes crazy, y acomete contra el público. Instinctively, I shove the Juvenile toward the vereda (él ya está más que aburrido, Mom, there's horseshit everywhere, this is boooring . . . se queja, not even realizing he could be in imminent danger) and move myself, casi detrás de la flimsy plataforma. El rogue horse spins and thrashes, hooves clicking sharp, bucking, nearly throwing his rider against the run-down wall of a building.

El único otro jinete notable, además del primero (que logra ensortijar su palito al menos dos veces más), es un delicado adolescente de unos 14 o 15 años quizás, riding an equally petite palomino. An incredible clattering of hooves announces him, such smallness in such an intense burst of speed. Just feet before the ring, el joven se pone de pie en los estribos, standing completely upright one perfect second extiende el palo y *zas*, he has it. El truco is not *only* to get the ring on the stick but also not to let it fly off (which it does with disheartening regularity) and, of course, not to fall off the horse.

It is late en la sultry noche porteña de barrio. We begin to walk away, right next to the foam-flecked horses (they sweat right down to their hooves; rico el olor). Nos damos cuenta de que la perspectiva desde el comienzo de la carrera es, si cabe, even more thrilling. From here, we can sense the anticipation of riders and their mounts; the horses turn and twitch, reluctant or bored, y los jinetes intentan contenerlos, inspirarlos. They take off like a shot, four legs pumping together, rider crouched down on the haunches and then rising up, some of them, nearly vertical. Algunos caballos fustigados to within an inch of their lives, it seems — *thwack* se escucha el crop — mientras otros run like hell, simplemente porque sí. No látigo required.

The dancers have moved from chacarera and samba to tango now; la plaza está más atestada que nunca. The night is just beginning para los vecinos de Mataderos, but an hour-long taxi ride awaits us (thrill of his life pal conservative, father of "three non-drug-taking teens" taxista que nos ha tocado). From the end of the earth — or at least, the end of Capital Federal — up through all the suburban and sleepy residential barrios that begin with "Villa," dropping off Gaby in Villa Urquiza, and finally back to Palermo. Palermo a secas. Our Palermo. Pero that ride, like they say, es otra historia.

26 febrero 2001
Buenos Aires

giannina braschi

PELOS EN LA LENGUA

EL BILINGÜISMO es una estética bound to double business. O, tis most sweet when in one line two crafts directly meet. To be and not to be. Habla con la boca llena and from both sides of its mouth. Está con Dios y con el diablo. Con el punto y con la coma. Es un purgatorio, un signo gramatical intermedio, entre heaven and earth, un semicolon entre la independencia y la estadidad, un estado libre asociado, un mamarracho multicultural. No tiene cláusulas ni subterfugios, no anda con gríngolas ni con muletas, no es artrítico, no se queja — aúlla como un perro al infinito y pide maná del cielo que caiga como lluvia — no se ahoga en un vaso de agua, no deja que le doren la píldora — no anda con yeso, saltando como un güimo con muletas de aquí pá allá — no es el canario que se balancea en el columpio dentro de la jaula comiendo los pistachos — se ha ido y se sigue yendo de todas las jaulas como Pedro por su Casa y no ha vuelto a mirar hacia atrás. No tiene 10 mandamientos porque no tiene pelos en la lengua, pero tiene huevos — yo los he venido poniendo desde toda mi obra que es una sola — y la llamo el manifiesto de los huevos poéticos — se hace mostrando los huevos, metiendo la pata, pisseando aquí y pisseando allá. Nace del fuego popular, del pan, de la tierra, y de la libertad. Es un perro realengo atravesando un puente entre el norte y el sur, entre el siglo XX y el siglo XXI, entre Segismundo y Hamlet, entre Neruda y Whitman, entre Dickinson y Sor Juana, entre Darío y Stein, entre Sarmiento y Melville — entre los dos yo's en choque está mi *Yo-Yo Boing!*

FRONTERAS

juan felipe herrera

❧ EXILES

and I heard an unending scream piercing nature.
— FROM THE DIARY OF EDVARD MUNCH, 1892

At the Greyhound bus stations, at airports, at silent wharfs
the bodies exit the crafts. Women, men, children; cast out
from the new paradise.

They are not there in the homeland, in Argentina, not there
in Santiago, Chile; never there no more in Montevideo,
    Uruguay,
and they are not here

in *America*

They are in exile: a slow scream across a yellow bridge
the jaws stretched, widening, the eyes multiplied into blood
orbits, torn, whirling, spilling between two slopes; the sea, black,
swallowing all prayers, shadeless. Only tall faceless figures
of pain flutter across the bridge. They pace in charred suits,
the hands lift, point and ache and fly at sunset as cold dark
birds. They will hover over the dead ones: a family shattered
by military, buried by hunger, asleep now with the eyes burning
echoes calling *Joaquín, María, Andrea, Joaquín, Joaquín, Andrea,*

en exilio

From here we see them, we the ones from here, not there or
    across,

only here, without the bridge, without the arms as blue liquid
quenching the secret thirst of unmarked graves, without
our flesh journeying refuge or pilgrimage; not passengers
on imaginary ships sailing between reef and sky, we that die
here awake on Harrison Street, on Excelsior Avenue clutching
the tenderness of chrome radios, whispering to the saints
in supermarkets, motionless in the chasms of playgrounds,
searching at 9 A.M. from our third-floor cells, bowing mute,
shoving the curtains with trembling speckled brown hands.
    Alone,
we look out to the wires, the summer, to the newspapers wound
in knots as matches for tenements. We that look out from
our miniature vestibules, peering out from our old clothes,
the father's well-sewn plaid shirt pocket, an old woman's
oversized wool sweater peering out from the makeshift kitchen.
We peer out to the streets, to the parades, we the ones from here
not there or across, from here, only here. Where is our exile?
Who has taken it?

stephanie elizondo griest

❧ LA EXTRANJERA

A FTER THAT NIGHT with Yuer in Tiananmen, I hit the road with hopes of finding a new life plan. But absolute freedom can be as paralyzing as confinement when you don't know what you want. I spent June and July exploring Mongolia, Uzbekistan, and Kyrgyzstan by jeep, horse, and foot and made it to Moscow in time to catch the Rolling Stones in concert. My old stomping grounds had changed more in my two-year absence than Corpus had in twenty. There were gleaming new shopping malls, richly restored cathedrals, Internet cafés, and trendy bars and restaurants staffed by *devushki* who were downright cordial. People looked better, too, more stylish and sophisticated. But while thrilling to reunite with friends like Elena and Valera, there wasn't terribly much for me to *do* there. I filled the days designing a press kit for a newspaper for the homeless and volunteering at a soup kitchen, wondering, "What next?"

Then, on August 17, Russia's currency collapsed. Bank lines grew longer as the exchange rate of the ruble plummeted further with each passing day. When rumors started spreading about ATM machines closing and Elena cut a hole in their mattress to store their American dollars, it seemed time to go. After a pit stop in East Berlin, I flew out to Istanbul with grand ambitions of selling carpets by day and belly dancing by night. Five days into my stay, however, my passport, credit cards, money, traveler's checks, and driver's license disappeared from the thigh pouch in which they'd been sealed for months. Exactly how remains a mystery — the police said someone probably threw a powder in my eyes that knocked me out while they mugged me — but I took it as a sign that my destiny awaited elsewhere.

Colombia, to be precise.

That's right. Whether out of love, loneliness, or just plain stupidity, I decided to give Mario — the full-blooded, soccer-playing, coffee-picking, sign-of-the-crossing Latino who decimated my heart — another chance. He had visited me in Asia before I departed and left an invitation burning in my ears: "Come to Bogotá and we'll open a coffeehouse together." You can't travel with a man on your mind: Mario so consumed my thoughts, I started passing up world-renowned museums to sit in Internet cafés and have cybersex. Resolving that the only way to ward off life's regrets is to pursue any and all question marks, I flew out to Colombia and discovered a stunning country locked in civil war: roads blocked, military posted, eyes untrusting and fearful. But this very real human drama was overshadowed by the one that promptly erupted between Mario and me. He'd drink, I'd yell, we'd fight, he'd leave, I'd cry, he'd return, we'd make love, and so forth. Looking back, I believe he *wanted* me to hate him, but nothing he did worked — not even abandoning me on a junkie-infested beach in Cartagena at one in the morning. In fact, the worse he treated me, the more determined I became to stay. It was such a beautifully fucked-up story, I wanted to see how he'd hurt me next.

So when Mario suggested we both move back to Austin to "start over again," I agreed. I got a job at the Associated Press, signed a lease, and happily prepared our love nest, envisioning late-night candlelit dinners, lazy Sunday brunches, and sex whenever I wanted. He arrived a few weeks later with plans of enrolling in culinary school (presumably to learn how to bake our future café's pastries). But our first night together in my new apartment, he sat me down, looked deep into my eyes, and said: "Stephanie, this isn't going to work . . ."

That's right. He dumped me. Again.

And after my contract ended with AP, I wound up back in Corpus Christi. At the washed-up age of twenty-five. Living at home with my parents. Lacking even the wheels to go cruising through the parking lot at Taco Bell.

Then came the fortuitous call from my good friend Machi, who was back in town for the holidays. Machi was the sort of Texan who wore cowboy boots under secondhand Levi's and drove a beat-up truck to yoga class. We first met at a conference for Hispanic journalists back in college, where we bonded over our substandard Spanish. She'd made amends over the years, however, winning a fellowship to study in Mexico and then immersing herself in the Latino community for her documentaries. We talked for hours that night, and before we hung up, she brought up the rapidly approaching end of the millennium. How was I bringing in 2000?

"Probably watching the Dick Clark special." I sighed. "You?"

"I'm thinking about going to Cuba."

"But . . . how would you get there?"

"Through Mexico."

"But . . . where would you stay?"

"In somebody's house."

"But . . . it's illegal!"

"Only if you get caught."

"But . . ." I stopped as it dawned on me that I had been jetting halfway around the world to see red when it was only ninety miles away. "Can I come, too?"

Though I had lived within 150 miles of Mexico most of my life and had family in Monterrey, I only vaguely knew of its border towns, which — from my limited vantage point — consisted primarily of sock-and-sandaled tourists haggling over souvenirs, senior citizens hoarding cheap prescription drugs, and college kids slamming tequila shots. So it was a treat to experience the country's interior as Machi and I worked our way south toward Cuba by bus, from the frenetic pace of Mexico City to the tranquility of Tepoztlán. Yet being around *puros mexicanos* — real Mexicans — made me feel grossly incompetent. Every word I had ever uttered in Russian or Mandarin had seemed like a trophy to me, something I had sought, studied, and conquered. In Spanish, however, my speech felt pocked with failures, as though everything I managed to say were an admission of what more I could not. Though I had invested time in the language that year, studying from workbooks and conversing with my *tías*, I dreaded using it — largely out of fear of the direction a conversation with a *mexicano* might take. *"¿Tu mamá es mexicana? Híjale,* what the hell happened to *you?"*

Machi, on the other hand, was eager to use the Spanish she'd learned over the past few years. She became our spokeswoman in virtually every transaction, from small talk to business negotiations, while I cowered behind, wishing a Kyrgyz shepherd would ramble by so I'd have someone to talk to, feeling more like an *extranjera* — or foreigner — than ever before.

After a few days of wandering around, Machi bargained a great deal on airline tickets at a travel agency in Cuernavaca and we jetted off to Havana. Somewhere over the Gulf of Mexico, paranoia struck. True, upward of fifty thousand Americans sneak into Cuba illegally every year, but it does entail a degree of risk. Under the Trading with the Enemy Act, any American caught spending money in Communist Cuba without Uncle Sam's explicit permission could — in theory — be slapped with fines of up to $250,000 and ten years in prison. We were also a little nervous about losing our passports. We couldn't expect much sympathy from the U.S. Interests Section (America's version of an embassy in Havana) if we weren't supposed to be there in the first place, could we? And what if we ran out of money? American traveler's checks and credit cards don't work in Cuba. We might have to sell our belongings (or our bodies) in a gutter somewhere.

By the time we landed at José Martí International, our nerves had seriously frayed. Machi's personal breaking point came when the airline attendant bade everyone *hasta luego* when they exited the plane — except her. "She took one look at me and said, '*Ten cuidado*' — Be careful!" she hissed. "What did she mean by that?!"

As we got in line at passport control, my entire body began to tremble. Cuban control officers supposedly didn't stamp U.S. passports when asked nicely, but what if mine misunderstood? Or asked for a bribe? Or had a vendetta against Americans? When our turn came, I pushed Machi ahead. She took a deep breath and, with a toss of her silky black hair, marched up to the window and relinquished her blue booklet. *Blam-blam* went the control man. Did he stamp it, did he stamp it? Machi grabbed her papers and disappeared through a little white door without looking back.

Great. My turn. My stomach now churning upon itself, I approached the booth and handed my papers to the officer, who had his back turned to me. *"Por favor, no pone un . . . ,"* I began the carefully rehearsed phrase. Then he turned around. His eyes were amber, his chin was cleft, his skin was a deep shade of copper. I smiled shyly. He gave a sideways grin. Then his hands — hidden beneath the counter — made that horrifying *blam-blam* sound. I hyperventilated. Did he stamp it, did he stamp it?

"No te preocupes, mi amor," he whispered as he returned my unmarked passport. Don't worry about it, honey. Then he winked and buzzed me into one of the few remaining bastions of communism in the world. It smelled of salt and sea and sex.

Before leaving South Texas, I blew $70 in long-distance calls to Cuba tracking down some guy named Jorge who — according to a friend of a friend — rented out a room in his house to foreigners at a fraction of the cost of a hotel. When we showed up on his doorstep in Centro Habana that afternoon, however, he had forgotten our reservation and rented our room out to some Swedes.

"Where are we supposed to stay?" we wailed.

"No problema," he promised, then shifted his eyes into the street as a caramel-skinned, spandex-clad woman in her early forties sauntered by. "Cecilia! Do you have any room for these girls?"

"¿Sí, cóma no?" she replied. Of course.

Machi and I exchanged glances. Could we really just go home with a random passerby? Seeing few alternatives, we followed her to a three-story nineteenth-century house regally designed with high ceilings, carved wooden doors, ornate light fixtures, and grilled ironwork but modestly kept with humble furniture and peeling paint. Vintage Chinese bicycles leaned against the outer wall of the courtyard while two floors' worth of neighbors' laundry dripped dry from above. Cecilia opened a padlock hanging on a door and let us peek inside. For $12 a night, she offered a king-sized bed, a dresser, a vase of plastic roses, and a bathroom with a sliver of soap. While we deliberated, she darted off to the kitchen and returned with two steaming glasses of coffee. *"Es negro como la piel y dulce como una muchacha,"* she quipped. It's as black as skin and sweet as a girl.

It tasted so good, it was also the deal maker. "We'll take it."

After stashing our stuff away, we ventured out to explore our new 'hood. With the exception of a 1956 Chevrolet carcass rotting on a curb, there wasn't a car in sight, enabling us to walk directly in the street instead of just along it. The residential area quickly gave way to a commercial strip where a bakery featured bread loaves as long and wide as the pickets of a fence, and a pharmacy sold medicine bottles with handwritten wrappers glued upon them. A dark, musty warehouse served as a melancholic farmers' market, where vendors sat listlessly behind bins of scrawny yuccas, plantains, guavas, and chiles and a butcher sold ham by the slice. Across the street, a long-lashed woman in a window cried out, *"Cerrrr-veeeee-zaaaa!"* until a customer stopped by. She whipped out a glass, poured him some beer, and plunked it on the sill; he chugged it down, wiped his lip, slipped her some pesos, and continued down the street as she washed the glass, wiped it dry, and resumed her barter cry: *"Cerrrr-veeeee-zaaaaa!"* Another vendor — a gorgeous old man in a beret — had scrawled his croquette menu on a piece of cardboard with a Nike decal stuck on it. When I pointed at the brazen capitalist symbol, he grinned good-naturedly and said: *"Es bonito."* It's pretty.

Up ahead glimmered the Atlantic Ocean, bordered by the famous stretch of limestone boulevard known as the Malecon. Locals strolled upon it in droves, many wearing T-shirts depicting a sullen Elián González crouched behind a chain-link fence. (The child refugee had been plucked from the sea two months before and was still living with his Miami relatives.) Lovers tangled into impassioned embraces while children dangled their legs over the seawall and portly women sold roasted peanuts inside rolled-up newspapers. We passed some fishermen just as one got a nibble and cheered him on as he reeled in a foot-long fish. After ripping the hook from the fish's gaping mouth, he jumped atop the seawall and treated the harbor to a victory dance punctuated with an energetic pelvic thrust.

We hadn't been on the Malecón five minutes when two guys our age asked to join us. Mine, Raul, introduced himself as a saxophonist from Camagüey and politely inquired about me. Uncertain how American journalists would be received here — particularly in light of the Elián fiasco — Machi and I had selected new identities on the plane ride over: Canadian grad students from Toronto and "some town out west you've probably never heard of." This wasn't the first time I'd lied about my nationality: after getting attacked by that *babushka* in the Moscow subway, I'd often claimed a Mexican heritage. That alibi wouldn't have worked in a Spanish-speaking nation, of course, but I thought my country's northern neighbor would make an equally good cover — until the interrogations started. Raul's brother, as it turned out, had recently opened a salsa discotheque in Toronto. Had I heard of it? What type of neighborhood was it in? What other good clubs were in the area? He planned on applying for a Canadian visa himself. What were Canada's immigration laws concerning Cubans? Could he enroll in a university right away? What about health care?

I answered his questions as vaguely as possible and then tossed one back at him: where could I buy one of those Elián T-shirts?

"Buy one?!" He laughed. "Nobody buys them. They are a gift from, you know . . ." He stroked his chin as though it had just sprouted a beard — Cuba-speak for Fidel Castro.

"Canadians think Elián should return home to Cuba," I volunteered.

"I don't," he said. "There is nothing for him to eat here. There is no freedom. There is no future. He's better off in Miami."

His frankness surprised me, but when I said as much, he shrugged. "Cubans aren't encouraged to talk with foreigners, but we do it anyway."

"Isn't that kind of risky?"

"How else are we supposed to know what's going on in the world? Our papers are censored; our media is controlled." He paused to nod at a police officer standing a few feet away. "You see that cop? If you told him that I was bothering you, he would take me to jail. Foreigners are treated better than Cubans — in our own country."

This was the open sort of conversation I'd dreamed of in Beijing, but having it my first hour in Havana made me nervous. I glanced back at the cop. Could he hear us?

"But these days will soon be over," Raul continued. "There is already a capitalist revolution under way. It won't be much longer before things change for good. I just hope I'm in Canada when it does. So, what do *you* think about Cuba?"

By that point, we had reached the Hotel Deauville, where friends of Machi's were staying. As she breezed into the lobby to find them, I turned to Raul. What was happening here? Had the Committees for the Defense of the Revolution (Castro's neighborhood watchdog groups) and the state security system caused Cubans to distrust one another as much as the Cultural Revolution had the Chinese and the KGB had the Russians, making foreigners a safe, sympathetic ear? Or did Raul have a more sinister motive? Soviet spies often tried to trick foreigners into bad-mouthing their system so they could get them kicked out of their country — did they do that here?

"It's more complex than I realized," I stated lamely, then bade him good night and walked inside the hotel.

Raul and his buddy watched me for a moment, then headed back to the Malecón. Another group of foreigners awaited.

lalo lopez alcaraz

LA CUCARACHA

LA CUCARACHA
LALO ALCARAZ ©94
S.O.S! SPRAY ON SPICKS! KEEPS ON WORKING FOR UP TO 2 ELECTIONS!
FRaid
ANTI IMMIGRANT BORDER SPRAY
187 FOR ME
INS AND GOP APPROVED!
9 OUT OF 10 RACIST POLITICIANS PREFER FRAID™ ANTI-IMMIGRANT SPRAY

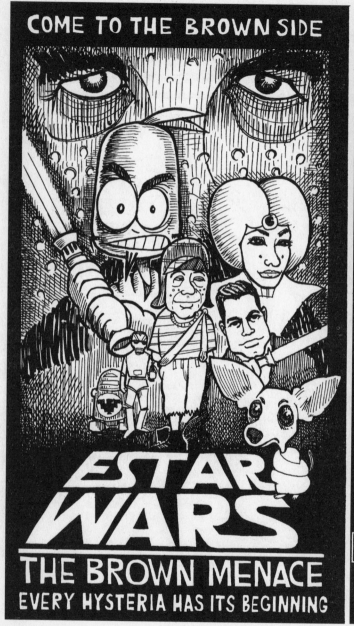

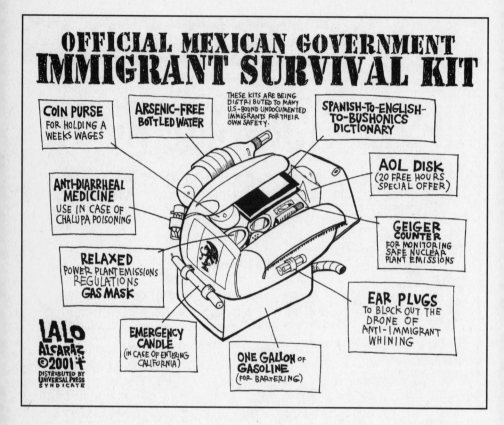

OFFICIAL MEXICAN GOVERNMENT IMMIGRANT SURVIVAL KIT

COIN PURSE
FOR HOLDING A WEEKS WAGES

ARSENIC-FREE BOTTLED WATER

THESE KITS ARE BEING DISTRIBUTED TO MANY U.S.-BOUND UNDOCUMENTED IMMIGRANTS FOR THEIR OWN SAFETY.

SPANISH-TO-ENGLISH-TO-BUSHONICS DICTIONARY

AOL DISK (20 FREE HOURS SPECIAL OFFER)

ANTI-DIARRHEAL MEDICINE
USE IN CASE OF CHALUPA POISONING

GEIGER COUNTER
FOR MONITORING SAFE NUCLEAR PLANT EMISSIONS

RELAXED
POWER PLANT EMISSIONS REGULATIONS
GAS MASK

EAR PLUGS
TO BLOCK OUT THE DRONE OF ANTI-IMMIGRANT WHINING

LALO ALCARAZ ©2001
DISTRIBUTED BY UNIVERSAL PRESS SYNDICATE

EMERGENCY CANDLE
(IN CASE OF ENTERING CALIFORNIA)

ONE GALLON OF GASOLINE
(FOR BARTERING)

U.S. TO OFFER IMMIGRATION INCENTIVES
FOR TERRORISM INFORMATION

hernandez bros.

THE KKK COMES TO HOPPERS

❦ THE PARROT CLUB MENÚ

L OCATED ON 363 Calle Fortaleza, in Old San Juan, Puerto
Rico, the Parrot Club is a restaurant on the edge. Designed in
blue, yellow, and peach, with a torch-lit courtyard, it offers its
clientele a tropical setting to enjoy the Nuevo Latino cuisine seasoned with local ingredients. What makes the place unique,
though, is its approach to Spanglish, which, according to the owners, is "the most fun way to describe our food." The menu features
an array of dishes — fresh ceviche, deep-fried crab cakes served
over a light passion fruit vinaigrette, a Caribbean-style flank steak,
and smoked chicken and goat cheese salad tossed with sweet plantains — described in a *mezcla sabrosa* of Spanish and English.

The Parrot Club

Cena — Dinner

*Welcome to The Parrot Club! Our dream was to create a place where
friends gather to taste exciting food, charlar, and tomarse un buen drink,
to take Latino into the nuevo millennium with familiar and new flavors,
classic latino music, and hospitality in an old and new setting . . .*

*The menu you are about to read is written in Spanglish, which we
felt was the most fun way to describe our food. If you need a translation
either way, please ask the server. All Parrot Club servers speak Spanglish
fluently! Buen provecho!*

Platitos y Ensaladas

Soup del día
$5

Mixed chips de viandas
$7.50

Our ceviches . . .

Fresh Fish Ceviche Nuevo Latino
$9

Vasito de Smoked Carrucho en Escabeche
$9

Veracruz-Style Shrimp y Scallop Ceviche Coctèl
$12

Ceviche Trio con Veggie Chips
$28

Our hot specialties . . .

Traditional Parrot Club Crabcakes Caribeños
$7

Spiced Calamari Frito con Chimichurri Aioli
$8

Ropa Vieja Blue Corn Tostada Napoleon
$12

Hot Bocalaitos Served with a Spicy Cool Crab Salad
$10

Risotto Nuevo Latino con Chicharrones del País
$9.50

Our salads . . .

Smoked Pollo & Goat Salad con Amarillos in Vinagre de Jerez
$12

Ensalada Caesar con Parmesan Fresco y Mofongo Croutons
$9

Ensalada Mixta con Warm Queso del País y Caribbean Vinaigrette
$8

Platos principales

Nuestra Famosa Blackened Tuna in a Dark Rum Sauce with
Orange Essence, Yuca Mahada, y Viandas
$24

Lamb Shank Barbacoa con Savory Ravioles de Queso
Cotija y Amarillos
$25

Seared Medallones de Mero (Grouper) con Aji Tapenade,
Roasted Red Peppers, y Papitas Nuevo Lyonnaise
$26

Grilled Latino Flank Steak con Timbale de Amarillos y
Portobellos, Tomato Chimichurri, and Viandas
$21

Tamarindo-Glazed Grilled Salmon con Sabana Salad y
Roasted Ajo-Apio Mash
$22

Pork Carne Frita con Guava Rum Glaze, Fufú
Cubano, y Chayote Slaw
$18

Jumbo Spiced Camarones (Shrimp) Pan Fried Servidos con
Bacon-Tomato Salsa, Arroz Blanco, y Jícama Salad
$26

Seared Black Sea Bass (Robalo) con Langosta, Leek y Scallop
Confit, over a Mofonguito con Ajo Essence
$27

Grilled 16 oz. Ribeye Steak Topped with Spiced Latino Butter
$24

Chicken Pinchos con Arroz Guisado, Habichuelas Negras,
y Chile Colorado BBQ Sauce
$18

The Parrot Club Torre Vegetariano
$16

salvador plascencia

❧ THE PEOPLE OF PAPER

Cameroon

She sat alone in her upstate New York apartment holding a jar of honeybees, pressing stingers into her forearms. At night, when the poison brought the fever, she peeled off her shirt and pulled down her panties, stretching, her feet pushing Saturn from the bed and onto the floor.

Underneath the bed: shoes, tangled bras, the smell of loneliness, and small mounds of spent and desiccated bees.

"Cami, what are these?" Saturn asked, holding two curled insects in the cup of his hand.

"I don't know," she said.

Cameroon kept the bees a secret, hiding them deep in her closet and covering the jars with towels. In the bathtub, while pretending to shave, she plucked the stingers from her arms. And the fever that kept her hot and sweating she blamed on the pneumonia she could never shake.

But at night a faint buzzing emanated from the closet doors. She slept, her fever warming the sheets and walls, melting the ice on the windows. As cliffs of snow crashed down, Saturn stepped out of bed, took the jars from the closet, and filled them with water, drowning all of the insects. In the morning, when she awoke, Cameroon tried to salvage the bees, but the stingers were limp and soft, unable to stab, and the poison she tried to suck from the ends was diluted by water and traces of honey.

"No more bees, I promise," she would say, the heat of her fever increasing, forming a halo at the crown of her head. And so Saturn lay in bed with her for weeks, holding her, feeling her body shake, and cleaning mouthfuls of chewed bread and fruit she had tried to eat. He brewed manzanilla tea and rubbed arnica cream on her belly and breasts; he squeezed out the thorns, using his teeth to pluck those that had gone deep into her meat.

The halo finally faded. Saturn left the room, only for a couple of hours, walking outside and over gray and salted snow, trailing dirt and melting ice into the supermarket, through the dairy aisles.

"I could have built you bookshelves," he thought, pulling the dedication page from his pocket, looking at the grocery list he had scribbled below the typed text.

He crossed "potato bread" from the list and placed the loaf in his basket. He crossed out other things too.

~~eggs~~

~~milk~~

"And for Liz ~~who taught me that we are all of paper~~," and then wrote:

"For Liz who fucked everything."

While Saturn unloaded his basket and the cashier tallied the items, Cameroon was in the apartment dialing. Twenty minutes, they said. And then they came, dressed in their wire veils, still holding their just-extinguished bee smokers. They traded two Mason jars of honeybees for three twenty-dollar bills.

This time she was careless — she made no attempt to hide any of it. He discovered dead bees on the carpet and in the trash bin, and others crawling up the curtains. He said nothing. He lay in bed, his back turned to her, the buzzing spilling from the Mason jar. Cameroon slowly silencing the whole jar, pocking her arms with bees pressed to her skin, singeing her hair, warming the room with the glow of her halo.

Natalia

Natalia had only one request: she asked that on their honeymoon Quinones would take her to a place where she could touch and eat

real snow. She had tasted shaved ice, covered in eggnog and sprin-
kled with crushed almonds and cinnamon, but machine-made ice
was never as soft or delicious as the flakes of a fresh flurry that
landed on her tongue as she watched the roaring falls of Niagara.

After thirty-five years of the perpetual summer of Ensenada,
Natalia wanted to feel the joy of wearing a sweater and drinking a
pot of hot coffee. She wanted, for once, to lie with Quinones and
not have the sheets turn into sweat rags; and she wanted goose
bumps that were raised not by embarrassment or nails scratching
on blackboards.

"We have lots of winters to make up for," she told Quinones.

Quinones had always known that he loved Natalia, but it was
not until he gave up sunbathing, the taste of tropical langostas, and
the sands of a warm coast that he understood the price of love.
What was supposed to be a weeklong honeymoon in the cold country was extended into a fifty-year residency on the frozen banks of
the Georgian Bay.

Jonathan Mead

After three years of searching, Jonathan Mead finally located his
daughter. The investigator provided him with the phone number
and descriptions of her hair color and its length (black and to mid-
back) and estimates of her height: around 5'6", 5'8", always wears
sneakers, except during heavy snow.

He had not seen his daughter since she was seven, and now, sixteen years later, he wanted what every remorseful and estranged father wants: to reconcile with the child he had abandoned. Jonathan
Mead held the piece of paper, imagining what it would feel like to
dial the number and hear his daughter's voice. He practiced what
he would say and the tone of voice in which he would speak, and
then began dialing.

Cameroon

When the first installment came, sealed with the saliva of million-
aires, Saturn did not use the money to fight Federico de la Fe and

EMF. Instead he forged war reports and sent them at regular inter-
vals to New York City, and he used the endowment to tend to Cameroon's bee stings and to alleviate his own sadness.

He filled a thermos with manzanilla tea and gave Cameroon two
jars of arnica cream that she packed between her sweaters and
pants next to an empty Mason jar. The doctors and curanderos recommended repose and wet towels — that is how you fight the
swelling and muscle cramps, they said — but Saturn opted for
the road. A route with no honey crates or beekeepers. But there
was another agenda: he knew that the true mission of Napoleon
Bonaparte was not always to conquer, but to travel. To see foreign
lands and forget the women who had hurt him. On the trip Saturn
would concentrate. He would touch Cameroon and look at her, calling her by the name that was hers. He would write his grocery list
on different paper, on sheets of paper that did not allude to anything but toiletries and edibles. He would not think of her or of the
white boy who colonized his memories. He who had spread his im-
perialism everywhere. All over her, spilling it on her chest and
stomach, coating her lips and throat, lining the esophagus and in-
testines.

"There will be no more of you," he said as if she were there.
"Only Cami, only Cami."

The first stop on Cameroon and Saturn's journey was what was ini-
tially known as the seventh wonder of the world but had been de-
moted by auditors to the ninth position, displaced by the Flamingo
Casino and the city of Needles, which claimed the largest thermometer on earth.

It was from the window of their hotel that Cameroon and Saturn
watched the crashing waters of the ninth wonder of the world, the
sound barely muffled by the soundproof windows of their honeymoon suite.

"People actually spend their honeymoons here?" she asked.

"Honeymooners and tourists," Saturn said.

"So what are we?"

"Just passing through."

~ ~ ~

When he went down on Cameroon he transferred everything that he knew about love onto her, no grocery lists or white boys in his mind. Just her softness and warmth, the taste of dissolving paper absent, but she was as white as *The Book of Incandescent Light*. He dragged his tongue across her and felt nothing but smooth flesh. When he reached her ear he whispered:

"Cami, you should let it grow."

"Why?"

"It's nice to feel something."

Then it was she who went down. The taste of foreskin filled her mouth; slowly she pulled away, handling it, and then folding back skin, hurting Saturn and exposing meat. No salted milk spilled. Not until the church-sanctioned missionary position was employed and the halo, which scorched the pillows and warped the headboard, was extinguished by the sweat of their bodies, only then did his starch come forth.

Saturn had not registered with the papal embassy for years, yet he retained a very Catholic idea of love. He followed the procedures faithfully, adhering to all church recommendations and the advice his devout great-grandfather had given him: caressing and never pulling hair, pinning 'em down and mounting, rocking gently, but never pounding — unless, of course, they specifically said to do so.

"Always from the front and never call her by the name that is not her name," his great-grandfather had said. After proper love there were symptoms: a sweaty forehead; the limbs sore and bruised; a philistine rawness on the foreskin; and a nearly insatiable and debilitating appetite, a hunger that had been specially invented for postcoital love, a hunger that never came to Saturn.

Niagara Falls was only the trailhead of the honeymooners' voyage, followed by the Caledon Hills, the incline of Kolapore, the limestone caves of Kimberly, terminating at the tip of the Bruce Peninsula. At the Niagara escarpments Saturn vomited a meal he could not recall eating and Cameroon purchased a sandwich to silence the growls of her stomach and then they drank water from the glacial melts.

At the end of the honeymoon trail, on the most northern part of the Bruce Peninsula, sat El Hotel de los Novios, founded by Natalia and Quinones Hernandez — a hotel that upheld the strictest honeymooner policies, accepting only those who could provide a marriage certificate no more than two weeks old, with rare exceptions granted for paper and platinum anniversaries. But no anniversary, regardless of its years, would take precedence over those newly wed.

Using the same ream of paper on which he had forged war reports, and with the help of Cameroon's penmanship, Saturn drafted a marriage certificate that he handed over at the reception desk.

The suite had no television, only a radio with an emergency weather station and two FM channels, each playing a constant rotation of love ballads. The bed was sturdily reinforced at its legs and dip, the linens starched, and the wedding lasso that hung above the bed was braided from four strands of rope. The bathroom was equipped with a French bidet and a wood-burning boiler, in which Cameroon put too much coal, scalding her shoulders and Saturn's chest when the boiling water spat out from the showerhead.

In El Hotel de los Novios, Saturn renounced the papal guidelines, folding and stretching Cameroon. She held on to towel racks and the backs of chairs, while he pretended to be impervious to her whimpers and cries. And she, as if to reciprocate, sat on Saturn, bending him and chafing him until his skin reddened and flaked, the friction sparking a halo that would burn through the front of his pants. And as an emphatic dismissal of the Vatican dicta, Cameroon and Saturn avoided any position that even hinted at the civility of love.

And though Cameroon had said she loved Saturn, whispering it over and over while underneath him — never when on top — she went into the washroom and sat on the bidet. She tossed a small log into the boiler and when the warm water spouted from the faucet in a low voice she recited the bidet prayer:

"I'm gonna wash this man right out of my hair, I'm gonna wash this man right out of me. My apologies to the Georgian Bay where he will go."

Natalia

Natalia and Quinones dedicated their married lives to each other and hotel management. And as Francophobes, never forgiving the French invasion of Puebla, they also dedicated much of their free time to dispelling many of the aphorisms Napoleon Bonaparte had popularized. Quinones helped Natalia with the hotel duties, replenishing bundles of wood and inspecting the authenticity of the marriage certificates, and when his duties were done, he sat at his mahogany desk writing to the French Museum in Montreal and to the Parisian Hall of Archives.

While he had yet to address Bonaparte's largest claim — "I believe love to be hurtful to the world, and to the individual happiness of men. I believe, in short, that love does more harm than good" — Quinones had argued against every other Napoleonic declaration.

So when Napoleon wrote, in his diplomatic letter to Alexander I, "All women in the world would not make me lose an hour," Quinones refuted, not by citing the names of all women in the world, a list that would take three months, six days, and two hours to read, but by simply writing one name: "Marie Louise."

And in response to Napoleon's assertion that he had "autre chose à penser que l'amour," Quinones submitted photographs of the uniform Napoleon's troops had worn and a diagram of their battle formations. Every uniform bore the same decorative pin that Marie Louise had given Napoleon when they first met, and when sent to battle, the troops were always deployed in the form of her initials.

The French, as always, were unimpressed, and aside from the occasional porcelain bidet that Quinones received, packed in Parisian headlines, there was never any official acknowledgment that they had read his letters. Quinones was never discouraged. In the morning he installed the bidets in the hotel's washrooms and then returned to his desk and wrote late into the night.

Natalia's critique of Bonaparte took a more subtle form, a critique manifested in the decor and menu of the hotel. There were no vanity stools to stand on and not a single topographical map hung on the wall, and in the kitchen the cooks were forbidden from ever preparing crepes or Napoleon's favorite pastry: the mille-feuille.

Jonathan Mead

He let the phone ring once and immediately hung up the receiver. He had rehearsed what he would say, how he would say it. He would speak with regret but not guilt.

There were run-throughs and simulations. Calling his own number to hear the tone of busy signals, calling restaurants after-hours for the string of endless rings, dialing ex-wives for the click and crackle of answering machines. Old friends for the sound of voice. Wrong numbers for terse goodbyes.

Cameroon

Saturn picked up the phone. At the other end the hotel proprietor requested that Saturn come down to the front desk.

"The marriage certificate . . ."

"Yes?" Saturn said.

"I'm afraid it's false. This is a hotel for honeymooners."

Saturn did not argue. He told Cameroon to pack her bags and with bags in hand walked down to the reception desk and returned the room keys and the knotted and tangled wedding lasso.

"Nothing against you. We are not to say who is in love and who is not. We just need something official that proves it."

"I understand," Saturn said.

On the drive out of the Bruce Peninsula, the clouds collapsed, covering everything, stranding Saturn and Cameroon underneath the white. They pulled the car to the side of the road, turned the engine off, and unpacked their bags, huddling into each other and wrinkled clothes. They shivered and did not sleep.

Saturn kissed Cameroon and called her by the name that was her name and for once felt the hunger pangs that he was supposed to feel, but did not know if it was love or signs of starvation.

"Your stomach is growling. When we thaw out we'll get some food," she said, and then touched his hair.

When the snowplows and thaw came they drove past a land that had disintegrated into a thousand islands. Once over the bridge, the earth consolidated and the spring weather began to encroach, melting snow from the roof of the car. They drove for the rest of the day until they reached the city of Philadelphia.

In Philadelphia, the redness from the stings subsided and the halo on Cameroon's head completely disappeared and Saturn finished plucking the last of the remaining thorns from her body.

"Why the bees?" he asked.

She said that when one is sad there are only insects or sex.

"Honeybees or fucking," she said.

Cameroon's sadness was not a biblical one like Federico de la Fe's, but it was a sadness that could not be suppressed by fire or by honeybees or by fucking. De la Fe's sorrow ran deeper, infecting even the tiny alcoves of his lungs, but there was always the possibility of a cure — the return of Merced. But for Cameroon no returns or reconciliations were possible. No way to forget a lonely childhood and the parade of fathers who tried to have a hand not only in her rearing but also underneath the elastic and hems of her clothes.

There were no indigenous bees in Philadelphia. They were imported from the South, from the islands of the Caribbean, some from the Florida panhandle, transported in punctured shoeboxes, in jars and screened crates. And she, with her empty Mason jars, her scarf blowing, and her feet on the banks of the Delaware River, waited for the beekeepers to come. They arrived wearing their wire veils and gloves, replenished Cameroon's empty jar, and walked away.

Natalia

In the fifty-year history of El Hotel de los Novios, a history that included three expansions and four different decorating schemes, Natalia and Quinones had uncovered only three fraudulent marriage certificates.

The first, though written in careful calligraphy and stamped with the justice of the peace's seal, was brought in by a fifty-year-old man who carried his suitcases and his thirteen-year-old bride in his arms. Though the certificate was authentic, the groom could not provide identification for his bride, and Natalia and Quinones were forced to turn the couple away.

The second was an Argentine couple whose marriage certificate was written with the cheap, faint ink of squids, in a cursive so illegible that Quinones could barely make out the newlyweds' names; on the required supplementary page, the names of witnesses had been purposely obscured with bird droppings. When Quinones tried to scrape the bird shit from the parchment, the bride protested, explaining that the witnesses could not be revealed without endangering not only the lives of those listed but also those who read the names. Natalia and Quinones left the names unexposed and the certificate invalidated, referring the couple to a motel that required no documentation.

The third came in the final years of their ownership, before Natalia had begun sniffing tanning oil and importing sand and coconut milk. The certificate was printed in sterile ink, the names of Cameroon and Saturn underlined and bolded, and all the required signatures neatly written on the dotted lines. The document was so convincing that Quinones could smell the scent of holy water emanating from the paper and see the oily stains of musk left by the priest's hands. And when he saw the couple, the bride tall, her face burned by cold and wind and a halo above her, the groom short like Napoleon, holding the luggage and snow umbrella, they seemed convincingly wed. And though Natalia was suspicious of Saturn's short stature and of the red of Cameroon's arms, she gave them a room on the third floor that faced the waters of the Georgian Bay.

At first, it seemed only a typographical error, but when Quinones reread the certificate and tried to find the location of the ceremony, consulting both maps and church directories, he came to realize that the place existed only in the imagination.

Natalia would have disapproved, but Quinones did not immediately evict the couple, waiting instead until morning.

Jonathan Mead

He let the phone ring. Four times and then hung up. He dialed again, fully aware that no one would pick up, letting it ring until his ear was warm. He had placed the call three days too late. His daughter was gone, in the passenger seat of a rented Buick heading toward the ninth wonder of the world.

Cameroon

Saturn watched Cameroon as she slept. The Mason jars were empty again and her arms were freckled with the thorns of insects. Two bees buzzed around the room, another tried to untangle itself from Cameroon's now full and unshaped muff, and a pile lay on the carpet torn in half, their stingers missing.

He watched as the bee threaded its way through Cameroon's hair, emerging on her stomach. He lifted the bee by its wings and pressed it into his arm. When the poison entered his body, suddenly swelling his veins and slowing the blood, all these things disappeared from Saturn's mind:

1. The war on Federico de la Fe
2. Cameroon
3. Liz

For once in a very long time Saturn felt the singularity that children sometimes feel when they are left alone on the lawn — as if there is nothing else in the world but the softness of grass.

dagoberto gilb

TOMATO POTATOE, CHALUPA SHALOOPA

L ET ME DESCRIBE plate #3 at every local Authenic Mexican Restaurant 50 years ago. Imagine an oval, particularly thick ceramic plate being hustled over straight out of an oven, so hot it can only be delivered with a potholder and a warning to never ever touch — it's a hot, hot plate each recipient, individually, will be uniquely told — that is set down a distance from the edge of the table so it won't burn chest hairs, or whatever, and the clothes in between. The refried beans are gurgling and the "Spanish" rice is reconstituting into its dry grain state, the peas and carrot chunks mutating away from the vegetable category, and the red sauce of the enchiladas is bubbling, the yellow and white cheese topping still sizzling from being on the verge of burning. Wait long enough so the plate can be handled. Then, go on, tip it sideways. Tip it upside down. Toss it to practice dexterity, letting it roll over and over, and catch it. Spin it on a finger like a top, food side down, or roll it on its edge across a long banquet table. Yes, the tablespoon of shredded iceberg lettuce and that thin, very thin slice of a too-green red tomato — colorful garnish — that nobody ever eats anyway, both of them wilted and dehydrated, will fall off. But the rest? Nope. It's a Mexican Frisbee!

The Mexican plate #3 was — and of course still is, more often than not — what Americans were served at Mexican restaurants miles north of the entire stretch of the border: tortillas or masa fried or soaked into lots of heavy oil or kneaded in lard, the least expensive ground chuck beef, fatty colored cheese packaged in huge, discount blocks. It is this food that Glen Bell, World War II Marine Corps veteran and owner of Bell's Drive-In hot dog stand ate and loved and riffed on until, in San Bernardino, Redlands, and Riverside, a desert agricultural region of Southern California, he established the first three fast-food taco stands featuring Mexican food, Taco Tia, which eventually was transformed into the mega-chain all America knows for its ad slogans "Run for the Border" and "*Yo quiero* Taco Bell" and its Chihuahua dog, not to mention those famed crackly tacos.

I remember when I first encountered what might be called hippie "fusion" Mexican food. I was in Isla Vista, California, a university community where a Bank of America was burned in a student riot that brought out the National Guard in 1970, an era and community where Mr. Kinko opened his first copy shop and that incubated the health and organic food rebellion, believing both would lead to the political contrary of what are now corporate enterprises. For someone like me who'd been raised in the big city, near rainbow-streaked, inky pools left from leaking oil pans, distracted by moonlit twinkles of broken half-pints and beer bottles smashed against a curb, the only green growth I really thought about was always in someone else's wallet. In Isla Vista, I saw lettuce and kale and collard grow in public hippie gardens. I was taught how to cut off fresh broccoli, and I learned to cook it too. I even got used to cauliflower if it had a good cheese sauce on it. But I sincerely thought things were going way too wacky when I went to an Isla Vista Mexican restaurant that had the bizarre cultural audacity to put alfalfa sprouts in a burrito. I grew up, for example, loving Chinese food, though not really those bean sprouts, but I didn't complain when I ate them — you just put enough soy and hot sauce over it all. But alfalfa sprouts in a burrito? *N'hombre, que pinche desmadre!*

Until I started liking it. And then I began to like the idea of it. I liked, for example, the idea of frijoles without that yummy bacon fat that was saved in the coffee can by the sink, or refried days and days after in a scoop or so of Crisco. I was changing with the times too, sure, but I had always loved fresh cooked mushrooms and corn served in butter or lemon, and avocado raw or mashed, and of course fresh jalapeños and serranos, and there was no store fruit made or invented — oh yeah, *grown*, on trees — that I didn't seek out. Where I came up, if you were a guy who made a point of eating that decorative slice of tomato — you know, intentionally and not by accident — there were dudes around that would ask you how hot pink your panties were. I was the kind of tough who'd shake his head at one of those *panzones*, especially if he wasn't too much bigger than me, and reach over and take the slice off his plate too.

Plate #3 is not the national plate of Mexico. Mexican food is diverse, if not one of the most complicated cuisines, competitive with Europe's. Even enchiladas aren't really a lasagna of cheese and *carne picada* and chopped onion wrapped in an oil-sogged tortilla; at its purest an enchilada is, first, dredged in chile (hence, "in chile" equals *enchilada*), then filled with what amounts to a taste of meat or cheese, which then, traditionally, gets a sprinkle of crumbly white fresh cheese, or *queso fresco*. Enchiladas and tacos are most often not primary meals. Fish is plentiful because there are ocean coasts on either side of the country. And vegetables, including *nopales*, and peppers, and squash. One of my favorite tacos was of sweet onions with *rajas de chile* in Matamoros. I love the ceviche both in Ensenada, Baja California, and Echo Park, Los Angeles. I love the huevos rancheros, with extra *chile de arból* over it, at Lucy's in El Paso. My favorite Mexican restaurant in Austin offers tacos *de espinaca* and *hongo*, and I'm sorry, that's not hippie, that's Mexican. I have eaten the best *pozole* ever in Mexico City, and *taquerías* there only cook straight off a grill near the sidewalk, no fried or ovened anything.

Mexican food is not, by nature, unhealthy — or not more so than French or even Chinese food is. Yet Taco Bell romanticizes the most fattening character of both popular American and Mexican food — it cannot be only a historical irony that this business symbiotically evolved out of and alongside the hot dog and hamburger culture (McDonald's Ray Kroc, a friend of Bell's, opened his first hamburger stand in San Bernardino, and Glen Bell's early business partner became the founder of the Del Taco chain, while Bell's wife came up with the ungrammatical German name for another friend's fledgling business, Der Wienerschnitzel). I would even go so far as to claim that plate #3 was and is not the most common meal in Mexican American homes, in the same way that chop suey was and is not in Chinese American homes. Inexpensive dishes are often created and eaten in the hungriest, make-the-best-of-it times, and poor people eat poor meals with poor products. But I'd even go a step further. That the #3 — well, maybe #5, with two beef tacos as well, the corn tortillas and the meat inside deep-fried — is what Anglos, not Mexicans, identified as Mexican food because the Mexican restaurants catered to them and their dinner money, as one in San Bernardino did to Mr. Bell.

But consider what has happened in the most populated Mexican American cities at and near the Texas border — El Paso and San Antonio. El Paso in particular is overwhelmed by fast-food and national chain restaurants and virtually nothing else. Even Chico's Tacos is a city institution most adored for its cheap hot dogs, burgers, and french fries, while the Hamburger Inn is known for the best of Sunday *menudo* — fresh oregano and dried chile and chopped onion and limes — on any late night. It might be that San Antonio has an equal number of chain food joints, but what has to be like three fourths of the central city's restaurants are making tacos, and seems like the competition is as much about who's the closest to 99¢. Breakfast tacos are always of egg and chorizo or potato or *papas con chorizo* or wienie or ham or country sausage or *machacado*. Lunch tacos can be *carne guisada, picadillo, chicharron,* country sausage, beef or chicken fajita, *carnitas, lengua, carne asada* — OK, one of guacamole, another of beans, but aside from that, and a spoonful of *tomate* blended for the *salsa de chile*, not a vegetable in the place, and there are no fruits for dessert. These are not tacos made with deep-fried corn tortillas. They are handmade on the spot and toasted on a grill and they are flour. They are good. The fluffiness of flour tortillas comes from the *manteca*. The fluffier they are, the more lard.

OK, though I do love healthy food, like everyone, I also love fluffy flour tortillas, the same as everyone does chocolate cake. I happen to love lightly fried corn tortillas — sprinkle salt on it while it's still hot, even a little *limón,* and I don't even need a filling. I love french fries fried with chorizo. I love too much cheese. There isn't a taco listed above I don't love to eat. I love fast-food burgers, especially if I can layer them with some slices of fresh or marinated jalapeño. I love Polish hot dogs. *Hijole,* I love fried bologna sandwiches with Tapatío hot sauce! I love tamales, green, red, or sweet. But. But, except, the problem is: it's the fluffiness portion again, and "the best" tamales are like 50 percent *manteca* fluffy!

While the filming proceeded on the latest version of *The Alamo* a couple of years ago, the gossip around the Austin movie scene was that there was trouble casting a Mexican army, which, in that other century, was especially hungry — which is to say, not so fat. I have not checked to see if the gossip was true, but you don't have to be looking for extras to notice, For example, I was in the sweetest hidden-away taco restaurant in San Antonio on a recent Sunday. Decorative tinsel frills of blue, silver, green, gold, and red crisscrossed the ceiling, the walls were lime green, the plastic tablecloths were blue-white, the dark carpet had lavender flowers, the chairs were orange vinyl, and there were probably seventy-five of them, and you had to wait for a table for *lonche.* The only thin person there was a woman maybe ninety years old with a walker. How many breakfast tacos can possibly fit between a tight belt and the memory of a small waist? How many flour tortillas? Let's not play around with it — just look at the schoolyards! Of course the explanation is not that there's such an overabundance of wealth we feast at a gluttonous Henry VIII banquet table. Some like to defend the bulk, calling it all a genetic propensity. Probably it is, especially while even that thin slice of tomato is avoided. It's that *lo barato sale caro.* That is, it's poverty, the food of the undereducated and underpaid, unexposed and untraveled ones who find *tacos de espinaca y hongo* weird and who find, in a taco of *huevos con wienie* and a Texas-sized Coke, the satisfying comfort of home.

Though it's really meant to be a drive-through experience, I recently spent an hour, 6–7 P.M., with a *muy* sugary sweet lemonade inside a South Austin Taco Bell. I will say, no offense, it brings on a strange motel-like experience. The music: Elton John, Natalie Merchant, Carly Simon, Bob Seeger. The patrons: a fat, graying, kind-looking white guy with a baseball cap and a mentally disabled Mexican American he clearly took care of, who was probably the same age, give or take. A very fat black couple. A way fat Mexican American guy alone. A Mexican American mom, a little heavy, and her cute overweight daughter, who went to refill her oil-drum-sized soda cup before they left. A family walked in, or what seemed like one. Mexican American, a mom and her three big teenage sons. Only one of the boys was a lot of belly soft; the others might just be called big kids. They were laughing, happy, which resonated in the punishing stillness that had been there. Just because that Taco Bell advertising push was driving me insane, as the cashier who sold me my drink, a scrawny white teenager with black-rimmed glasses, came near to pull out the full trash bag and replace it with a new plastic liner, I asked him to tell me what a chalupa was. You see, BTB — that is, Before Taco Bell — I thought I knew what a chalupa looked like, but then I am dumb. He described the meat and the cheese and lettuce and that it was inside a fried shell. I mean, I asked, how's it different from a taco? It's bigger, he said. That *is* exactly how it seems in its beautiful photo-shoot poses: just like a taco, which beside the big chalupa looks like a little boy, while his daddy is a hefty, NFL pro, grown up. So, I asked, how's the shell different from the taco's shell? It's thicker, he answered.

This South Austin Taco Bell is in a compact neighborhood of very rich, rich, middle, lower-middle, poor, and homeless. All the racial cross-section and mix is seen here. Sharing the same asphalted area is, on its east, an old-school McDonald's, and on its west a Goodyear Tire and Car Care Center. Across the street is, among others, a Radio Shack and a Dollar Store and a popular Family Thrift Store, a Rosie's Tamale House (not so great) and a Mandarin Chinese place (kind of too sticky and spooky dark inside to even trust the takeout). It's not more than a couple of blocks away from good Mexican restaurants. La Nueva Onda specializes in breakfast tacos and *fideo* bowls. Curra's serves the best from the interior of Mexico, like *pibil* and *mixiote,* maintaining the finest tequilas, and it's not that far west to Polvo's, where lots of vegetables come with most *platos,* or from the meat market Moreliana's, where tacos here are like tacos across and the *chile de aguacate* makes both Mexicans and non-Mexicans want to celebrate with a *grito.*

What I'm saying is that when I went into the Taco Bell the next time, for lunch, it was willful. I couldn't remember what one of those tacos tasted like. Like everyone else, I had relented, to be polite to others, once or twice in my teenage years. So long ago, it seemed like BTB. And here's the truth — I was afraid I would outright like the taco. I mean, I know I shouldn't, but, bad, I sneak a Mega Grab Doritos now and then and I eat too many tortilla chips at Polvo's before I get my favorite fish dinner and I used to really like cheap hamburgers and so how could I not think, if unhealthy like the aforementioned, I wouldn't like a taco that would be a combo of all those with some curls of cheese and ribbons of iceberg lettuce and a few tomato chunks that were now a settled source of a union dispute? I arrived at the same time as a cute, thin Chicana did — I opened the door for her and she ordered first. She was eating there. I'd say, by her voice, she didn't know Spanish. At my turn I ask this cashier, just to hear his answer, what a chalupa is. This cashier I swear is the same black dude at the corner up the street at the highway on-ramp who up and back walks a cardboard sign, "Anything Will Help." He turns and points to the image of a big chalupa on the framed plastic menu. What's in it? I ask. When he starts to read to me, very slowly, the description off the menu, I stop him. I order one chalupa and one taco, to go, and I wait, listening to Norah Jones. At the drive-up window, the young woman with the headset is talking English comfortably into the mike but switches into a more comfortable Spanish with another woman employee I can't see, who speaks Spanish so strong I'd bet she probably struggles with English. A black woman announces my number, knowing it's mine before I can find first the receipt and then the number on it, winking, and I grab a handful of the "fire" packets of hot sauce and throw them into the "Spice Up the Night" bag and set myself up once I get home.

How's a Taco Bell chalupa not like a Taco Bell taco? It is a lot big-ger, maybe by two. The beef one I bought had sour cream in it. But the shell, well, it is not corn like the taco's but is a thick white flour pita bread that has been fried on the outside so that it keeps its *U* shape but isn't hard inside. The main filling in both was the meat, the beef, what would be *picadillo* on a Mexican food menu. I ate them both, and let me tell you unvaguely, directly reflecting the complete and utter surprise that I myself did not anticipate, how genuinely awful the meat was. Spiced, if you'll excuse the expres-sion, somewhere between very lousy chili and the worst jar of spa-ghetti meat sauce, only a lot less good, it was so bad it doesn't even matter for me to say I didn't like the taste of that chalupa shell much or that the taco's shell wasn't nearly as good as the cheapest generic grocery store tortilla chips, because those are complaints along the lines of griping that Wal-Mart doesn't have a fine enough selection of clothing. I won't even bother to be polite and say that I liked the sour cream, you know, to think of something nice to say. Because it doesn't matter. Both the chalupa and the taco were so sincerely awful, a food thinking so outside the bun, that I can't even praise the few chunks of tasteless, if still possibly a little healthy, tomato.

But putting that all aside — I know, but putting all that aside any-way — there is something uniquely American happening because of the Taco Bell phenomenon. The people working there describe exactly the diversity of the American culture, even as the economic accident it is, which creates a public workplace where a Mexican national who speaks English poorly works with a nerdy white kid and a honey-talking black woman, where the manager, with two young children, might be named Jim or Ernesto or Tamiqua. And so what if this food's no more Mexican than a hamburger is from Hamburg, Germany — lots of people think it is, and if they think they like Mexican food, and then they want to try tacos at real Mexi-can restaurants, they may learn that they like not only the food but Mexican people and Mexican culture. That is not how it has been in even the recent past. It represents a positive when other American people might come to understand how *American* Mexican Americans are — seeing that mom and her three sons talking, laughing, eating the same bad chalupas as they do and not knowing any better. It's an Oprah's Book Club bringing culture to the dinner table — OK, so maybe to the coffee table in front of the tube, or maybe through the driver's window and spilled onto the car seat.

Taco Bell's seasoned ground meat isn't *picadillo* because it isn't Mexican. The taco, and its filling, is American now. Like spaghetti really isn't very Italian, like potatoes are not only for the Irish, like French bread isn't French, like a kosher dill pickle isn't only Jewish anymore, a taco from Taco Bell is what food from Mexico can never become because of its variation and specialties in different regions not only on the other side of the border but even on this, the American side: burritos, huge in popularity and girth in California, are exotic in borderlands Texas and New Mexico, while breakfast tacos, craved by all who live in a city like San Antonio, go virtually unheard of from El Paso to Los Angeles. Taco Bell's non- or panregional taco crosses every state line and carries across the country an idea, if not the reality, of an American culture that comes from Mexico. It is, in other words, an American food. Tacos in those crackable, mass-produced shells (which Mr. Glen Bell claims to have pioneered, if not patented), purchasable in sealed, airtight plastic, sold in grocery stores in Maine or Montana, are now no more ethnic than pizza, than a submarine sandwich. Tacos are as everywhere as hamburgers and hot dogs, hot-and-sour and soy sauce, ketchup and salsa. This is an American taco born into a culture without any relatives in Mexico or in the borderlands anymore, that mispronounces a few words in Spanish the same as it does a couple in Italian or Greek or German.

And Taco Bell's success is not only as an implosion of a not very healthy glop, but has to have been the commercial inspiration of at least two new regional fast-food chains — Taco Cabana in Texas and Baja Fresh in California — which dare to feature what would have once-upon-a-time been an exotic, *Mexican* Mexican taco. And that fusion of Mexican culture and the healthy hippie — which bloomed sunflower big into a demand for a nouveau gourmet — is transforming the architecture of food in the Southwest and Texas. In Austin, for instance, where Bush lost big-time in 2004, menus posted outside chic restaurants bear Mexican dish names as stylized as if they were French- or Italian-influenced. And what was unheard of when Mr. Bell first ate plate #3, Mexican restaurants themselves, owned by Mexican immigrants who stay near the cash registers and in the kitchens, no longer look to hire petite waitresses from Tamaulipas or Monterrey but tattooed, slacker-hip white dudes who wear ball caps and cool T-shirts and say "dude" at various times as part of their personalized service.

One last thing, just for the record. That freaking "chalupa" is not a *chalupa!* The word "chalupa," like the word "taco," draws up a specific, historical image and it's one that does not look like a taco any more than it does a chili dog or a steak sandwich. If any old Mexican word can be attached to Taco Bell's latest creation, they might as well call it an enchilada. Enough of the customers won't know any different, most won't care, and in time restaurants will have to explain what those items on a plate that used to be called enchiladas are. Since this chalupa doesn't have Mexican corn in it, why not name it after a Spanish dish, like paella, an exotic name there, or, like a car, give it the name of a famous Spanish city, like Toledo, maybe with a little vowel variation on it, so it might be called a Tolido Taco. Or take it on like Mrs. Bell would. Something like Taco Perro.

michael jaime-becerra

❧ PRACTICE TATTOOS

I F I MAKE seven free throws in a row, Violet Cervantes will like me. I've made ten straight before, but now the rim is hard to see because it's late and the courts at Kranz have no lights. It feels like I've been out here for a couple of hours, but still I don't wanna go home because my mom and Gina were fighting over Gina's boy-friend when I left. Knowing my mom, she won't get over this guy Max having his ears pierced. I shoot the ball and miss. It bounces left to another court, the rim on this one all crooked and bent from someone hanging on it. OK, if I make six in a row, Violet will like me.

I shoot and make it. Then two. Three. Four in a row. I'm about to make number five, but I stop because I hear yells and the smash of a bottle from the other end of the grass field by the basketball courts. It's probably cholos. Even though my mom makes me go to church with her twice a week because she says I make her feel safe, I'm so skinny that there's no way I could stop a bunch of drunk cholos from killing me if they wanted to. I turn around and shoot at the rim way on the other side, thinking of Violet, hoping the shot goes in. When the ball misses, I run after it and wonder where to go next.

Gina's dragged the phone into her room to talk to Max, laugh-ing loud and making lots of noise because our parents aren't home. The cord's stretched straight from the phone jack by the couch, down the hall, under the door to her room. It looks like a tightrope, and I step on it, arms out for extra balance. One step

91

and the cord pops out from the wall. Something bangs on the other side of Gina's door. I close my eyes, keep my arms stretched, and imagine that I'm falling, that a net will be there to catch me before I hit the ground. I open my eyes and Gina's staring at me, puppy dog slippers on her feet, green towel around her head like a genie. She calls me a fuckin' weirdo, then slams the door to her room.

I'm weird? I'm not the one with black nail polish on my toes. The one whose friends all think they're punk-rock Draculas. I mean Gina's boyfriend, Max, all he wears is black. His pants are all tight and he always wears a leather jacket like it's glued to his back. Last month, when we went to see *Beverly Hills Cop*, I saw him and his friends pushing his green Tercel at the mall. It was almost summer, and the bus I was on had air conditioning. Just looking at him pushing that car out in the heat and wearing that stupid jacket made me sweat. Max is weird, but at least he's not Junior, Gina's last boyfriend.

Junior always scratched and picked at his face. He was superskinny too. One time I saw him with his shirt off and his stomach was all caved in like it was trying to eat itself. Him and my sister were together for like six months. For Gina that was like six years. When he would come and pick up my sister it was always a big deal. Gina said it was because Junior lived over in Pico Rivera and he had to take three buses to see her. I remember him biting his lip as he waited by the door for my sister. Junior always had this shitty, pissed-off look on his face, like he just came from a fight he had started and lost.

The last time anybody talked about Junior was also the last time I saw my mom drive the car. Math homework was kicking my ass that night. My mom answered the phone and listened for a few seconds before saying Junior's name and making the sign of the cross. She took the pencil from my hand, suds dripping onto my book as she leaned over to write in the margins. The dishes stayed in the sink, and my mom had me recopy her sloppy directions as she looked for the car keys and her purse. My mom's always been afraid to drive, but there she was, going fast and crazy, running a red light and honking at the screeching cars like it was their fault they were in our way.

We flew through Whittier Narrows and got to the bowling alley in about ten minutes. The big signs advertising 36 LANES and THE SLO-POKE LOUNGE colored everything red. My mom drove around the packed parking lot, and I went inside to look. The place was chilly from too much air conditioning. I went up to the front desk, and before I could talk, the guy behind the counter put down the pair of shoes he was spraying and told me to get in line. Instead, I checked the pay phones and thought a couple times about going into the ladies' room. I wandered down to one end of the building, bumping into people while I looked for Gina's face. A bowler hollered in a lane nearby and kicked at the air like a ninja as the people around him laughed. I said Gina's name over and over as I tried to remember what she had on when she left the house.

After a while I went back outside and walked around the building. I could hear my mom before I even saw the two of them. The car was in front of an orange dumpster, driver door open, engine still running. One of the headlights shone on Gina. She was plopped on the ground, and it looked like the Spanish words flying from my mom's mouth were punches that kept my sister from lifting her head out of her hands. My mom finally stopped her yelling when she saw me standing behind her.

She told Gina to get in the car, and we both sat in the back and didn't say anything. Gina had mascara stripes down her face and she kept her hand tucked tight against her neck. Her eyes followed the cars that passed us as our mom drove home. We stopped at a signal, and the bright lights from the Mobil station by our house flooded the car. Gina took her hand from her neck, and I could see blood on her palm, a dark shiny spot the size of a dime. My mom stepped on the gas and I tried to mind my own business as the car ducked under a freeway overpass. Later on, I found out this was Gina's last fight with Junior, that he had used her neck as an ashtray before dumping her at the bowling alley. The car groaned from my mom's foot, and Gina stared at her hand, sorta smiling before rubbing it into the sleeve of her shirt.

THIS IS WHAT I KNOW ABOUT VIOLET CERVANTES:

1. Her dad owns Paisano's Pizza. Every day she goes straight there after school. When I pass by on the way home, she's already working.
2. Her, Yvette Valdez, and Isabel Zaragoza got caught smoking in the girls' bathroom right before Christmas vacation.
3. Last year she was going around with Sal Torres, but she broke up with him. Rico told me she slapped him across the face at Yvette's party because Sal stuck his hand up her shirt and everybody saw.
4. Sometimes, mostly on Fridays, she wears these blue socks that have white stars on them.
5. She sits across from me in Clack-clack's class. In Mrs. Aispuro's class, she sits in the front row by the chalkboard. Violet pays attention and writes a lot of stuff down.
6. She's way better than me at math. Whenever we take tests, the people who get A's get their picture taken. The photos are pinned to a wall covered in red construction paper with a sign of a cartoon pencil saying GREAT JOB! One time I got an 89 on a test. Mrs. Aispuro said to try harder next week, but that's the best I ever did. The next time Violet gets her picture taken, I think I'm going to steal it.

~ ~ ~

Gina has purple hair! She's standing in front of me, putting on her makeup, with this purple fuckin' hair. Max is outside, honking the horn on his piece-a-shit car. I ask where's she going and she says to tell Mom she went to the movies with her friends. Yesterday Gina was all excited because she won tickets to a concert off the radio. I ask if she's going to see one of her stupid KROQ groups. Gina says the name of the band, and I say, "Social who?"

She looks up from the dark lipstick in her hand and repeats herself real slow, like I'm an idiot for not knowing what she's talking about. "Social. Distortion. They're opening for the Jesus and Mary Chain."

"Mom'll love that one," I say, but Max honks again.

Gina kisses a Kleenex, throws her makeup in her bag, and mumbles something about Max needing to calm down. She checks herself in the mirror one last time. I tell Gina she looks like a Muppet and she tells me to fuck off.

I pour a glass of water and reach into the freezer for ice cubes. I drop three into the glass and rub one on the back of my head until it starts to melt between my fingers. Tomorrow I'll probably have a bump from that foul, but at least I made the basket and we won the last game. My dad tells me to turn off the light in the kitchen because he's watching TV. I pick up my ball, and as I start to my room, I stop and listen. Besides the television, I can hear Gina's voice in the bathroom. She's explaining about her hair, how it isn't that big a deal, that it'll probably wash out in a week. Two at the most.

"Besides," she tells my mom, "tú también te lo pintas."

I sorta laugh at that one and walk closer to the half-open bathroom door. My mom does get her hair dyed black every two weeks at Brenda's Hair Salon. The color's so dark I always imagine Brenda painting it on with a brush, the dye thick and steaming like the tar my dad uses to stick roofs to people's houses. My mom tells Gina it's not the same thing. She says she doesn't come home looking like a monster.

Gina says, "God, it's no big deal," and then I hear a smack.

"Don't bring God into this," my mom says. "Ni digas el nombre de Dios con esa greña."

The faucet turns on and I can hear water splashing in the bathtub. There's the sound of people pushing and Gina whining. Someone slams someone else against one wall before bouncing them to the other. Gina screams and my mom keeps shouting in Spanish, You're not my daughter, looking like this you're not my daughter. There's the big crash of bodies falling, and my dad yells to keep it down. I step into the bathroom and they both look up at me. My mom's on top of Gina, teeth clenched, one hand on my sister's neck, her other one trying to push the crown of purple suds on

Gina's head under the running water. The faucet is pointed toward the wall, and water splashes all over, and blood is coming from Gina's forehead. The blood mixes with the dye and the suds from the spilled shampoo, making this kind of syrup on the rim of the tub, and some of it hits me when my mom points and tells me to shut the door.

I step out of the confessional and my mom takes my place inside. The door closes behind her with a thud. It's Monday night and the church is empty. It's only us, the priest in the other half of the confession box, and a nun who's sweeping up around the altar. The priest gave me a short penance, and I kneel to start my first Our Father. Halfway through I stop. If we had come on Thursday like normal, I wouldn't be missing the Laker game right now. I start praying the names of the Lakers instead, calling out the starting lineup in my head. I say their names over and over, faster and faster. Each name speeds up in my brain until all the players become a blur of whispered words and uniform numbers.

I get up and slide back against the pew. After a while I start counting the stations of the cross. I squint and make out seven candles around the altar. I throw my head back and count sixteen iron lamps hanging from the ceiling. I take out my wallet, inspect my three dollars, and rearrange the papers and cards inside. The nun has started sweeping the pews across from where I'm sitting. She looks at me and I smile, all embarrassed like she caught me doing something nasty. The door to the confessional opens. My mom kneels and does a quick sign of the cross. She adjusts the black leather bag on her shoulder, pulling out a yellow scarf. She uses it to wipe at her eyes, then ties it around her head, hiding her face as she hurries outside.

I dribble with my left and carry my trophy in my right hand as me and Rico walk into Paisano's Pizza. It's Saturday, and both Violet and her older sister Leti are working. I put the trophy on the counter and hold the ball with my foot. Violet's filling tiny plastic containers with Parmesan cheese. Leti's talking on the phone. There's a sign that says WE ONLY USE FRESH INGREDIENTS behind them. Violet takes Rico's order, and I smooth my wrinkled money on the counter, the bills damp from being in my shorts the whole tournament. Rico gets three pepperoni slices and a root beer. I ask for cheese pizza, two slices, and I make sure to say please. When Rico sees that I don't have a drink, he says he'll lend me the money so I can buy a Coke. I tell him thanks and take his money and pretend to read the menu on the wall because my face has turned red.

Violet gives me my change and I sit with Rico at one of the two tables facing the street. Leti hangs up the phone and gives the order to her dad. Mr. Cervantes reads the slip of paper before shoving it into his apron. He tells Leti to write neater as he slides a pizza in the oven, closing the heavy steel door before going back to the kitchen. A few seconds later, two cholos walk in. One is big and tall, like six-foot-something. He looks like a bear standing on its back legs. The other one is tall too, only thinner. His head is shaved and his nose points out like a Doberman's. As they stand at the counter, I can read the tattoos that branch out from their tank tops and stretch across their shoulders. The Bear orders two Cokes with extra ice. The Doberman taps a cigarette on the counter while Violet gets the drinks. Leti takes their money. She says there's no smoking in here, and the Doberman smiles and tells her to relax.

Mr. Cervantes comes back out from the kitchen carrying a stack of cardboard. He drops it on the counter and stares at the cholos as they take their drinks, his eyes practically pushing them out the door. The cholos leave without saying anything, probably because Mr. Cervantes looks like he could pick up the pizza oven and throw it at them. Mr. Cervantes tells Leti to bring our food, then tells Violet that those delivery boxes aren't going to fold themselves. Violet pulls her hair into a ponytail and wipes her hands on her apron. Leti brings our plates of pizza, then sits next to Violet, and thin white boxes start to form between them.

Rico folds two of his slices together to make a sandwich. He takes a big bite and fans air into his mouth because it's hot. He swallows and starts talking about the Laker game and I answer without paying attention. I listen to Leti ask Violet if she liked either of those guys, if she saw all those tattoos, if she thought the Doberman was cute. I take a bite of my pizza but don't chew. Violet shrugs and says, I guess. Both of them giggle at the same time and I want to leave.

The door plays "La Cucaracha" when Gina opens it, and she dances past a wall of fish tanks as I step inside. The place smells like one of the animals had an accident and the owner just covered the floor with straw instead of mopping the mess up. We're there because she says Max picked up a stray dog and she wants to buy it a collar, a cool one with spikes so the dog can look punk. Gina needs money. She said she'd take me to Max's house if I lent her the cash to buy a collar for the stupid dog, because Max has a tattoo gun and she can talk him into doing me for no charge.

The man working has a thin mustache that reminds me of the guy who controls the Tilt-A-Whirl at the Epiphany carnival. He says hi and to let him know if we need any help, then goes back to scooping fish out of a tank. There's a big brown iguana in an aquarium by the cash register. He scratches lazy at the glass like he hasn't accepted that he's going to spend the rest of his life behind it. A radio plays salsa music and the guy working starts singing to the fish as he chases them around in the water with his blue net. He pours them into plastic bags, fills them with a squirt of air from a big green tank, and spins them around with his hand like miniature dance partners.

Gina finds the collars. She calls me over to decide between a black leather one with silver spikes and a brown one that's thicker and decorated with studs.

"Get whichever one's cheaper," I say.

I don't tell her that I've been saving this money for two weeks, skipping lunches and washing our neighbors' cars. Gina picks the black one, looks at its price tag, and asks me for twenty bucks. I give her the money, and she presses the spikes against my cheek and says, "See, they're not even sharp." Gina tells the guy working that she thinks she's ready, and he turns the knob on the air tank and spins another bag of fish before he heads to the cash register. As my sister pays, I wonder if that tank has the kind of air that makes your voice all squeaky and high. The guy's not looking, so I stick the tube in my mouth and turn the knob. My cheeks puff with air and I can feel it push down my throat and burst through both my nostrils. I cough and drop the tube. It lands in a bucket of saw-dust and I have to cover my eyes as it clouds up around me. The guy yells and Gina starts laughing and we both run out the door. I sprint all the way down to the liquor store, where I start walking, popping my ears until Gina catches up. She tells me I shoulda thought of that sooner, that maybe we coulda got the collar for free.

Max lives in a rented garage. There's a bed and a dresser, a radio with tapes piled on top, and a long couch that's so dirty it looks like it's covered in camouflage. There's a table with a glass top held to-gether by stickers and strips of duct tape. I sit on an aluminum beach chair, and Max is across from me, his chair creaking as he flips through a notebook full of scribbles. He isn't wearing a shirt, probably to show off the practice tattoos he's been giving himself, or maybe to give them air so they can heal. There's a skull on Max's chest that's either laughing or shouting. It's hard to tell because the ink is dark and the skin around it is all raw and red.

I ask Max about his dog, and he looks up from his notebook and says, "Ask your sister. She's the one who left the gate open."

Gina gets up off the couch and leans over Max. "Again, for the thousandth time, I'm sorry. Besides, you didn't really want him anyway," she says, kissing Max on the neck. She traces her finger across Max's tattoo. He flinches and pushes her away, then he says that he's sorry. He grabs my sister's hand and pulls her close for a quick kiss. After that, Gina walks away and turns on the TV. She twists the knob through a few channels and takes a bag of Polly seeds from her purse, sticking a few in her mouth before sitting on the couch.

"Is this how you want it?" Max asks. The page he shows me has Violet's name written out in curly letters, the V in that style you see on diplomas. It's a little big, longer than my hand, but I still tell Max yeah, and reach behind my shoulder and say, "Put it right here."

"Who's this Violet girl anyway?" Gina asks. I tell her she's my girlfriend. Gina splits a seed in her mouth and picks the small shell apart with her fingers. "If Violet's your girlfriend, how come she never calls the house?"

I tell Gina that Violet can't get through. "You're always on the fuckin' phone."

Max tells me to take off my shirt and to sit on the floor near the couch. I do both. Gina's watching channel 34, an old Mexican movie about a charro who wears a wrestling mask. Max sits behind me, and the charro shoots about ten shots from a revolver, killing all the bad guys except for the one holding his girlfriend hostage. I can't really tell what happens next because Max tells me to put my head down. He rubs my shoulder with alcohol and it's so cold that I get chills. He wipes me with a towel, then starts to draw an outline on me with a marker. He tells me not to move. I can feel the tip of his pen curving up and down my shoulder blade as the movie goes to a commercial. The marker tickles, but I make myself concentrate on the ads to keep from laughing. When the charro comes back, Max says that I'm ready.

I lift my head and the charro is singing on his horse. The horse rears up, hooves kicking at the air, and some lady hugs herself and says for him, she'll wait forever. Max pushes my head back down and turns his tattoo gun on. It makes this angry mechanical buzz like Max is holding a metal bee. "Hold still," he says, and I think of Violet giggling, and right before the needle touches me I scoot away.

Max asks what's wrong, and my sister laughs. She flicks a shell to the small mess on the floor. "I knew you wouldn't do it."

"He's just nervous," Max says. He turns the gun off, goes to his dresser, and comes back with a bottle. It's dark brown with a train on the front. "For relaxation," he says before taking a long drink to help me believe him.

I think I'm going to die right here, on the sidewalk, coming home from church. I want to sleep. My head is pounding. All through mass, when the people were singing, I wanted to take two pillows and stuff them in my ears, lean over on the pew, and close my eyes.

Now my mom wants to stop at La Dulzura, the bakery over on Penn Mar. This morning I told her I was sick, that I ate something bad at Rico's house, that his mom can't cook, because it always makes my mom feel good to know she's better than other parents.

La Dulzura smells like sugar and flour, and the heat from the oven in back hugs you when you walk in. My mom takes a number and we wait. All the pan dulce actually looks good, probably because I didn't have breakfast and last night, when he drove us home, Max had to pull over three times so I could puke. Afterwards Gina gave me some gum and called me a lightweight. This morning my mom woke me up fifteen minutes before she wanted to leave. Time to brush my teeth and comb my hair. I grabbed the only clean church shirt I could find, my white one from like two years ago that fits me all tight.

The lady calls our number and my mom gets half a dozen bolillos to make my dad sandwiches for work. Then she starts picking pan dulce. She gets two empanadas for herself, a concha with yellow sugar on top and another one with chocolate. She gets one of those pink things with raisins and coconut that Gina likes. My mom tells me to pick something, and I look in the glass case for one of those Neapolitan cookies. I lean over, and my shirt gets all tight like it's going to rip apart. I ask the lady if they have any cookies de tres colores. She says no, so I get an elote instead.

My mom pays and we leave, and when we get outside she tells me to take my shirt off. I swallow and ask, "What?"

Her voice gets loud and slow. "Quítate la camisa."

I try to laugh and start walking, but my mom grabs me.

I unbutton my shirt and look around. Two guys sitting outside the liquor store across the street watch me. Even though I didn't get the tattoo, the outline Max drew is still there. I'm standing with my shirt in my hands, my chest getting all goose-pimply from the cool morning air. My mom gasps and makes the sign of the cross. I'm about to explain, but she slaps me across the face. Her nail scratches my eyelid. I rub the pain a few seconds. When I take my hand away, the guys across the street are blurry, but I can still tell that they're laughing.

The rest of the walk home is quiet, and I stay behind my mom the entire way. I don't bother explaining because she won't listen to anything now, and besides, no matter what I say, I'm fucked once we get home. When we come to our street, I'm surprised to see Max's green piece-a-shit parked where he left it last night, and even more surprised that my mom doesn't notice. She unlocks the front door, we step inside the house, and we both hear the same noises. It takes her a few seconds to figure out that they're coming from Gina's room. My mom leaves her purse in the doorway, keys in the knob, and marches down the hall, switching both bags of bread to her left hand before opening the door. I look over my mom's shoulder, and Gina's right there in the middle of the floor, on the carpet, naked. Max's face is between her legs and she's groaning, one foot turning a slow circle in the air, the other playing with the waistband to Max's chones.

"Oh shit," I say, and Max turns around, his eyes big with surprise, his chin all wet with drool. Gina screams and pulls the sheet off her bed to cover up. My mom jumps on top of them, swinging the plastic bags of bread to beat them apart. Max reaches for his jacket. Its zippers scrape against the wall and the pictures wobble as he squeezes past me and heads for the door wearing only his boxers. My mom yells about rape and calling the police. She hurls the bolillos for my dad's lunch at Max and they bounce off him like those fake rocks in Godzilla movies.

My mom and Gina argue inside the house, but I follow Max outside. He's trying to get the Tercel started, but it just coughs and whines. He gets out and starts to push it into the street. Gina comes outside wearing shorts and a T-shirt, the laces to her monkey boots untied and dragging. She carries some clothes that she throws in Max's car. My mom's right behind her as Max gets it rolling. The engine catches and they get in. I'm waiting for my mom to stop her, but instead she stays at the curb like she's chained to the house, quiet like our street is someplace unknown and dangerous.

So I go after them, racing at full speed and staying close enough to read the numbers off Max's license plate until they reach Parkway. By then the car's exhaust is choking me. I run through the intersection and there's the squeal of brakes and I turn as a gold Cadillac skids to a crooked stop right in front of me, smoke coming up from its tires as it rocks backwards. The driver jams his hand against the horn, but instead of moving, I turn back toward Fineview, where Max is driving Gina away. The air around me stinks of burned rubber, the Tercel a shrinking green dot. I yell my sister's name, but the Cadillac keeps honking, the horn so loud that Gina couldn't hear me if I was riding in the backseat. The scratch over my eye burns.

daniel chacón

⟋ GODOY LIVES

J UAN'S COUSIN wrote what he knew of the dead guy. He was
from Jalisco. Not married. Some called him *maricón* because
they suspected he was gay, but no one knew for sure.

The age of the man was the same as Juan's, twenty-four, and the
picture on the green card strikingly similar, sunken cheeks, small
forehead, tiny, deep-set eyes that on Juan looked as if everything
scared him, but that on the dead guy looked focused, confident.
"You could use this to come work here," his cousin wrote.

It was perfect, Juan thought, if not for the name written on the
green card: Miguel Valencia Godoy.

Godoy? Juan wasn't even sure how to pronounce it. His wife,
Maria, held the green card in her small, work-gnarled hand and she
looked at the name, then at Juan.

"Goo doy," she said.

He tried: "Guld Yoy."

Patiently, she took a breath. "Goo doy."

He practiced and practiced. It got so the entire family was saying
it: Maria, their four-year-old boy, Juan Jr., and even the big-eyed
baby girl came close with "goo goo." Only Juan couldn't say it.
Some nights Maria kept him up late, pushing him awake as he
dozed off, until he said it correctly three times in a row.

When the day came for him to leave, he kissed her goodbye,
shook his son's hand like a man, and kissed the baby's soft, warm
head. The treeless dirt road stretched into the barren hills, reaching
toward the nearest town seven miles away where he would catch
the bus to Tijuana.

"I'll be back," he said to Maria.

"I know you will," she said.

"I'll send money when I find work."

"I know you will," she said. She placed an open palm on his face. "You're a good man, Juan. I know you'll do what's right."

He looked into her eyes, disappointed that he could not find in them a single tear. She smiled sadly, like a mother sending her child off to school.

"Go, Juan," she said. "Don't make this harder than it needs to be."

"I can't help it." He wept.

She hugged him in her strong, bony arms. She smelled of body odor. "Don't do this. Be a man," she said firmly.

He pulled away from her, wiped his tears, and said, "I'm going."

"Again," she said.

"Duld Woy," he sniveled.

"Goo doy. Again."

"Goose boy."

"Juan, if you don't get it, things will be bad."

At the border, he nervously stepped across a red line painted on the sidewalk. He stepped past warning signs that ordered people to turn back if not able to enter the U.S. Inside the building, big and bright as an indoor sports stadium, he was surprised at the number of Mexicans waiting in line to get to the U.S. side. Still, most of the people were white, holding bags of souvenirs, colorful Mexican blankets, ceramics, bottles of tequila. He looked at the heads of the lines to see which U.S. immigration officer he should approach.

People who knew had told him that the worst immigration officers in the U.S. were the ones of Mexican descent. Pick a white officer, he had heard, because the Mexican American, the Chicano INS officers had to prove to the white people that they were no longer Mexicans. He had heard in the mountains that they would beat people up or sic vicious dogs on them, laughing as the bloody flesh would fly in all directions.

There were three open lines, three officers, a white woman and two white men. He chose a young man with a shaved head whose line moved fast because he barely looked at the IDs held out to him, just waved everyone through, bored, like he didn't want to be there.

Juan knew that this would be easier than he had imagined. With a confidence he had never felt before, he said to himself, slightly out loud, in perfect pronunciation, "Godoy."

When he was two people from the front, something terrible happened. A tall Chicano officer tapped the white agent on the shoulder and said something. The white guy smiled, stood up, and left, leaving the tall Chicano to take his place. This Mexican American was mean-looking, well over six feet tall, with massive shoulders and legs thick as tree trunks. His green INS uniform stretched like a football player's. Set below his flat forehead, above his chubby cheeks, were small black eyes that darted suspiciously from face to face. His hair was cut short to his head, sticking straight up, and he didn't smile.

Juan wanted to get out of the line, but he was next.

The Chicano looked down at him. "Why should I let you through?" he demanded in English.

Juan didn't understand a word except for *you*, which he believed meant him, but he assumed the officer had asked for his green card, so he held it up.

And smiled.

The Chicano looked suspiciously into Juan's eyes. He grabbed the card from his fingers and looked closely at the picture, then back at Juan.

"What's your name?" he asked in Spanish.

Juan took a deep breath and said, "Miguel Valencia Goo Poo."

"*What?*" asked the officer, chest inflating with air.

Juan was sure he'd be grabbed by the collar and dragged out.

He tried again: "Miguel Valencia Godoy."

"What's that last name?"

Sweat trickled down his back.

"Godoy?" he offered.

"Where are you from?"

"Jalisco," he remembered.

The officer put the ID card on the counter and said, with a big smile, "Cousin! It's me!"

He had said it in Spanish, but the words still had no meaning to Juan.

"I'm your cousin. Francisco Pancho Montes Godoy."

"Oh?"

"Don't you remember me?"

"Oh, Pancho, of course," said Juan, weakly.

"You lying son of a bitch," said Pancho. "You don't even recognize me. Come on," he said, coming around the counter. "I know what to do with guys like you." He picked up the duffel bag as effortlessly as if it were a purse and led Juan across the vast floor of the building, through crowds of people, into a little room with chairs, a TV, and magazines in English. Pancho dropped the bag, turned around, and said *"Un abrazo,"* holding out his long and thick arms. He hugged the breath out of Juan. He smelled of freshly cleaned laundry. Then he held him at arm's length to get a better look.

"You haven't changed. You wait right here. When I get off, I'm taking you home. You can see my wife and kids." He started to walk out, but something struck him. He turned around. "Oh, I just thought of something."

"What?"

"Really. It just occurred to me."

"What did?"

"I have a special surprise for you, Miguel."

"What surprise?" asked Juan.

"You'll see," said Pancho. "A surprise."

Juan waited about three hours in that room. One time he tried to escape, but when he opened the door, Pancho, from behind the counter, looked right at him and winked.

At last, Pancho opened the door. He was now dressed in street clothes, 501 jeans and a T-shirt with a faded image of Mickey Mouse. He looked like a giant kid.

"Come on, cousin," he said. "I'm taking you home."

Like a lamb led to the slaughter, Juan followed through the parking lot, looking between the rows for an escape route, Pancho's shadow stretching across the hoods of several cars. Pancho grabbed him by the arm with a strong grip and escorted him to the passenger's side of an oversized Ford pickup. Juan pictured Maria wearing a black dress and veil, standing over his grave, not weeping, just shaking her head, saying, "Dumb Juan. Why can't he do nothing right?"

He climbed up into the cab, using both hands and feet, like a child climbing a tree. He had to get out of there quick, find his real cousin, the one who had sent him the dead man's green card, and work his ass off so he could send Maria money. She needed him. His family needed him.

They drove through town, the truck so high off the ground Juan thought that surely this must be what it was like to be on a horse. He held on to the rim of the seat.

"Hey, cousin. Listen to me," Pancho said. "You'll never guess the surprise I have for you."

"What is it?" Juan asked.

Pancho laughed an evil laugh.

"You'll see," he said.

"Can you give me a hint?"

"You won't be disappointed. So, tell me, where have you been these last years?"

"I'm not married," Juan said, remembering another detail about Godoy.

"Oh?" Pancho asked.

"Never found someone I loved," he said.

"Well, here you'll find plenty of women. Lorena has a pretty sister. Lorena turned out to be the greatest wife in the world."

Juan wanted to say, no, that Maria was the greatest, but he couldn't.

He had seen her at an outdoor dance in the *zócalo* of a nearby town one sunny Sunday afternoon. She was the prettiest girl there, wearing a white dress that fell just above her knees, her cinnamon-colored legs smooth and shapely. She was seventeen. All afternoon guys stood around her like giants, boys with large shoulders, black cowboy boots, and white straw cowboy hats that shined in the sun, while Juan, a skinny, sickly looking boy barely eighteen, watched her from behind the balloon vendor. Still, Maria noticed him.

As was the custom, the unmarried young people walked in a circle at the center of the plaza, girls in one direction, boys in another, and although several girls were available, most of the boys eyed Maria, and when they passed her, they threw confetti in her long black hair, or they offered their hands to her, but she walked by each of them, looking at Juan the entire time. He, in turn, looked over his shoulder at the tiled dome of the cathedral, convinced she was looking past him. Since she was rejecting so many others, he decided it wouldn't be so bad when she rejected him, so he was determined to throw some confetti in her hair. When she was right beside him, he raised his clenched hand, but when he opened it, he realized he had nothing. *What a fool I am!* he cried to himself. But Maria brushed out the confetti already in her hair and offered him her hand. So excited, he wasn't sure with which hand to take hers, extending one, withdrawing it, extending the other, so she took control. She grabbed his arm and led him away from the circle.

Pancho pulled the truck into a gravel lot lined by a three-foot-tall chain-link fence that surrounded a large front yard and a small house. Two dogs barked at the truck, a German shepherd and a big black lab. "Here we are, *primo*," he said. "This is home."

Pancho opened the fence and the dogs jumped on him for affection, but then they stopped and seemed to wait for Juan to enter the yard, their tongues hanging out, tails wagging, whining as if unable to contain their excitement.

"Do they bite?" Juan asked.

"Don't worry, they only bite strangers," said Pancho.

"That's good," Juan said. The dogs surrounded him, sniffing his crotch, his legs, the Michoacán dirt caked on his boots.

The men entered the house, which had purple shag carpet and a velveteen couch and love seat. The painting above the TV was a velvet likeness of the Aztec warrior with the dead woman in his arms. The place smelled of beans cooking.

"Lorena," called Pancho. "He's here." Then he looked at Juan. "I called her and told her you'd be coming."

Lorena, a strikingly handsome woman in a jean skirt, which came above her knees, and a white T-shirt that hugged her voluptuous body, walked in, wiping her hands on a dish towel. Standing next to each other, she and her husband looked like the perfect couple, him tall and broad-shouldered, a little chubby around the middle and on the face, and her tall, big-boned, wide hips. She had a long jaw like an Indian and long black hair tied in a ponytail.

"I don't believe it," she said. She ran up and gave Juan a big hug. Her flesh was soft and pillowy, and she smelled of fresh onions. She held him at arm's length. "This is such a wonderful day. Imagine," she said. "Just imagine."

"Imagine," Pancho said, his hands on his hips, smiling big.

Juan wasn't sure if Godoy had ever met Lorena, so he wasn't sure what to say. He said, "Imagine."

"I have your room ready for you," she said. "Do you want to wash up or rest?"

"Later," said Pancho. "First he has to meet the girls."

He led Juan down the hallway. Framed family pictures lined the walls. At one metal frame with multiple photos, Pancho stopped and pointed to two little kids dressed like cowboys, holding toy guns and trying to look mean. "You remember that?"

It was Pancho and the dead man as kids. Juan looked closely. The similarities between that child and how he remembered looking as a child were so great that it spooked him, as if he had had two lives that went on simultaneously. He almost remembered that day playing cowboys.

"That was in Jalisco," Juan said.

"That's right. On Grandfather's ranch. Remember that ranch?"

Juan pictured acres of land, a stable with twenty of the finest horses, and a garden where the family ate dinner, served by Indians, on a long wooden table. "Do I," he said dreamily.

"And all those horses," Pancho said, sadly delighted. "Oh, well, come on. We have plenty of time to reminisce, but first I want you to meet the girls."

Juan expected that he was referring to Lorena's sisters, but when Pancho opened a bedroom door, two little girls, five-year-old black-eyed twins, sat on the floor playing with dolls. They looked up at their father. "Hello, Daddy," they said in unison.

"Come here, sweethearts. I want you to meet someone."

Obediently they rose and came to their father, standing on either side of him. "This is your *Tío* Miguel."

Both girls ran to Juan and hugged him. "Hi, *tío*. We love you."

They smelled of baby powder.

Lorena insisted he go to bed early because of his long journey, so after dinner — chili verde with fat flour tortillas — she led him into the extra bedroom and clicked on a table lamp, an arc of light appearing like a holy apparition across the white wall. Their shadows were so tall that their heads touched the ceiling. She showed him the shower and where they kept the towels. When she bent over to explain how to use the stereo, her T-shirt hung open, exposing her cleavage. She slowly kissed him on the forehead, soft, wet lips, and she left him alone. As he lay in bed he felt himself aroused. As much as he tried to picture Maria, he couldn't stop seeing Lorena, nor could he help but fantasize about what her sister looked like. He reached in his underwear and felt for himself, but on the high part of the wall, above the shadow of his horizontal body, in the arc of light, he saw an image of Maria as if wearing a veil. He turned off the lamp.

The next day Pancho woke him early and said it was his day off and he'd show Juan around.

"And tomorrow I'm calling in sick. We have so much to do."

As they drove through the city, Juan said, "I need to work, *primo*. I need a job."

"What are you going to do?" said Pancho.

"I have some connections in Fresno," said Juan. "I thought I'd go there and pick fruit."

Pancho laughed. "That's wetback work."

I *am* a wetback, Juan thought. But he said, "I'm not experienced enough at anything else."

"Miguel. Miguelito," said Pancho, shaking his head. His chubby cheeks were slightly pockmarked from acne as a teenager. "I got it all figured out, *primo*. Don't worry."

They drove out of town onto a narrow two-lane highway lined by tall pine trees, until they reached a clearing, a vast green ranch set in a glen, beyond which the ocean lay over the horizon like a sparkling blue sheet. They entered a white gate with the name of the ranch, Cielito Lindo, and drove on the paved driveway until they reached a three-story Spanish-style hacienda.

"What is this place?" Juan asked.

"You'll see."

A white man in his fifties walked out of the mansion. He wore tight jeans and a flannel shirt tucked in and was in good shape for his age. His gray hair was balding on the top. He smiled as he approached Juan, extending his hand. "Welcome, Miguel. My name's BD. Pancho told me all about you and the funny thing that happened at the border." Although he spoke with an American accent, he spoke Spanish well.

"Yes, it was very funny," Juan said.

"What are the chances?" BD said.

BD led them around the mansion to the stables, white wooden buildings with so many doors extending on the horizon that it looked like a mirror image of itself. People led horses in and out of the doors. They entered one and saw horses proudly standing in their stalls, white and black Arabians, their nostrils flaring as if aware of their own worth. A Mexican man was brushing one of them, and as he stroked her silky neck, he cooed how beautiful she was.

"Memo," BD said to the man.

Memo looked up.

"This is Miguel Godoy. He's going to join our team."

"It's very nice to meet you," said Juan.

"Guillermo Reyes," the man said, extending his hand to Juan. "Godoy, you say? Is that a Mexican name?"

"Of course it is," said Juan.

"Well, the name itself isn't," said Pancho. "But our family is pure Mexican. Although we're the first generation of American," he said, proudly putting his arm around Juan.

Memo's eyes scrutinized Juan. "Are you from Michoacán?"

"No, hell no. He's from Jalisco," said Pancho, offended by the thought.

"You sound like you're from Michoacán," Memo said.

Over iced tea under a white gazebo, BD explained how he became part owner of the ranch when he was Pancho's age, twenty-five, and he had invested money in the land with four other partners. Over the years they built the country club, the stables, and bought twenty more acres on which their customers rode the horses. Some of the horses they took care of for the rich and famous. BD, who worked as an INS officer with Pancho, would retire in a few years a rich man. "I'll spend all my time out here."

"See, cousin, that's the secret of success. You spend your lifetime investing. Right now I'm thinking about buying into an apartment building. We'll invest our money together, cousin, and we'll be rich."

"What money?" Juan asked.

"What money," Pancho repeated, laughing.

Juan's job at the ranch, BD explained, was to take the horses out of the stable for the customers, make sure the customers mounted safely, and then return the horses to Memo or another stable hand when the ride was over.

"But I don't speak English," Juan said.

"What a great way to learn," Pancho said.

"I don't know anything about horses," Juan said.

"He's being modest," Pancho said. "He has a gift."

When BD told Juan how much he'd be earning, Juan had to hear it again to be certain he had heard right.

"And the best part of it is," said Pancho, "tax-free. Cash."

That evening Lorena's sister, Elida, an eighteen-year-old with light brown hair and golden eyes, had dinner with the family. She was so beautiful that Juan couldn't stop sneaking looks at her, and she frequently looked at him and smiled shyly, which made the little black-eyed twins put their tiny hands over their mouths and giggle. When Pancho broke out with the stories about Miguel as a child, how brave he was and how everyone knew he'd be a great man, how girls used to follow him around, about the fights he'd get into with older and bigger boys, Elida looked at him with a stare that bordered on awe. Juan relished the stories, picturing it all and almost believing that he had done those things. After dinner, while the family was drinking coffee and the little girls were eating their dessert, Juan stood up and said he'd like to get some fresh air. He looked at Elida and asked if she would join him.

She said she'd love to.

On the patio they sat on the swing. The full moon shone like a cross in the black sky and reflected in Elida's large eyes. Her face was smooth. The sweet smell of her perfume rose like curls of smoke and swam into his nose, reaching so far into him that they massaged his heart. "Can I touch your face?" he said.

"My face? That's funny. Why for would you want to do that?"

Her Spanish wasn't good, but she had probably never been to Mexico.

"Because it's the most beautiful face I have ever seen."

She lowered her eyes. He kept looking at the smoothness of her skin, down her thin neck — a birthmark at the protruding bone. Her breasts.

"OK," she said. "You can touch."

He looked up.

He reached out his hand, opened his palm, and as if he were touching something sacred, he slowly felt the warmth of her face. Passionately, she pressed her cheek into his hand and she closed her eyes and sighed. "That's nice," she said, opening her eyes and looking into his.

Lorena called them inside to watch a movie they had rented. Side by side on the love seat, they glanced as often at each other as they did at the TV. When it was over, Elida said she had to get home. Juan walked her to the car. She opened the door, but before she got in she turned around, bit her bottom lip, and peered at him with eyes that spoke of desire. "I guess I'll see you later," she said.

"You will."

He watched her pull onto the street, her taillights disappearing into the darkness.

When he went back into the house, Pancho and Lorena were waiting for him, standing side by side, big smiles on their faces.

Although it hadn't been two days, these two seemed so familiar, so much like family. It occurred to him that he could keep this up for a long time, maybe forever. Maybe they would never know. Juan, quite frankly, was having a good time.

What was the rush to work in those hot fields, making less in one month than what he'd make in a week at the stables? He could still send Maria money.

Maria.

She hadn't even cried when he left. She was probably glad he was gone.

"Well, cousin, tell us," Pancho said, as if he couldn't stand the anticipation. "What did you think of Lorena's sister?"

Juan laughed, heading toward the hallway to his bedroom, and he said, as if the question carried its own answer, "What did I think of Lorena's sister."

Life was great.

He made plenty of money, much of which he spent taking Elida to restaurants. He was beginning to learn English, and Pancho wanted them to invest in real estate together, as a team. When Juan reminded him he didn't have much money, Pancho assured him it would work out. "I don't think that'll be a problem," he said. One day at work, feeling good after a night with Elida, wherein they went further than they ever had, although not all the way, he was friendly and joked with the customers in English. Around midday, he got this urge to have lunch with someone, to click glasses with an old friend. In the stables he searched for Memo but couldn't find him, not in the country club or walking around the grounds. Finally, as he was walking around the back of the stables, he saw him at a picnic table, eating lunch with his family, his wife and two kids, a little boy and a little girl. They weren't talking as they ate, but it was such a picture of happiness that for the first time in a long time, he thought of his own kids, Juan Jr., the baby, and he felt a great loss for his Maria.

What was she going to do without him? The right thing to do would be to take the money he had already earned, perhaps earn a little more, and send it to Maria. Wherever she was at that moment, whatever she was doing, there was no doubt in her mind that he was going to come back. He had to quit seeing Elida.

Later that night they were walking along the pier in San Diego when he decided to tell her it was over between them. He said, "I think you should know something."

Elida stopped walking and looked at him. Her eyes filled with love and hope. Anticipation.

"I love you," he blurted.

They kissed.

Later that night in her small bedroom plastered with glossy Ricky Martin posters, they made love. Her parents were out of town. Afterwards, as he held her smooth body in his thin arms, the smell of her perfume mixed with the scent of the peach candle flickering on her nightstand, he told her that he never wanted to be without her. And he meant it. He was in love.

When he got home, Pancho was sitting on the couch waiting for him, his big legs crossed, his arm extended across the back of the sofa.

"What's up?" Juan asked.

"Remember that surprise I told you about?"

"What surprise?" asked Juan.

"When I first saw you at the border. I told you I had a surprise for you."

"Oh yeah," said Juan.

"Well, tomorrow I'm going to let you have it," he said, standing up.

When Juan woke up the next morning, Pancho had already left. He found Lorena in the kitchen cutting a melon into bite-sized slices. She told him that Pancho had gone to get the surprise. As she served him a plate of the melon and a cup of strong black coffee, she saw the concern in his face. "Don't worry so much," she said as she sat at the table opposite him.

He remained silent, worried.

"You do like it here with me and Pancho, right?"

He was distracted, but he still said yes.

"Look," she said, feeling sorry for him, "I think what Pancho's doing is wrong. I told him so. If you're not prepared for it, things could be difficult."

"What are you talking about?"

"The surprise. I told him not to do it this way, but he wouldn't listen. Sometimes he doesn't think things out fully. This is one of those times."

"What's the surprise?" asked Juan.

"OK, I'm going to tell you," Lorena said. "But only because I don't think it's right what he's doing."

Pancho went to the Greyhound bus station, she said, to pick up Godoy's mother, who had been living in El Paso. He was bringing her here so she could live with Miguel, her only living son.

The world fell on him. It was over. A mother would always know who her son was. "Don't worry," said Lorena. "She'll be so happy to see you. She never stopped being your mother."

After eating a couple of pieces of melon and drinking coffee, Juan said he wasn't feeling well and wanted to lie down. When he got into his bedroom, he quickly pulled the dirty duffel bag from the closet and started packing everything that would fit. He grabbed the cash he had already earned and stuffed it at the very bottom of his socks and then pulled on his boots. He had to be gone before Pancho got back. He would lose out on a few days' pay, but better that than lose his life. He was ready to go, when he heard a knock on the bedroom door. He stuffed the bag in the closet and jumped into bed, pulling the covers over his body. "Come in," he said.

Lorena walked in, disturbed. She pulled the chair that was leaning against the wall and scooted it close to the bed. "There's something else. And this is it. I mean this is really it. This is why I'm telling you what Pancho's doing. I think you need to be prepared."

"What?" he said.

"It's been a long time since you've seen her." She paused, as if the words were too difficult. "Miguel, your mother is getting very senile."

"How senile?" he said, perking up.

"She forgets things sometimes. People sometimes. And . . ."

"What? What?"

"After your father disowned you — and she still doesn't believe the story."

"The story?"

"About you and that other boy. She doesn't believe it. None of us do."

"Uh, that's good."

"But after he disowned you, she never gave up on you. She knew she would see you again. She's been saving things for you. After your father died, he left, well, quite a bit of money."

"How much?"

"A lot, Miguel. You don't even have to work if you don't want. She's been saving it for you. I only tell you this because I want you to be prepared. I told Pancho it wasn't a good idea to not tell you first. But he was just so excited about the, you know, the . . . Well, he wants you to be happy."

"What if she doesn't recognize me?" he asked.

"She's senile. It just means we'd have to . . . What am I saying? She will."

Juan sat up on his bed. "Well, then, I'll look forward to meeting her. I mean, seeing her again."

Lorena left the room. Juan paced back and forth with a burst of energy. When he heard the truck pull up onto the gravel, he said to himself, "Here we go." He looked at himself in the mirror. He saw staring at him Miguel Valencia Godoy. Clean-shaven, handsome, lean-bodied, confident. But then he glimpsed something that bothered him, a dull gleam in his eyes, something that didn't belong to him. Insecurity. It was Juan. He shook it off and went out into the living room to see his mother.

aleida rodríguez

LEXICON OF EXILE

> Animals seem to fill their skins, trees their bark,
> rivers their banks, so beautifully, that we cannot
> help but see in their wildness a perfect at-homeness.
> — SCOTT RUSSELL SANDERS

There is no way I can crank a dial,
scroll back the scenery,
perch *sinsontes* outside my windows
instead of scrub jays and mockingbirds and linnets.

There is no way the brightly lit film
of childhood's cerulean sky, fat with meringue clouds,
can play out its reel unbroken by the hypnotist's snap:
You will not remember this.

There is no way I can make that Pan American plane
fly backward, halt the tanks of the Cuban revolution,
grow old in Güines, smelling the sour blend of rice and milk
fermenting in a pan by the chicken coop.

There is no way I can pull the harsh tongue
from my mouth, replace it with lambent
turquoise on a white sand palate,
the cluck of coconuts high in the arc of palm trees.

The trees fingering their dresses outside my windows now
are live oak, mock orange, pine, eucalyptus.
Gone are the *ciruelas, naranjas agrias,*

the *mamoncillos* with their crisp green shells
concealing the pink tenderness of lips.

Earth's language is a continuous current,
translating the voices of my early trees along the ground.
I can't afford not to listen.
They find me islanded in Los Angeles,
surrounded by a moat filled with glare,
and deliver a lost dictionary of delight.

A lingual bridge lowers into my backyard,
where the Fuju persimmon beams in late summer
and the fig's gnarled silver limbs become conduits
for all the ants of the world; where the downy woodpecker
    teletypes
a greeting on the lightpost and the overripe sapotes fall
with a squishy thud; where the lemon, pointillistically studded
with fruit, glows like a celebration; where the loquat drops
yellow vowels and the scrub jays nesting in the lime
chisel them noisily with their hard black beaks
high in the branches, and the red-throated hummingbird —
mistaking me for a flower — suspends just inches from my face,
deciding whether or not to dip into the nectar of my eyes
until I blink, and it sweeps all my questions into the single sky

luis alberto urrea

🦅 TIJUANA COP

H E FLICKED ON THE SIREN. It whooped satisfactorily, sounding like a television show. *"Muévete, pendejo"* (Move, asshole), he muttered to the cars that blocked his way as he maneuvered the Río de Tijuana thoroughfare. I glanced at the speedometer: we were doing eighty-five miles per hour, slaloming around the traffic. He steered with his left hand, his right arm casually thrown over the back of the passenger seat. I stared at his wrist hairs as I slid around in the back.

"Hey," he said, glancing back at me with a big grin. He wore aviator shades that completely hid his eyes; his mustache drooped past the corners of his mouth. "I bet you never thought you'd be riding in the back seat of a Tijuana cop car!"

"Not on purpose," I said.

It began innocently enough, with me babbling in abject terror.

I was getting my boots shined in one of those step-up shoeshine stalls you find all over Tijuana. It was like going to confession — the little booth had a wooden seat, and the only things visible to passersby were my feet. The gentleman buffing my left boot was wiry and bright with sweat. I settled in with a copy of *¡Alarma!*, Mexico's premier blood-drenched tabloid. As usual, it was full of satisfyingly lurid pictures: massacred cops, massacred drug dealers, car-wreck victims, cult murders, train-killed bodies.

We were on the corner of Ninth. A tan-clad arm flashed into the booth, its hard fist closing on my wrist. *A cop!* I jerked: *Oh my God! I'm busted!* For what, in retrospect, I don't know. I had wanted to meet a Tijuana cop, and had asked my relatives to arrange it, yet here I was blanching white and going utterly dry-mouthed. I had forgotten everything.

"What are you doing here, you son of a bitch," his voice snarled.

The shoeshine man, not knowing what was going on, backed away from my foot and sat on his haunches, watching. His face was completely blank.

"Ubb," I offered. "Ubba, ubba," I explained.

The cop's face peered in at me. I could see myself in his shades. He started to smile. Then he laughed. He asked me how I was doing. This apparently passed for humor among Tijuana's finest.

They are aware of their reputations. They cultivate their reputations. After all, nothing is more *macho* than causing immediate fear. They swagger, they beat people, they demand bribes, and they shoot. Members of my family have been officers of the Tijuana police force, yet I cut a wide swath around their brothers-in-arms, as does anyone with any sense.

Still, imagine being a cop in Tijuana. The mind reels. Here is a man called upon to preserve order in the most celebrated bastion of chaos on the border. This man is expected to enforce traffic laws in a country whose roads are haphazard at best, where stop signs often appear either twenty yards before an intersection — which is merely a dirt path straggling down to the road — or immediately after. There are no stop lines. No one minds the speed limits. And if he gives a gringo a traffic ticket, the gringo drives home and shows it to his friends and they have a good laugh and throw it away.

He works a city of famed vice: cascades of liquor, prostitution, child porn, drugs, even a healthy black market in fireworks and faux perfumes. His beat is visited by more gringos than visit Disneyland, and he has to judge which of these tourists are actually here to do harm, which are here to find innocent bargains, which have cocaine stuffed in their underwear, which carry knives, which are stoned or drunk or psychopathic.

His world is governed by laws that are effectively the reverse of ours: in Mexico, you are guilty until proven innocent. This leads to an enforced, endemic paranoia: of course you're lying — only a good lawyer will make anybody think otherwise. Add this policy to the already embattled and embittered mentality of a beat cop, and then stir in a Mexican loathing and resentment of gringos, and you're dealing with a difficult situation, at best. As a walking ambassador of American goodwill, you will invariably fail to impress.

And then, of course, there are the bribes. Mexicans call them *la mordida* (the bite). (American kids called cops "pigs" in the sixties, and Mexican kids called cops "dogs.") *La mordida* is not a private vice of the Mexican police. Anyone who has dealt with our friendly neighbor knows this. The phenomenon is too complex to dissect here — suffice it to say that it's a culture of patronage, with a long tradition of graft. It is a social Darwinist's dream, where the strong rule, and their strength is often measured by how much money they can extract from you for the most basic human need. It is a symbolic world where the money you pay out demonstrates your respect for the official and the official's position of merit, honor, and service.

In the case of the cops, add poverty.

Most police will tell you that no cop is paid enough. In Tijuana, as late as the early eighties, cops pulled in a whopping salary of twenty dollars a week. As if that weren't difficult enough, Tijuana cops buy their own guns. Motorcycle cops buy their own motorcycles. A handsome .357 Magnum with ivory grips and a Harley hog cost a bit more than any average officer can afford. Guess where they get their extra budgets.

I pulled myself from the shoeshine stand and was embarrassed that my knees shook. *Man,* I thought, *what a wimp.*

His shirt was open at the neck, showing black hair curling over the top of a brilliant white undershirt. The inevitable *Dirty Harry* Magnum rode high on his right hip. He wore knee boots polished bright as mirrors. Stripes ran up the sides of his tight pants.

"I just got a call I have to investigate. Want to come?"

"Yeah," I said.

"Let's go," he said, spinning on his heel and marching toward the police station.

We hopped into a cruiser, and he clicked on the radio, muttered his name, his destination, and a series of numbers.

"Hey, Pepe!" he called out the window. "I'm taking your car!"

"Fuck you!" Officer Pepe yelled back. Everybody laughed.

"Pinche Pepe," he said.

We wove down the street, impatiently honking at slow cars. Pedestrians on the corners gawked at me in the back with the same slack-faced look of dread I suddenly realized I had on my face every time a prisoner was whisked past me in the back of one of those cars.

"Look at this," the cop was saying. Cars refused to allow him through the intersection. "Nobody gives a damn about the law!"

He hit his siren, gestured, waved his arms.

"¡Policía!" he snapped out the window. "Get out of the way!"

Tijuana's downtown gridlock suddenly broke, and we shot through.

"Nobody loves a cop," he said.

"Don't say I said so," he said, "but there are a lot of crooked officers on this force."

"Really?" I said, trying to sound bland.

He shrugged, raised both hands. The car steered itself for twenty feet. "That's life. What did you expect? This is Tijuana."

We came upon a gap in the center island.

"Hold on," he said.

Before I knew what we were doing, he threw us into a power slide, sideways through the gap. The car fishtailed in front of oncoming traffic, then the tires bit into the road and we shot off in the opposite direction, still going a respectable seventy-five.

"Not bad, eh?" he said.

"Wow," I said.

"I'll show *you* who can drive," he said.

"No! Please!" I cried. I thought twice about making any jokes about police cruelty or torture of suspects. Instead, I said, "Tell me more about corruption."

"A few years ago," he said, "we were getting a lot of hassle from the San Diego police. We had car thieves working on our force. San Diego told us, 'Look. You can't do this. You can't steal American cars. You're cops!'"

He glanced back at me. "Lots of these *cabrones* have new Toyota pickups. Where do you think they got them?"

We slowed abruptly and left the main road, cutting up a hill at the north end of Tijuana. We passed under a narrow railroad bridge and hit rough patches of dirt.

"Those crooked cops," he said, "make it hard for us who want to be honest. Some of us are good cops. But now all of us get investigated all the time."

We were heading up into Colonia Libertad, the notorious *barrio* where illegals and *coyotes* gathered every night to go into the canyons. Lawlessness had enjoyed a vogue in those hills for so long that police didn't care to venture there at night. My guide said, "Watch out up here. These people are animals. They don't give a shit about anything. If they catch us in a dead end, they'll hit us with rocks. Stay with me and keep your mouth shut."

"Yes, sir," I said.

Apparently a bus had run over a guy on a motorcycle. Someone called it in to police headquarters, but nobody knew how long ago. When we got there, the twisted bike was lying in the dirt. It was a small Japanese machine. The bus had backed out of a blind drive, climbed over the bike and the rider, and continued backing out.

"You didn't see him?" demanded the cop.

"No," said the driver.

"You didn't *feel* him?"

"No."

The cop rubbed his face, looked around. "Where's the cyclist?"

Everybody shrugged.

"Is he dead?"

Shrugs. "Maybe." "No." "I don't know."

Mud around the crushed bike could have been blood. Then again, it could have been oil or gas or urine.

"Did an ambulance take him?"

"No," said the bus driver. Then, "A car. One of the neighbors."

Clearly angry by now, the cop took his name and address. "We'll be coming for you," he said ominously.

The driver's eyebrows shot up in alarm, but before the cop could be reasoned with, he was back in his car. On the hill, *cholos* yelled slang insults at him: "Hey *chota*" (a nickname for "cop"), *"fuck you!"*

Grimly, he backed out and floored it, pelting the crowd with gravel. They skipped and danced in his cloud of dust.

"We're going to the city hospital," he said. "It's a butcher shop. Don't say anything when we get there, because they don't like people seeing their emergency rooms. I'll tell them you're a detective."

We arrived on the emergency ramp in a burst of lights.

"Walk fast," he said, hitching up his gun belt.

I followed him at my best police-inspector clip. We stormed through the doors, brushing past a concerned orderly who wanted us to halt. On our way into the bowels of the hospital, however, we were accosted by an old nurse. She held up her hand and commanded us to stop. "What is your business?" she asked.

"Investigating an accident," the cop said.

"And this gentleman?"

"Detective."

I looked too much like a gringo.

"Sí, señora," I said in my best Spanish.

Like a relentless gnome in a Monty Python skit, she badgered us. "Does he have ID?" she demanded of the cop.

"Ma'am," he said, exasperated, "he's *undercover!*"

This arcane police word seemed to work on her, and she relented.

"Follow me," she said.

Although there were surely no flies in the hospital, they remain my overwhelming impression of the place. I imagine big-assed flies bumping into everything. Dust and dirt formed small wedges in the corners, dirty bandages were visible on the floors of rooms standing empty, middle-aged women lay on stretchers in the hall obviously suffering from something that was not readily visible. We glanced into the various emergency cubicles as we went down the hall. Innumerable fascinating scenes were enacted in each, but no biker. The last stall featured the nightmarish vision of a nurse leaning over a boy's face with pliers of some sort. She had latched on to something and was trying to work it out. He writhed and shouted, flat on his back, arms and legs strapped down. She paused in her efforts and looked up at us, plier handles still firmly in her grip. The cop blandly stared at this tableau, then looked at me and wiggled his eyebrows up and down. "Interesting," he said.

Outside, he said, "Well, who knows where the motorcyclist is." We got in the car. "Fuck him. Let's go."

So we went back to the station.

I entered with some dread.

"Keep out of the way," he said, going in to make out his report.

A small group of Americans was seated on a bench. One of the women had slivers of glass in her face; she was dabbing at the blood with tissues. Various cops milled around the bench looking down at the kids. The official *policía* translator hovered over them. He was a smarmy disco king in a shiny silken shirt and slicked-back hair.

"Hello, frien'," he said to them. "Hello, baby."

"Please," the cut woman said.

"Baby," the translator said, "you go to jail." It sounded as though he were asking her if she attended Yale.

"Everybody," he said, gesturing at the lot of them, "going to Yale!"

He beamed, as though they had just won a raffle.

"They have to be investigated," the cop said behind me. He must have filed a short report.

"But they're hurt," I said.

"That's what happens in a car wreck, *amigo*."

Too dazed to be terrified, the gringo kids slumped on the seat, looking stringy and tattered.

"She needs help," I said.

The cop pursed his lips. He took a better look, apparently suspicious that she was faking the glass in her face.

"Hmm," he said.

"Don't worry, frien'," said the translator. "No problem!"

I didn't dare speak to the kids. I had no idea what codes of behavior and protocol I might be breaking. I certainly didn't want to join them in Yale.

The cop went to talk to the captain, who stepped out of his office and scowled at me, then at them. This was obviously highly irregular.

"Martínez!" he snapped at some distant officer. "Get this girl some medical attention."

He vanished back into his office.

All the cops seemed shocked by this development. They stood there staring at the kids on the bench. One of them finally detached himself from the mob and tenderly took the young woman by the arm and pulled her up. Then he looked around, wondering what to do with her. They turned and disappeared into the interior of the station, and the translator was cooing, "OK, baby. Is O-K."

Dark was falling. He was going off-duty.

"I'll give you a ride to where you're going," he said. We wandered back over to Pepe's car and got in again.

"You can sit in the front," he said.

He took off his shades, worked his crackling neck, rubbed his eyes.

"What a job," he said.

We backed out, cruised slowly. His eyes compulsively scanned the sidewalks, flicked from door to door, lit fleetingly on faces as we passed.

"A Salvadoran got his tongue cut out over here," he said, pointing to a corner. "How do you like that? Right down the street from the police station. *Pinche* gang of *cholos* get hold of this poor guy and cut out his tongue. What do you do with people like that?"

Next block.

"This old man came up to me this morning. Some crazy *pendejo* killed his dog over there." He pointed. "He pulled the dog out of the old man's truck and kicked it to death." He shook his head. "What are you going to do," he said.

It was fully dark by now.

"That's a great disco over there," he said. "You should try it." Marko's Jet-Set Disco.

"You have a strange job," I said.

He smiled.

"It's not so bad," he said. "Hey! You know my favorite thing about being a cop?" He pulled over and stopped, turned around in the seat to face me. Tijuana's one last honest cop.

"What?" I said.

"Disco patrol."

"Disco patrol?"

"Yeah. It starts at two or three in the morning. We hang around on the side streets, watching for American women driving alone." He was really smiling now. "These dumb broads come down here by themselves to dance and pick up Mexicans."

"Oh, really," I said.

"So they come out of the discos and head for the border, and if they're alone, or there's two of them, I pull them over."

"Ticket," I said.

"Exactly. I turn on my lights, hit the siren — it scares them. They pull over. I get out of the car, mad as hell. I tell them they ran a red light."

"And you charge them a bribe?" I offered.

"A *bribe!*" he barked. "Don't make me laugh. I tell them they have to go to jail. I arrest them. Then I get them in the car. Then I pull out my lariat." *(La reata.)* He pantomimed laying a penis clearly nineteen inches long across the steering wheel.

"I tell them, 'Suck on this and you can go.' And you know what? Gringas are sluts — they always suck my lariat."

"Oh," I said.

He drove me to my destination in silence.

When we got there, I said, "Do you let them go?"

He said, "Of course I let them go! I'm a cop, not a monster."

culture clash

❦ THE MISSION

T HE BEGINNING of the play is set in eighteenth-century San Francisco, California. The upstage center area is used as the Mission courtyard. The downstage center area is flanked by a very contemporary apartment, which must not be exposed for the opening "Serra Overture" scene.

Serra Overture, 1776

Darkness.

Four Mission bells toll and a Native American funeral chant is heard. Moments later two Indios enter carrying candles. They cross center stage and salute the Four Directions, then turn upstage toward the altar/pedestal.

The Indios bend down and each light a candle on the floor; then they each light a candle on the second step of the pedestal. They are precise in observing their ritual. Following the lighting of the candles, the Indios kneel, each holding a candle at eye level. They blow the candles out.

The funeral chant music segues into European religious music. As this music builds, the lights slowly expose Father Serra on his pedestal — first his feet, then his legs, then his face, and then his hands outstretched to the heavens.

Father Serra descends a step at a time, assisted by the Indios, who remain on their knees until Father Serra passes before them. The Indios rise, turn toward the audience, follow Father Serra a step downstage, and kneel again to receive communion.

An overly dramatic narration is heard:

VOICEOVER: October 9th, 1776. The sixth mission under the direction of Father Junipero Serra was completed in California. San Francisco de Assisi was the crown jewel of all the missions in the Brave New World.

One man, one vision, one million Indios wiped out by murder, disease, and torture. And at least five known cases of the dreaded jock itch.

(*One of the Indios scratches his crotch area. Father Serra grabs the Indios by their ears.*)

Father Serra loved his little savages. No Indian was buried before his time. And by the grace of God, he set out to make these naked creatures "Men of Reason." The beloved Mission Dolores was built next to the Stream of Sorrows, known today as the San Francisco Bathhouse of Sorrows. Thousands of tourists lose their collective chonies there each year in the barrio streets of their mind, de chamberline, hear my rhyme, tecate with lime, commit a crime, do the time, OK, that's enough. Ladies and gentlemen, the anatomy of a Culture Clash — The Mission!

(*Music swells, underscoring Father Serra's following monologue.*)

FATHER SERRA: Oh, my little brown ones. What mischief have we been in today? My little savages, digo, my little sheep. When I found these little creatures, they were living in the cracks of the earth. Now they say no to crack! Verdad!

(*With that, Father Serra yanks the Indios' heads back by their hair.*)

I took away their pagan dances and gave them true culture! La opera, el ballet, los Gypsy Kings! I took away their primitive tongue and taught them Español, and you better speak Spanish now, my little ones, before English becomes the official language! I took away their religion; now they fear God! And, with a little help from the whip, the gun, and the cross . . . (*He pulls a large blade from a cross*) they respect me, despite my lisp.

One day the world will recognize me. In fact, I was almost canonized by the Pope himself. Yes, I'm feeling a little smug about the whole affair, and why not? The guilt I have instilled in these Indios is the very same guilt passed on to future generations of Indios, mestizos, and struggling Latino actors. I founded twenty-one California missions. My favorite is Mission Dolores in San Francisco of a sissy, digo Assisi, I envision a city here with great bridges, of pyramids, of Forty-Niners, and of Giants. One day they will name hospitals and schools after me. One day they will construct a stupid statue of me on Highway 280! Yet there are people who question whether I have performed any miracles. My friends, let me show you un milagro.

(Father Serra slaps his hand in a command. Indio #1 instinctively rolls forward like a trained dog.)

Parate! Bestia!

(Indio #1 stands.)

Sing, my little neophyte. Sing, my little California raisin!
INDIO #1: Fa la la la la la . . . *(Turns to Father Serra for approval)*
FATHER SERRA: You were flat like a tortilla. Donde esta mi whip? Sing again . . . sing . . . sing!

(Father Serra begins to flog the Indio with a leather whip.)

Sing, sing, sing! *(He is in a flogging sadomasochistic frenzy.)* Stop! Stop! Vale, vale, you have reached your flogging quota for the day. Go!

(Indio #1 turns back upstage to join Indio #2. As he turns, he exposes to the audience a perfect tic-tac-toe game on his back from the bloody flogging.)

FATHER SERRA: Oh, I don't know what to do with these Indios. I give them books, college, and I still get ring around the collar. Oh well, I guess I'll go to the Friars Club and have a smoke. Why do I speak like Count Chocula? (*Walks upstage to the Indios. To Indio #2:*) And I better not catch you spray-painting graffiti on the mission walls! (*Turns to Indio #1*) And as for you, do not worry about your back. A little lime juice will help.

(*With that, Father Serra whips Indio #1 on the back again. Indio #1 contorts in pain. Father Serra crosses himself.*)

And God bless you, son. And remember (*chanting*), Dominus Pizza delivers!

(*Father Serra exits. Indio #2 helps Indio #1 from the ground; they struggle. Indio #1 is singing, half dazed from the whipping. Indio #2 slaps some sense into him.*
Indio #1 speaks to Indio #2 in exaggerated sign language. Indio #2 responds with faster sign language.)

INDIO #1: Wait, wait, my brother; you always go too fast.

(*Indio #2 slows down. Then the Indios stop signing and start speaking in mock English accents.*)

Yes, what you say is true, my hardened-nippled brother. Father Serra is . . . an asshole!
INDIO #2: Why do you refuse to speak in our own language? You are assimilating, and why must you pretend to be a singer? You have told me on numerous occasions that you want to be a stand-up comedian.
INDIO #1: What you say is true, but the friars do not allow me to tell jokes in our native tongue. Why, just last night at the Monks' Lounge, I told a joke in our language and I received fifty lashes! Would you like to see the joke? (*He gestures the joke in native sign language.*) Do you like it?

INDIO #2: Yes, but I saw that on Indio Star Search last night.

INDIO #1: I remember a time not long ago when we didn't have to hold in our tummies so hard. A time when our people were proud and unafraid.

INDIO #2: We used to pray to the Grandfather Spirit and we respected Mother Earth.

INDIO #1: And then the Spaniards moved in, high atop their horses, and they tried to fix up everybody's hut and put our children in Montessori schools. And there went the barrio!

INDIO #2: And now our days are filled with hard labor, endless hours of work, pesticides. And we have no medical or dental benefits. Oh, why couldn't César Chávez have been born now?

INDIO #1: Hark! My foolish Jerry Garcia–looking brother, these Spaniards do not understand nonviolent protest. They will kill us for sure! What we need to do is mount an attack, a revolution! We must educate the others. (*Secretive*) I know a printer in Berkeley who can print us 10,000 flyers for a bushel of corn and a pair of Birkenstocks! What is it, my Three Dog Night–looking brother? Why does it appear that you are smelling freshly laid buffalo manure?

INDIO #2: Oh, my large-buttocked friend, the flogging has gone to your head like bad peyote.

(*Indio #2 slaps Indio #1 on his flogged back.*)

INDIO #1: Ouch!

INDIO #2: Sorry. What I am trying to say is that our brothers from the south tried an insurrection and it failed. This is our destiny. History is not on our side. (*Singing*) Que será, será. Whatever will be, will be.

INDIO #1: The future's not ours to see . . .

INDIO #2: Que Serra, Serra . . .

INDIO #1: There you go again with that Doris Day existential buffalo crap again. I have no time for your Kafka novel. You are falling for the Spanish Manifesto. I will mount a revolution myself. Because, my Credence Clearwater Revival Brother, at the end of this tunnel of death, I see a light!

INDIO #2: Light, my brother?
INDIO #1: Bud Lite! *(Pulls out beer can from a sack)* No! There.
INDIO #2: The exit sign?
INDIO #1: No, higher.
INDIO #2: Hi-yer?
INDIO #1: Hi-yah.
INDIO #2: Hi-yah?

(They perform a mock Native American chant and dance.)

INDIOS #1 AND #2: Hi-yah, hi-yah, hi-yah, hi-yah.
INDIO #1: Stop that! See, high above the ridge. A thousand points of light, a burning bush, and a dead quail. Surely it is a sign. I must warn the others, I must go. *(He exits.)*
INDIO #2: My brother, my brother . . . My heart bleeds for him. Too many floggings, too much MTV. I must transcend this reality. I must call upon the Grandfather Spirit and make contact with future generations and warn them of the evil and slaughter to come.

MELODRAMAS

nelly rosario

❧ INVASIONS, 1916

G RACIELA AND SILVIO stood hand in hand on El Malecón, sea breeze polishing their faces. Silvio hurled stones out to the waves and Graciela bunched up her skirt to search for more pebbles. Her knees were ashy and she wore her spongy hair in four knots. A rusty lard can filled with pigeon peas, label long worn from trips to the market, was by her feet. Silvio's straw hat was in Graciela's hands, and quickly, she turned to toss it to the water. The hat fluttered like a hungry seagull, then was lapped up by foam. Silvio's kiss pinned Graciela against the railing.

It was a hazy day. The hot kissing made Graciela squint against the silver light. Beyond her lashes, Silvio was a sepia prince.

— That yanqui over there's lookin' at us, he murmured into Graciela's mouth. He pulled out his hand from the rip in her skirt. Graciela turned to see a pink man standing a few yards away from them. She noticed that the yanqui wore a hat and a vest — he surely did not seem to be a Marine. When she was with Silvio, Graciela forgot to worry about anyone telling on her to Mai and Pai, much less panic over yanquis and their Marine boots scraping the cobblestones of the Colonial Quarter.

Passion burned stronger than fear. Graciela turned back to Silvio.

— Forget him. Her pelvis dug into his until she felt iron.

Graciela and Silvio were too lost in their tangle of tongues to care that a few yards away, the yanqui was glad for a brief break from the brutal sun that tormented his skin. With her tongue tracing Silvio's neck, Graciela couldn't care less that Theodore Roosevelt's "soft voice and big stick" on Latin America had dipped the yanqui the farthest south he had ever been from New York City. Silvio's hands crawled back into the rip in Graciela's skirt; she would not blush if she learned that the yanqui spying on them had already photographed the Marines stationed on her side of the island, who were there to "order and pacify," in all their debauchery; that dozens of her fellow Dominicans somberly populated the yanqui's photo negatives; and that the lush Dominican landscape had left marks on the legs of his tripod. Of no interest to a moaning Graciela were the picturesque postcard views that the yanqui planned on selling in New York and, he hoped, in France and Germany. And having always been poor and anonymous herself, Graciela would certainly not pity the yanqui because his still lifes, nature shots, images of battleships for the newspapers had not won him big money or recognition.

— Forget the goddamned yanqui, I said. Graciela squeezed Silvio's arm when his lips broke suction with hers.

— He's comin' over here, Silvio said. He turned away from Graciela to hide his erection against the seawall. Graciela watched the man approach them. He had a slight limp. Up close, she could see that his skin was indeed pink and his hair was a deep shade of orange. Graciela had never seen a real yanqui up close. She smiled and folded her skirt so that the rip disappeared.

The man pulled a handkerchief from his vest pocket and wiped his neck. He cleared his throat and held out his right hand, first to Silvio, then to Graciela. His handshake swallowed up Graciela's wrist, but she shook just as hard. In cornhashed Spanish the man introduced himself: Peter West, he was.

Peter. Silvio. Graciela. They were all happy to meet each other. The man leaned against the seawall and pulled out a wad of pesos from a pocket in his outer jacket. His eyes never left Graciela and Silvio.

— ¿So, are you with the Marines? Silvio asked in an octave lower than usual, and Graciela had to smile secretly because her sepia prince was not yet old enough to wear long pants.

The yanqui shook his head.

— No, no, he said with an air of importance. His thumb and index finger formed a circle around his right eye. Graciela looked over at Silvio. They wrinkled their noses. Then more cornhashed Spanish.

With the help of a Galician vendor, Peter West explained, he had accumulated an especially piquant series of photographs: brothel quadroons bathed in feathers, a Negro chambermaid naked to the waist, and, of course, he remembered with the silliest grin Graciela had ever seen, the drunken sailors with the sow. In fact, the sun was not so mean to him when he wore his hat and jacket. And fruit was sweet, whores were cheap.

Graciela reached for the pesos before Silvio did; after all, Peter West had thrust them in her direction when he finished his convoluted explanations. But he quickly pulled the pesos away, leaving Graciela's fingers splayed open.

With the promise of pesos, Graciela and Silvio found themselves in the Galician vendor's warehouse, where Peter West had staged many ribald acts among its sacks of rice. How happy they had been to help this yanqui-man push together the papier-mâché trees, to roll out the starched canvas of cracked land and sky. Silvio straddled the tiger with its frozen growl while Graciela pried open the legs of a broken tripod to look in its middle. When West lit the lamps, Graciela and Silvio squealed.

— ¡Look, look how he brought the sun in here!

Silvio shaded his eyes.

— This yanqui-man, he is a crazy.

Graciela's whisper rippled through the warehouse when the fantasy soured. The pink hand tugged at her skirt and pointed briskly to Silvio's pants. They turned to each other as the same hand dangled pesos before them.

— ¿You still want to go away with me, Mami, or no?

Silvio's whisper was hoarse.

Graciela's shoulders dropped. She unlaced her hair and folded her blouse and skirt. In turn, Silvio unbuttoned his mandarin shirt and untied the rope at his waist. Graciela folded her clothes along with his over a pile of cornhusks. In the dampness, they shivered while West kneaded their bodies as if molding stubborn clay.

They struggled to mimic his pouts and sleepy eyes. Instead of wrestling under heavy trees by Rio Ozama, or chewing cane in the fields near bateyes, or scratching each other's bellies in abandoned mills, or pressing up against the foot of a bridge, they were twisted about on a hard couch that stank of old rags. Bewildered, they cocked their necks for minutes at a time in a sun more barbarous than the one outside. Their bodies shone like waxed fruit, so West wiped them with white powder. Too light. So he used, instead, mud from the previous day's rain.

"Like this, you idiots."

Where his Spanish failed, West made monkey faces, which finally made Graciela titter — only to reveal gaps where her teeth had been knocked out in a fall from a cashew tree. She found it difficult to sweetly gaze up at the beams of the warehouse as he had instructed. Her eyes remained fixed on the camera.

Then Graciela and Silvio watched in complicit silence as West approached the couch and knelt in front of them. Graciela's leg prickled with the heat of his ragged breathing. One by one, West's fingers wrapped around Silvio's growing penis. He wedged the thumb of his other hand into the humid mound between Graciela's thighs. Neither moved while they watched his forehead glitter. And just as they could hear each other's own sucks of breath, they felt piercing slaps on their chins. West ran to the camera to capture the fire in their faces.

As promised, the yanqui-man tossed Silvio a flurry of pesos. Graciela rubbed caked mud from her arms while Silvio, still naked, wet his fingers to count the bills. Graciela wondered if he would hog up the money, then go off to porches and storefronts to resoak her name in mud. As she wiggled her toes into her sandals, cigar smoke made her bite the inside of her cheek.

— Me amur, ¿qué pase?

This time the knotted Spanish was in Graciela's hair, the grip on her shoulder moist. Before she could demand her own flurry of colored bills, a crash echoed throughout the warehouse. Glass and metal scattered across the floor. The photographer ran toward the crash and in his frenetic efforts to salvage the film plate did not bother to strangle Silvio.

Graciela and Silvio ran from the warehouse and hid behind barrels along the dock, suppressing adrenaline giggles.

— You liked it, she said.

Silvio made a fist, then pointed to the pockets of his shorts.

— ¡Gimme my earn, you! Graciela hissed. She clutched at his pocket. A puff of hair flopped over her eye.

— You liked it too, he said.

They wrestled, the strange arousal they had felt in the warehouse pumping through them again.

— I'll hold it for when I come for you, Silvio said in between breaths.

Graciela had to trust Silvio. She tied up her hair into four knots and ran to the market, where she should have been, before Mai sent her brother for her. Silvio kept his head down to try to hide the recently-paid-man brightness in his eyes. He should have been home helping his father with the coal. Graciela and Silvio did not know they had just been immortalized.

Absentmindedly, Graciela plucked four pieces of yucca for barter from the vendor's selection. Silvio's narrow back had disappeared into the market crowd in a swagger that thickened the dread in Graciela's throat. She was about to hand the vendor a lard can's worth of pigeon peas, only to realize that she had left it at the warehouse.

— Devil's toying with my peas.

Graciela bit the inside of her cheek. She turned away and fled.

— ¡Ladrona! the ever-suspicious vendor yelled into the crowd, but today, as usual, no one listened.

Away from the mass of vendors, fowl, and vegetables, Graciela's chest heaved under the stolen yucca and her hair unraveled again.

Once her stride slowed down, she banged her forehead three times with the heel of her hand. ¡Sugar! She was supposed to buy sugar, not yucca, which already grew in her father's plot. Graciela sucked her teeth, almost tasting the molasses hanging heavy in the air from the smokestacks eclipsing the hills.

— Graciela, your mai looks for you.

A woman with the carriage of a swan and a bundle balanced on her head walked from the nearby stream. Her even teeth flashed a warning as she stepped onto the road.

— Mai's got eyes all over me.

— You be careful with those yanqui-men ahead, the swan woman responded with a finger in midair. Then she walked toward the whistling ahead, bare feet sure and steady.

Graciela shaded her eyes. Tall uniformed men in hats shaped like gumdrops sat on the roadside. They drank from canteens and spat as far onto the road as they could. Graciela squatted in the dense grass to see how the fearless swan woman would move safely past them. The yanqui-men's rifles and giant bodies confirmed stories that had already filtered into the city from the eastern mountains: suspected gavillero rebels gutted like Christmas piglets; women left spread-eagled right before their fathers and husbands; children with eardrums drilled by bullets. Graciela had folded these stories into the back of her memory when she snuck about the city outskirts with Silvio. The yanqui-man in the warehouse seemed frail now, his black box and clammy hands no match for the long rifles aimed at the swan woman.

"Run, you Negro wench!" The soldier's shout was high-pitched and was followed by a chorus of whistles.

A pop resounded. Through the blades of grass, Graciela could see the white bundle continue down the road in a steady path. The woman held her head high as if the bundle could stretch her above the hats. Another pop and Graciela saw the woman drop to the ground. The soldiers milled around the screaming and thrashing in the grass. Some already had their shirts pulled out of their pants.

Behind the soldiers, Graciela scrabbled away in the blades of grass. By the time the pack of men dispersed, they had become olive dots behind her. The yucca grated inside her blouse. Twigs and soil lodged in her nails. Half an hour later, with all four hair knots completely undone, Graciela was relieved to catch a glimpse of donkeys and their cargo, vendors with their vegetable carts, a rare Model T making crisscross patterns on the road.

The air was tight as she pulled herself up and ran past neighbors' homes. No children played outside. Graciela did see horses — many horses — tied to fenceposts along the way. She could not shake the urge to yawn and swell her lungs with air.

The main road dropped into a dustier, brushier path, leading to the circle of familiar thatched cabins. Two horses were tied to the tree by the fence. Graciela could not hear her mother yelling to her younger brother, Fausto, for coal, or the chickens clucking in the kitchen. Fausto was not sitting on the rickety chair making graters from the sides of cans, saying, — Mai was gonna send for you, stupid harlot.

Instead, from the kitchen came the clatter of tin. As Graciela moved closer, the stench of old rags flared her nostrils again. Inside, Mai knelt by a soldier whose fists entangled her hair and had undone the cloth rollers. Fausto, a statue in the corner. A man wearing his mustache in the handlebar style of the yanquis calmly asked Mai where her husband hid the pistols and why he was away in the hills. Mai's face was marble as she explained that her husband had no weapons, he was a God-fearing farmer, and there was her daughter at the door with yucca from his plot, see how dirty she was from working so hard with her beloved father, come Graciela, come bring the fruits of his sweat so these gentlemen can see how hard we work.

Graciela stepped forward with thin, yellow-meat yucca she was too ashamed to say her father had harvested. The interpreter shoved Graciela against the cold hearth and jammed his face against hers.

Must be cane rum coloring his bloodshot eyes, she thought, Devil toying with her peas again, trying to stick pins in her eyes to make her blink.

— Pai don't got pistols, he only got cane rum, Graciela said.

Her eyes still on the man, Graciela pointed to a shed outside. The man twisted the ends of his mustache. With the same fingers he clamped Graciela's nose and held it until there was blood, which he wiped against her blouse.

— Now you've got my aquiline nose, he said, then sucked the

rest of her blood from his fingers. This overeager display of barbarism fueled in Graciela more anger than fear. Mai, Graciela, and Fausto watched as he helped the yanqui-men load their horses with bottles of cane rum. Before taking off, they rinsed their hands in the family's barrel of fresh rainwater.

The mandatory disarmament of the city and its outskirts left a trail of new stories that would find their way back to the eastern mountains. By 1917, the country fell prey to young American men relieved that their incompetence had landed them in the tropics instead of Europe, where fellow soldiers had been dropped into a bubbling world war. For the next eight years these men sparked a war, equipped with sturdy boots, uniforms, and rifles, against machetes, rusty revolvers, and sometimes bare feet. It was a battle between lion and ant. And when an ant pinched a paw, the lion's roar echoed: in Mexico, Panama, Cuba, Haiti, Dominican Republic.

A passionate creditor, Woodrow Wilson, demanded that the country's debt dollars be paid back in full while World War I shook across the ocean. At roughly 23°30' north longitude, 30°30' west latitude, Graciela and Silvio could not distinguish the taste of gunpowder from salt in the air of El Malecón.

Graciela's swollen nose stung as she peeled away the yucca's husk. Yellow and gray veins tunneled through the tuber's white flesh.

— ¡Sugar! I send you for sugar, and you take the morning with you, Mai said, panic still twisting her voice.

For a moment Graciela wished that the soldiers had worked harder on Mai, had left her eyes swollen shut so she could not notice Graciela's unraveled hair.

Of course Graciela could never reveal that in the two hours she had been gone the sea salt was good against her skin, and so was Silvio, and that she was even able to earn some extra money . . .

Mai blared about hard-earned peas, and money for coal, money for shoes, money for sugar, about what green yanqui soldiers do to girls with skirts aflame, how lucky they all were to have been spared. Mai whacked her daughter on the back with a cooking spoon, squeezed the tender cartilage of her ears, wove her claws into Graciela's knotted hair. And Mai sobbed at only having her own flesh and blood with which to avenge humiliation. Excuses for the lack of peas, or money, or sugar on the table were postponed until the following day, when Pai returned from the bush with better crop and a heavier whipping hand.

Pai did emerge from the bush with better crop, but with hands too blistered by a week of harvesting to draw out confessions. He unearthed the pistols from under the water barrels and, with a furrowed brow, oiled them in the privacy of the outhouse. Graciela was perversely relieved by his preoccupation with who had snitched him out to the yanquis, and she carried on with her household chores, rag-doll dramas, fights with Fausto. Whenever she thought of Silvio buying tamarind balls with their money, Graciela bit the roughened inside of her cheek.

— Get yourself a whipping branch, Pai said days later to Graciela after he had devoured an avocado. He sat in front of the house repairing his only pair of shoes while she reluctantly climbed the cashew tree. As she handed over a thin branch, Graciela saw where mercury still stained the cuts on his hands.

— I told you to get a thicker branch, girl, he said.

After she had chosen the branch and wet it as he had instructed, Graciela followed Pai to the back of the house; Mai had already laid out the rice and stood a few feet away with her arms crossed. Without being told, Graciela removed her dress and knelt on the grains.

— You beat her good so she learns, Mai said to Pai. Then she disappeared into the kitchen, where Graciela could see her spying between the wood planks.

The first strike of the branch burned across the back of her thighs.

— Cry hard, girl, and satisfy your mai.

Pai thrashed the dirt around them. Graciela kept the smirk that she knew could make Mai's voice turn to pieces of breaking china. Finally, Pai cut the branch across the soles of her feet and hurled it to the bushes. Exasperated, he set a brand-new lard can full of peas on her head.

— Girl, you stay there till you lose that insolence.

Rice grains cut into her knees and the can of peas ignited a migraine. Still, Graciela would not confess; nothing she could have said would put her in a favorable light. Better to withstand the bursts of pain in her knees than to tell of her travesties with Silvio and multiply the existing worries in the household.

To numb herself Graciela sang songs, counted to ten twenty times, made popping sounds and saliva bubbles, concentrated on the caterpillar by the outhouse. Her thighs pressed tighter to hold back urine. After the breeze had chilled her raw skin, she began to itch where Paï's forgiving whip had left inevitable welts. A bug tickled her ankle. A sneeze crippled her side.

— ¡Move and I shoot! Fausto said. He wore a gourd on his head, pointed a long piece of sugarcane at her, and revealed his own gaps for front teeth.

Two lizards copulated behind the barrel of rainwater. And suddenly Silvio waved pesos across Graciela's mind. He had not snuck around to their grove of cashews with his telltale whistle since the day of the yanqui. The clouds above Graciela did not move. In her agony, her anger and longing for Silvio became interchangeable.

Had Pai known of what she did with Silvio, he would have let the whip open her skin. He might have had Silvio hunted like a guinea hen. Might have scared him with a fresh-oiled pistol. Or turned him over to the yanquis.

With the frozen clouds and the sun baking circles in her head and the can of peas tumbling to the ground and the rice grains up against her flushed cheek, Graciela decided she would hunt for Silvio herself and make him put a zinc roof over her head.

felicia luna lemus

TRACE ELEMENTS OF
RANDOM TEA PARTIES

TRIPPED over a seam in the trailer's chrome floor. Real quick,
before I could do any serious damage, I introduced myself, sat
down in the kitchen nook, and did my best to mumble out
socially appropriate words between no-blink stares. Fireworks, I
watched her lick maple frosting off her fork, all flat-tongue sticking
out the way Nana used to slap me upside the head for doing. I was
beyond smitten. Story's name was Edith and she got to Amy's
trailer half an hour after Nolan and I showed up for the Fourth of
July tea party.

I might as well tell you right now that this is really about my girl
Weeping Woman, Nana, and me. My best boy, Nolan, she says listening to me is like letting a drunk drive you to a gala event — no
indicators given at turns and the windshield wipers are always on.
Buckle up, doll. I promise I'll try not to tangle your quinceañera
dress. We'll get to the ballroom soon enough.

My girl Edith: smarty-pants Mission District glamour homegrrrl
moved down to Los Angeles on her leopard-print motorcycle. Edith
and her amazing sex-radical dancer thighs, she had a homemade
guitar string tattoo on her bony wrist and there was usually a
healthy touch of orange-red lipstick near the gap between her top
front teeth. When she entered a room, sweet thick crisp green lilac
perfume sharpened the air.

That Independence Day, only a few weeks after I'd moved to
Los Angeles, Edith dug into my chest, took my sucker heart in
her teeth, dared me to trust her, and promised to walk away. Two

days later I got up the nerve to ask Amy for Edith's phone number. I called Edith. We made a coffee date. And when I showed up at the café, she laughed a rather icy laugh and pulled a cigarette from her monogrammed silver case. Taking time like starlight in slow motion, she placed her cigarette in this crazy sleek sterling holder and stared at me, demanding I take her lighter from the table. I wondered if she had one of those cigarette finger rings that Gloria Swanson used to perch to her lips, all talon hands. Sitting across from me was one of the few women in the world who could look fabulous perfect with such an insane gadget. My stalling, my thinking, it was annoying Edie. Once my fumbling finally brought her flame to life, she tilted her head back slightly, still inspecting me, and took a drag. Exhaling blue smoke in my direction, she announced that over the phone she had thought I was the other girl.

"Do remind me her name . . ."

I stuttered, "Oh, Nolan. She's out of town with her boyfriend." A total and complete lie, but I wasn't about to play nice and share my newfound bliss. "I can have her call you when she gets back if you want."

She bit down on the holder's dark brown Bakelite mouthpiece and smiled toothy sly.

"That won't be necessary."

And so began an affair as confused as its first date.

By our third date, I knew what made my girl Edith pleased. Saran Wrap. She loved the stuff. Edith would bind my entire body in Saran Wrap before even licking my elbow. Let *me* tell you, clear microwaveable stretch 'n' cling wrap is not sexy. Especially not when it's the generic purple kind she'd watertight me in. But for Edith I gladly let myself be polyurethane girl from chin to toe. Still, I felt like a desperate and misguided mamasita, all gussied up in kitchen paraphernalia to greet her hunka-hunka at the door and try to cook up some loving. I've read about stuff like that in *Good Housekeeping* at the dentist's. You know, the path to your sexual happiness is through his digestive tract, that sort of thing. It's strange for two chicana dykes to live *Good Housekeeping* lust, but the way Edith's eyes shimmered when she'd airtight me with the Saran, I was willing to do anything to see that wild glow.

After bouts of all-night hygienic sex and pints of the dairy-free sherbet Edie seemed to have with her at all times, we'd break up and get back together again and then break up but still meet to go to a movie and get our sex on again and then get back together again but be exclusive sexually but not monogamous dating-wise. The entire time my tiny twin mattress was smack-dab next to my apartment's front door. See, Edith was always cold and I got scared by how lemon-lime Otter Pop her toes could get, so I dragged my bed to the wall furnace right next to the triple bolts and doorknob and it stayed there the whole messy six months we tortured each other.

Every time when we were near pass-out exhausted, Edith began to talk. My pupils tired, trying to make contact in the pitch-black dark, my body twitching with a need for sleep, she told me her existentialist rationale of why the "we" of she and me could not be. Each night my response was the same, "Yes, Bird." Edith had eyes as endless brown as an orchard oriole's. "Yes, Bird."

She was right. It was nearly impossible to "be" when we were just this side of falling asleep. The brink of dreams was the only time she ever talked and she didn't really want answers, so all I had to do was give her my one easy-to-remember-even-when-about-to-fall-asleep line and let her continue to get the tension out of her mouth. Soon we'd sleep all tangled up in each other's limbs on my bed barely wide enough for one of us.

That girl, she was dreamy. A dreamsicle. Creamy. Dreamy.

We only talked when I was asleep. Our relationship existed as I slept beside her. My eyes closed. Calm breathing. She'd talk. We'd wake.

Come morning, she'd still be cold but it was usually me doing the sniffling, my left knee bruised though no physical mark was visible. See, I was down on my knee, begging for my Edie. Me, a young gent without a ring to offer her because she already wore it. Edith took the ring but never said yes, so there I knelt, with only myself to offer and what I had to offer was not enough.

Night again. My hand cupped the curve of her waist as she once again articulately delineated the impossibility of us, her right side in the thick cushion of my feather bed. "Yes, Bird." Quills jabbing at my shoulder through the pink sheets, I shifted to reach for her.

Body in my hands. Inside. Nipple hard against my lips.

May I eat you alive?

I was spinning pleasant dizzy and then Edith broke up with me "for real this time," she said. She started leaving home-baked goods, muffins and sweet bread and stuff that tended to be under-cooked in its middle, at my front door, once with instructions written on a schmaltzy Hallmark card to meet her at the dressing rooms at Macy's for a slice of heaven. A week after Macy's, I found a "secret admirer" note drenched in flowery tobacco perfume on my doorstep, inviting me to meet at Crystal's bar. An hour after closing time, three in the morning, an entire roll of Saran Wrap and some wax paper too, Edith explained yet again why we couldn't ever be together.

I woke the next morning with my Bird by my side and she asked me how I slept. Maybe it was the way the wall heater turned up to high made the air sandy, but for whatever reason, right then my nose started to bleed. No, I take that back, my nose was gushing as furiously as a fire hydrant does when kids break it open with a wrench. I was a sudden mess. I bled onto Edith's wrist as she reached out to touch me. My blood was on her wrist and the Saran Girl, she didn't even flinch. I answered her question.

"I slept wonderfully. Thank you very much. And you?" I ran to the bathroom.

Returning with a bundle of toilet paper at my left nostril, I smiled under the rough wad turning crimson. She stared at the blood on her right forearm and smiled slow. She slept well also, thanks for asking.

I went back to the bathroom and tilted my head over the sink. The marbled cream counter splashed bright red. Letting blood. Purification rite. Drip. Splash. Drip. Splash. Bubbles of oxygen surrounded the drops as they joined the expanding dark puddle. Blood thickening in the sink but fluidly leaving my left nostril. My face lacking its glow, all pasty olive-green pale. Drip. Splash. Drip. Splash.

I returned to bed and my Bird Edith had flown away. She was like that, Edith was. A wisp of wind would blow in through the window, Edith would disappear, leaving the scent of lilacs to haunt in her wake.

Tiring of our game, there came a point when I threatened to move far far away and bail on Edith for good. My Betty Crocker Bird started crying real cruel like people do when they want you to take all their pain and then some. She said quietly and between her teeth, "You simply do not up and move without discussing your plans with your girlfriend first."

Her eyes glittered mean like I'd seen them do once when she was dancing in her majorette getup and a guy sitting at the catwalk licked his palm and reached out to touch her. The only thing he made contact with was the baton when Edith knocked him out clean cold. I knew to proceed with caution. The plain truth seemed safe enough.

"Ex-girlfriend, Edith. Ex-girlfriend. You broke up with me last week, remember?"

She stared at me and clenched her jaw until her ears turned chalk white.

Lord, I knew to watch my back with that woman then. The topper was how she wanted to hug me and then handed me a fresh loaf of prune nut bread when we said goodbye. Now, look, I know about the poison apple. It isn't just Disney Snow White or Adam and Eve with the little snake in the garden. Forget for a moment that it's probably more historically accurate to say it was a pomegranate, not a Red Delicious, staining Eve's hands a mess. Keep things simple, we're talking Poison Apples. No doubt in my mind that food can be tainted with intent. This is old-school simple truth. I'd learned it from Nana and she learned it from Mamá Estrella, who probably learned it from her mama. Scared for what poison it might leak onto me, I took the loaf of bread from Edith because I figured if I didn't she'd throw it at me, hard. That and because, though I hate to admit it, I still wanted to get back together with her again, just a little bit. I mean, that gap between her teeth and those sharp minxy eyes and the way we tangled up so sweet when we slept. But I didn't let myself eat the bread. That would have signed the pact in blood. On my kitchen's faux wood counter is where the bread sat until I lost enough fear to throw it moldy and uneaten in the trash.

That Tuesday trash day I found Edith in the street going through my apartment's garbage bin. Crumpled-up foil balls were piled at her side. She was looking for the bread. Seeing her with her orange lipstick and her obsessed hunt, I forgot that I'd promised myself never to talk to her again.

"Hello, my sweet chocolate pie."

Edith dropped the torn-open black garbage bag held in her yellow dish-glove hands and leaned against the bin poised and scolding as if I'd interrupted the rising sun.

"Chocolate pie, Leticia? Why pie? And chocolate pie at that? Tell me, just what the hell is chocolate pie supposed to signify, Leticia Marisol Estrella Torrez?"

Nobody but family scolding when I was a kid ever pulled such a sneaky trick as throwing down my full name. The game was in motion.

"You rather lemon meringue or minced meat? Eh, Ms. Inmaculada Edith Contreras? Maybe key lime, or caramelo? Not apple, I can tell you that much. No, I couldn't call you apple pie even if you begged like a good little pie should."

Edith tore off her rubber duck yellow gloves and threw them to the ground. She wiped angry tears from her high Dolores del Rio cheekbones, smoothed spit curls at her temples into place, and stomped her vinyl go-go boots self up to the apartment I had rented in what I was beginning to realize was a futile attempt to outrun my Weeping Woman and Nana.

luisita lópez torregrosa

❦ AN ISLAND OF ILLUSIONS

THE BOX LAY ON MY LAP. I did not want to open it. Angeles sat across from me, in the torn leather chair in the room in Edgewood, Texas, where my mother had kept her books, her photo albums, and the trinkets she had picked up in her travels. I had arrived just a few hours before and had walked around the house as if it were a church, slowly, gazing up at the pictures my mother had chosen to hang on the walls, looking at her bed, at her bottles of Arpège and her felt-lined jewelry box, staring unbelievingly at her faded red robe still hanging on the back of the bathroom door.

My mother's room had not been touched. The bed was made, the rose-colored bedspread smoothed around it, not a wrinkle in it, the way she had left it. Beside her bed, on her night table, she had a framed picture of my grandmother, a picture I had always loved, my grandmother in a gray and white housedress with dark stripes. Her face was powerful, nothing frail about it. It was the face of Spanish doñas, those Goya faces, smileless, almost ruthless, eyes long lost in some past. Next to the picture was a paperback edition of Toni Morrison's *Beloved,* a book I had recommended to her. It lay there as if it had just been bought, no pages turned. Closest to the bed and my mother's pillow was her latest crossword puzzle, which she had clipped from a newspaper. It was unfinished. I wanted to take it but didn't dare touch it. I couldn't touch any of it.

I glanced up and down the hallway, where her diplomas were hanging in the same frames I remembered, and the picture of her I most loved, taken when she was twenty-three, just before I was born. It was in a cluster of family pictures. I stood before it the way I stood, when I was very young, before the statues of the Virgin Mary, the way I later looked at posters of movie stars.

I want a copy of that, I said.

The house where she had lived for the last five years of her life was full of people, more people, I was sure, than had ever been in it when she was alive. Townspeople, neighbors, her husband's relatives, people I had not met or had forgotten. My sisters were already there, and my brother, and my aunt, Angela Luisa, with her son, Jacobo. I was startled to see him, immaculately dressed in a dark business suit, resolute and somber, standing at her side, just a step behind her, attentive but distant, at her elbow but not quite touching it. I wouldn't have recognized him now except for the close-set eyes and foxlike face, the same look he had when he was a boy.

One by one they came to me.

But, nena, you look the same, my aunt said. It had been many years, more than two decades since I had last seen her.

You look the same, too, I lied, throwing my arms around her, relieved to see someone who had shared my mother's life, who had shared our childhood.

She said, I came because I knew that if I didn't come you and your sisters and brother would not have anyone here that was real family. I embraced her again. She was right. The sadness in her, the sorrow that had to be in her after losing her only sister, her older sister, seemed muted, cut off. She had never been one to show much emotion.

When I was a child, she had been a spire to me. She was a writer, a journalist, the center of attention in rooms crowded with powerful men whom you read about in the papers, and with women in demure cocktail dresses who kissed her on both cheeks. She had been my model, tall and light-haired, unadorned yet shining in her silk scarves, elegant like a swan. But she didn't look the same, how could she? She was seventy-four years old, two years younger than my mother, and she was less agile and a bit stooped. Her hair was a blond gray curled by beauty parlor hot rolls, combed in tight waves. She had on a silken dress with long, flowing sleeves, the sort she would wear to a theater opening. Her strand of pearls was draped loosely around her old woman's neck. But she had the brightness about her that I remembered, her glow, her playful smile, and the warmth she seemed to hold mostly for Angeles and me.

Your mother, she said, taking me aside, should have lived the life I had (she meant fame, travel, awards all over the walls), and I should have had hers.

I didn't believe her, didn't believe that she would've traded lives with my mother, but I did believe that my mother would have wanted my aunt's life. This was a comment, I thought, meant to suggest something about my mother more than about my aunt, and she said it as if revealing a secret, something she had thought about all those years. It felt like the point of a blade touching briefly, coldly, against my skin, before it fell to the ground.

When she embraced me again, she let her long, ringless fingers rest on my shoulder, and stood back to look at me. I wanted to scream, Where is she, where is she?

Angeles came out of a room, and we held each other for a very long time. She looked older than I, her hair a sea gray that was oddly almost black like the depths of the sea. She held me like a doll, tight to her, and her tears touched my face, making it impossible for me to cry. Holding her was as close as I could ever get to holding my mother again, but we still played the roles we had played since we were children. She cried, I didn't.

She looked so tired after a twelve-hour flight, arriving only to learn that she was too late, that our mother was already dead. She felt so small in my arms, even though she was bigger than I, and I brushed back her hair.

She laughed suddenly, pulling away from me, and took me to the room where she had been hiding from the crowd in the living room and in the kitchen, where my mother's second husband, Leon, a Texan with the bearing of a onetime football quarterback, was receiving the townsfolk.

We didn't want to have anything to do with those people, in-laws we didn't know, the mayor of the town, the beautician, the store-keepers, the women who set up bingo games in the annex of the church, who belonged to the ladies' auxiliary and put up notes on missing pets on the town hall's bulletin board — the people who had been my mother's everyday acquaintances, people who called my mother a Good Samaritan, so ready to help with all the town's activities.

Your mother was so kind to our community, they said with little variation as they filed in, carrying pies and casseroles, the usual in those parts. She was so good to our town, so interesting, so charming. We will miss her so.

Angeles looked around and said, Who are these people?

I found a chair, and Amaury swayed toward me, his eyebrows raised in anger.

Where have you been? You're the last one to arrive.

I couldn't come any faster, I said, brusque, lying.

He knew. I glared at him, turning away. He had that way about him, saying the wrong thing, miscalculating, and he reminded me of my father.

I've been here since yesterday, he said, an accusation. I took the first flight out of New York.

He was the good son, he was saying, and I was the selfish daughter. He was wrecked, his face darker than I remembered, the limp in his right leg more pronounced. When he was a boy, maybe four years old, he fell off a swing and broke his arm. I let him lie on the ground while he cried. It was Angeles who came running to him. She still did that, and now, when he needed to stop crying, she came to him again. They cracked a joke that I didn't get. I was separate; they separated me from them. We smoked, we had Lone Star beer. We let the ashes fall on the floor and the bottles pile on a table.

Angeles refused to go out to the kitchen and meet all the people and thank them for coming. But I went; my aunt insisted. I found room at the kitchen table, and sat quietly, thanking strangers who took my hands and looked at me with blurred eyes. Are you the journalist? I smiled, nodding.

Your mother talked about you all the time, the ladies said.

I knew that; she talked about all her children, always pulling our old pictures out of her wallet.

In front of me, on the table, was a bowl of fake fruit (Mother loved fresh fruit — why would she buy waxed apples, pears, bananas? I wondered). Scoops of potato salad and slices of honey-glazed ham were put on a plate for me and I pushed it aside. How could I eat? Finally, it was time to go view the body.

I'm not going, I said. Angeles is not going. Amaury is not going.

The others — Carmen, Sara, and Olga — all went, parceling their cars, dragging their husbands and children with them.

Angeles and I stayed in the den, and Amaury stayed with us. Together, we thought ourselves a trinity — the three oldest, the ones who really knew the story. We were our parents, their reflection. Angeles more than any of us.

Now we were going through my mother's things, her boxes, plain shoeboxes, all unmarked. We were looking for anything of hers. Angeles had already gone through the box on my lap, holding each letter, some many years old, in her own childlike handwriting. She took the letters out of envelopes, glancing over them, and putting them back in the box, in order, just as they had been placed there by my mother.

She said nothing when she handed me the box. She reached for a cigarette and lit it with the burning butt of the one she had just smoked.

Mother wanted to be cremated, Angeles said finally. It's in there, in her handwriting.

I opened the box. I found the note, on top of the pile of yellowing papers. I read it quickly. I never saw this before, I said, injured.

I did, years ago, Angeles said.

Why not me? I said, our little jealousies rising above the pain.

The letter was undated, not addressed to any of us. Mother wrote it on plain drugstore stationery and she had folded the single page in half. The ink was fading, the paper stiff. In handwriting that still retained her fluid slope, but was now a little more crooked and shaky in her old age, she had written that she wanted her ashes spread in her garden.

So why was she not cremated? I asked. Amaury looked at the floor. He didn't know. He had just read the letter for the first time.

Angeles whispered, It's too late. She's already embalmed, everything had been arranged before we got here. We didn't know.

But why is she being buried here? I said, repeating myself, helpless, furious that I had not known before, that her wishes had been ignored. Why were we not asked? What does she have to do with this town? She belongs in Puerto Rico, I kept saying, a meaningless thought since she had not lived on the island for thirty years. But it was the dream I thought she had, a dream I had for her. It was her home, I said. It was our home.

We were born in a place of no particular consequence, on an island of certain beauty, at the intersection of two cultures, where the Atlantic meets the Caribbean, a place of crosswinds and hurricanes, jumbo jets and puddle jumpers, a stopover for travelers going by sea or by air to one or another tourist resort in the American tropics. Island colonies, all of them, outcrops of sunken landmasses, dead rims of ancient volcanoes, pieces of land conquered and abandoned, hot, sensuous, primitive, ocean-lapped and wind-lashed. Places like this island have no history, their beginnings pulverized by time and indifference, their moments of heroism and cowardice passing unnoticed by the grander world.

We have known voyagers in armor, and voyagers who happen upon us, travelers who come to invent us, enamored of islands and of their moist seduction. Poets are born under the susurration of coconut palms, in the black nights of the islands, and out of the incomprehensible beauty around us, out of this brilliant palette, come these people, who over centuries of copulation have shed and grown layers of skin and color, a people indefinable, irreducible, passionate and unforgiving, penitent and superstitious, rootless, insular, without horizons.

A people confined by water, surrounded by the infinite, with nothing but dreams.

They dream they came from a land across the water, from a continent of magnificent riches and ancient races, a place they could only dimly remember so many centuries later, but that gave them a strength in the blood, a way of moving and talking, a music older than any memory. They dream they came in royal galleons, across cold purple seas, to conquer lands of fabled treasures, a red earth engorged with gold and silver, and endless shores of sands without footprints. They came, those in armor and those in tricornered hats, the barons and dukes, the knights and masters of empire, sailing under the silken banners of a kingdom, to plunder and Christianize, to spread their seed, to take.

Blood flowed in rivers, and in the openmouthed bays of the islands, deathless stone monuments were built to the conquest. Fortresses in Habana, in Santo Domingo, in San Juan, all proclaimed Spain's sovereignty, and cathedrals proclaimed the triumph of the Church over the primitive and uncivilized. In the cities spawned by the Spaniards, once scattered settlements of fruit-laden jungle and sheltering palm trees where the Taínos had made their bohíos and tended their yuccas and corn and cassavas, in nearly every new capital of the West Indies, the face of history became Spain. The French came later, and the English, and the Dutch, and the Africans in chains. But the bloodlines were to Spain, the passions and fatalism and poetry, the madness and the isolation, the irrational pride, the treachery and cruelty.

Those dreams, that history, became transmuted in time, embellished, living on in a few, the historians and artists, the poets, and in the families who claimed ancestors from the arid mountains of Galicia, from the vineyards of Andalusia, from the Mediterranean coast of Catalonia. And in those stories, the life of the island became ancient and romantic, filled with treasures found and lost, with nobility and bravery.

Illusions are the breath of life in a place of little importance.

The northwestern coast of the island runs jagged against the pounding surf of the Atlantic, a moody sea along that coast, heaving high, rugged waves against rocky beaches the color of bones. Ships and sailboats and adventurers cruise those waters, finding anchor and shelter in the seaside town of Aguadilla, where, they like to say, Columbus first landed in Puerto Rico, stopping for water at a spring that is now the center of the town's Parque El Parterre. The town has its Mediterranean airs, and retains some of the architectural curlicues and social snobbery of colonial times.

Out of this storied town, where family name and position determined destinies, came my mother's family. She was born there, in September 1918, when the Great War was devastating Europe and the island was a colony of the United States. She was a middle child, one of three children. The three of them, a boy and two girls, were born into a family where nothing but brilliance was expected, where certain things were assumed — manners and social graces, discipline and studiousness, and in time, good marriages.

My grandmother, a woman of the Old World, had been brought up by governesses and tutors, had grown up at dinner tables frequented by men who would one day figure in history books. She was the oldest in a family of six girls, daughters of Josefa Muñoz Rivera, who in a picture my grandmother kept in a gold-leaf frame on her dresser seemed forbidding and severe, with a stern, dour look. It was a face rounded by middle age, with hardened eyes, and hair so dark it seemed dyed. Doña Josefa's ancestors had come from Spain in the eighteenth century and settled in the central mountains of the island. Her grandfather, Luis Muñoz Iglesias, a captain in the Spanish militia, had gone into politics after making the months-long journey from Castilla la Vieja, a province north of Madrid. One of his sons, another Luis Muñoz, became a mayor and had five boys and three girls, among them Josefa, my great-grandmother. His oldest boy, Luis Muñoz Rivera, became a journalist, a poet, and a nationalist (the history books call him a statesman). Josefa did what women of that time usually did, marry and have children.

Josefa's oldest daughter, my grandmother, Monserrate Guevara Muñoz, was born in Aguadilla, and grew up with the privileges and comforts enjoyed by only a few on the island. Along with this came the emotional distance from her parents that was the custom in families whose names were passed on to the next generation like heirlooms.

I can't see my grandmother ever being an infant or a child, play-ing freely, getting dirty in the mud with other children. But I can see her at the piano, her back straight, shoulders high. I can see her embroidering a dress, and dancing in a white gown, the hem of which she would hold up with a long, manicured hand. She was a striking young woman, long-necked and lean, who held forth in any conversation, sprinkling bons mots and charm on the serious talk of politics and theater she grew up hearing around the dining table in that house where her father, Agustín Guevara Santini, a marshal of the courts, was a quiet force.

When she was in her early twenties, still living in Aguadilla, she married a shy and bookish lawyer and journalist, Angel Torregrosa, a slight man with wavy light brown hair and owlish eyes that were made more owlish by his wire-rimmed reading glasses. There are no letters and no family stories about a great passion between them, nothing to tell us that their marriage was the culmination of a soulful love affair. It was a proper marriage, a matter of accom-modation and tradition. He was an inch shorter than she and stoutly reserved, son of a family of note, whose father, Luis Tor-regrosa, a pharmacist, was, like many men of his class at that time, more politician than businessman. He served in the parliament and helped establish the Republican Party.

The strain of politics ran thick in my grandfather's blood. Even before my mother was born, Angel Torregrosa was publishing a weekly newspaper of political debate, fighting for the end to Ameri-can colonialism and for independence. They were the only Tor-regrosa family on the island, tracing back their origins to Tor-regrossa, a Catalan village near Barcelona.

My mother once tried to trace the family's history and she got as far back as the nineteenth century, when the Torregrosas left Spain, not to escape persecution or to find fortune but, according to lore, to minister to the New World colony in the name of Spain, to claim land and farm it, to educate the people and improve health services. They were professors, lawyers, and pharmacists, and they spawned a family of professors, lawyers, and doctors.

In the town in the mountains of the Cordillera Central where my grandparents moved after having their three children, the town where my mother grew up, Don Angel was a considerable figure, a judge and a writer, and, oddly for a man of introspection, a theater producer, something of a dashing impresario, friend of the actors and writers who came through town to stage plays in the theater he supported for years.

When my mother grew old, in her last years, this was the town she most longed for; this was her Puerto Rico, where she grew from a child into a fierce girl of fixed ideas and grandiose dreams, where she learned to ride horses and had boys circling her on the dance floor. Her roots, she said, ran deepest there, in those mountains.

She dreamed that one day she would build a house at the top of one of those hills, and she would stand in her garden in those cool mornings of the hills, drinking her black coffee, looking out to the Caribbean Sea on the far horizon to the south.

The town, Cayey, was surrounded by hills of coffee and tobacco farms and pineapple fields hoed and planted on the skirts of the mountains. On the higher ground, near hilltops that seemed unreachable from the spinning two-lane road that cut through the island north to south, campesinos tended their banana and vegetable patches and lived in one-room houses they built of wood and scraps of tin, tiny houses that seemed like pin-sized spots of yellow or blue, so high up in those hills they could touch the clouds.

Cayey was built like all the other towns on the island, around the plaza. The plaza was the center of the world. The layout of the town reflected the rigid social structure that predated even colonial times: the farther from the plaza, from the municipal buildings and the church, the poorer the houses, the poorer the people. The best homes fronted the plaza, their trellised verandas looking out on the social and commercial life of the town, on the church and its processions, on the strollers and the soft glow of globe-shaped streetlamps, on the ferias of music and dancing.

Sitting on their balconies as the sun went down, even in the heat of breezeless days and on rainy dusks, the flies gathering on meriendas of sugary coffee and cakes, the women chaperoned the passing of the day, watching out for their husbands to come home and keeping an eye on the children playing hopscotch and jumping rope in the plaza in that hour when the children were allowed out, just before dinner and bedtime. For it was women who sat on those porches, mothers, grandmothers, greeting visitors, telling their tales, chattering about the things women chattered about, loves and children, weddings, and the situation with the servants.

My grandmother's three children were exactly two years apart, a perfect scale. Children to her were adornments, the inescapable obligation of women. In this house voices were not raised, and disapproval was shown not with screams but only with a raised eyebrow and a glowering stare. My mother, her sister and brother, all had nursemaids and cooks, and they took piano lessons and learned to recite verses and to perform in public.

They were model children, my grandmother claimed, setting for me an example. But then, pausing for a minute, she would turn to me and whisper, Except for your mother.

I learned to enumerate all my mother's sins: she was moody, disobedient, stubborn, bossy, opinionated, and, worst of all, she couldn't sit still. Children are meant to be looked at, not to be heard, my grandmother said repeatedly, another of the old sayings she seemed to have for nearly every occasion.

Grandmother painted my mother as half genius, half tyrant.

Your mother was too smart, too quick with that mouth of hers, didn't like to study but got the best grades, everything came too easily to her, and she had no patience for anything that wasn't perfect, for anything that wasn't the way she saw it. She believed she was always right, and she drove Angela Luisa to tears. Poor Angela Luisa, she was so meek, so quiet, she did everything your mother wanted. She made her dresses, she brushed her hair, she put on your mother's makeup, she ran errands for her. She was always there, in the background.

Your mother was such a terror — she said this with a sigh not of resignation but rather of admiration. Look, one day your mother left school and went to the stables and got on a horse and we didn't know where she was for hours. We couldn't find her anywhere. That was the time, my grandmother said, building up the story like a fairy tale, when your grandfather hit her. Grandmother raised her right arm high to show me how Grandfather had done it. That was the only time he raised his hand against any of his children, she said. I couldn't see my grandfather hitting anyone, least of all my mother.

But this was not the time, she said, when your mother was thrown off her horse — that was later. Her boot was caught in the saddle and the horse ran wild and dragged her down a rough field, her head bouncing off rocks and pebbles, bleeding, unconscious — that time, we almost lost her, she almost died.

These stories about my mother were recycled, embroidered, woven from vaguely remembered episodes and stray moments shaped out of half-truths, dimmed and shaded by pride and hurt, and the layers of years, like all memories.

Sometimes, when the rain came in the afternoon and we had nothing to do but sit on the porch, Grandmother would come out of her bedroom with her pack of old photos: Mother and Angela Luisa in sailor dresses, their hair cut the same, in a bob with bangs, looking almost like twins; Mother, Angela Luisa, and José Luis, teenagers posing for a formal picture, my uncle in suit and jacket, the girls in grown-up dresses; my mother, maybe sixteen years old, wearing a long party dress, her mouth slightly open in a smile, her eyes gazing directly at the camera.

Your mother was a beauty, my grandmother would say. She said that often.

She would pull out more pictures. Here was my mother in her riding jacket and tight, knee-high black boots, and in ball gowns, posing with her girlfriends, my mother standing at the front, everyone else radiating around her. She was already a full woman, her breasts clenched in a corset, her hair falling over part of her face, her eyes riveting with promises.

Her lips were shaped perfectly, as if they had been drawn on her. They were rich, defined. Even without the red lipstick that she usually wore, her mouth had a way of speaking its own language, pursed or tightly closed, crooked in disapproval, carelessly open in laughter.

On the theater stage, she was a star, carnations falling at her feet. She was not yet eighteen, still in high school, when she founded with her brother the Farándula Bohemia, a theater ensemble that for several years toured the island. Grandmother kept the old newspaper clippings and read them to me, and I saw my mother, in front of the crimson velvet curtain, her hands raised in triumph, welcoming the applause, her head thrown back. But eventually she left the theater company and left, too, a wreckage of smitten boys who serenaded her with moonlight songs, who brought her gardenias and azucenas, who swept her around dance floors.

She left Cayey for the University of Puerto Rico. She was going to study law.

A few years later, my grandparents moved to San Juan. My mother had already finished her undergraduate degree and had entered law school. My grandfather went to work for a government agency and published newspaper articles on politics and theater and adoring biographies of men he admired. They had an apartment near the university, just off the Avenida Muñoz Rivera, a modest flat where my parents came to live after they were married, where I first lived. This was where my grandfather, still wearing his suit and tie, would pick me up and, putting my baby feet on his buffed cordovans, would dance with me in his old man's shuffle.

He was a man of habit, spending his evenings secluded in his room, reading, writing, and, a family story has it, drinking. One day he came home from work with a terrible headache, took to his room, and was found hours later dead of a brain hemorrhage. He was not sixty years old.

Widowed suddenly, my grandmother left the apartment where he had died and with us moved to El Vedado, a neighborhood of old Spanish-colonial homes and smaller bungalows. We had a large house of constant breezes and the shade of big trees, a one-story house that was yellow like my grandmother's amapolas. It was a house, like all of my grandmother's houses, that seemed always to be full of company, aunts and cousins and distant relations. She didn't live there very long, perhaps two years, before she built a house nearby, on Calle Pérez Galdós, but I remember the coolness of floor tiles in that old house where I learned to walk.

Now and then I see flashes of rainy afternoons at Pérez Galdós.

My grandmother has her long dark hair pulled up in a bun, her loose, faded dress falls down to her bony ankles, and she's sitting back in her rocking chair, reading the newspapers to me. She read the obituaries, pointing out this or that person she had known. For hours she would tell me these stories of our family, nationalists and journalists, writers and poets, names given to avenues in San Juan, to town streets, to public schools and parks and plazas. I grew up with their names and faces in my head, men with heavy mustaches and spectacles, austere men in dark regalia, whose sepia portraits appear in the histories of the island.

My grandmother's house, built near the Avenida Eleanor Roosevelt on a lot in a new section of El Vedado, was designed by my mother, who had an eye for architecture and liked to walk around in her heels in the unplowed lot, imagining floors being laid down and walls going up. This house, which would be my grandmother's last home, had two stories and it was square and flat-roofed in the tropical style, with a front porch that butted a rectangle of grass edged by flowers my grandmother planted. They were her favorite yellow and red hibiscuses, pink poinsettias, and shrubs I could not name.

Grandmother lived on the ground floor. It was a big flat with two large airy bedrooms, a small maid's room, and a sunny living room with crank-up slatted windows. She kept her old caned chairs there, the ones she had inherited from her mother, and her upright piano and her radio. To the side, she had a small dining area that looked on a small side porch, and a kitchen that caught the breezes when the door to the outside was opened, letting in light and the voices of neighbors from across the wall that separated our house from the building next door.

Every morning Grandmother was up before sunup, in her slippers and apron, making coffee, pouring it through the damp cloth filter. She and Mother were reading the papers, drinking coffee from little cups, by the time Angeles and I woke up and got dressed. Mother left early for her job at the Justice Department, taking the bus to Old San Juan. Usually my father was away at the United States Army barracks, where he, a chemical engineer who knew nothing of war and was too old to go to the front, was serving his tour of duty shuffling papers at a desk job.

All day long I had Grandmother to myself.

She was a tall woman, with a long narrow back slightly stooped by age, a deeply featured face with a hooked Roman nose, and the bluish freckled skin of someone who never sat in the sun. Her skin was wrinkled tight around the bones of her forearms, and her frame was fragile and flat, but her face, lean and creviced, with high cheekbones, loosened when she laughed, a birdlike fluttering around her favorite visitors.

On the days she went out, she wore her hairpiece. She kept it in a bottom drawer of her mahogany armoire, where her dresses were hung high, too high for me to reach. The closets in her house were for us, not for her. She would not put her things in a closet, a place without the wood scent that I could smell on her clothes. Her hairpiece was a thick round bun, like a crown, which she said had been made from her own hair. She let her long, fine hair fall down to the middle of her back. Then she would wrap it around the hairpiece with long hairpins and combs. She took great care. She powdered her face, she splashed on blush, and she wore a silk camisole over her bare, flattened, sagging breasts. In the flesh-colored stockings she always wore and her stacked-heeled black leather shoes (her feet were so big), with an heirloom brooch pinned to her blouse and her hair up in that soigné style, she looked head to foot like the matriarch she was, even taller and stronger, with an air of command in her face.

Almost every afternoon, around sundown, we had company, Grandmother's sisters and her cousins. She brought out glasses full of chilled tamarind juice, or cups of freshly made coffee, and a platter of white cheese and membrillo. Standing on the ledge of the porch, by the bank of daffodils and azaleas Grandmother watered at daybreak and at dusk, I spotted the visitors coming down the road and announced them to my grandmother.

One day I saw a strange woman rounding the street corner, walking in our direction in a hurry, appearing out of the rain like a mad ghost, dressed in black, the hem of her flapping dress touching the pavement. Her hair was a wild mass of wiry gray, her skin parchment white. She carried a leather-bound book of uncut pages, what turned out to be a collection of her poems.

Her unexpected appearance was a big occasion. My grandmother reddened with excitement, taking down from the shelves of her glass-fronted china cabinet her porcelain espresso cups and saucers, the ones with the blue birds and blue mountains, waterfalls and rivers and tiny Chinese houses with concave roofs. Seeing my grandmother so excited, I wanted to know who the woman was. Grandmother turned to me, putting her long index finger to her lips, quieting me, and said that this wild woman who would flit in and out of our house over the years was her cousin, a poet. Clara Lair she called herself, her pen name.

Grandmother held the book of Clara's poetry on her lap, fingering the leather jacket. She called Clara una lumbrera, a brilliant woman, a light in the firmament, a word that brought images of suns to my mind. Clara didn't stay long, ignored me as if I weren't there, and then flew out, gone as suddenly as she had appeared.

She's a little mad, Grandmother said to me later, smiling. Insanity runs in the family.

Our other visitors were not quite so mad or quite so lumbreras. Mostly they were my grandmother's sisters.

Nana was a spinster who so hated being touched by children that she squirmed and jerked back when I kissed her cheek. She sat stiffly, hands folded on her lap, in the wooden recliner by the porch table, sipping black coffee, her lips pursed, barely touching the cup. She had a government job, in the Treasury Department, in an office where she kept the books. Every day she wore her work uniform, the same round-collared, buttoned-up-to-the-neck pink cotton blouse and dark blue skirt that covered her knees. Her face was heavily caked, a chalky pink blush that she put on like a mask, stopping just below the hairline, leaving an odd thin line of white skin showing between her forehead and her hair. I was fascinated by that line, that bare space; I wanted to touch it.

Seven days a week she rose at dawn and went to mass, walking the mile to the nearest church in a black mantilla. She rarely missed a day. The Church and baseball were her passions, the only ones I ever knew about.

Every now and then, Grandmother let me go see Nana in her one-room flat in the building next door that was owned by another of my grandmother's sisters, Isabel, the rich sister, who had married sugar money. Nana had a half refrigerator with a bottle of milk and almost nothing else in it, and she had a bedside table where she kept her prayer book and a rosary of worn black beads. There was little else in that narrow room with the shuttered window, a single bed, a radio. On those evenings that she and I spent together, we didn't talk very much. We listened to the ball game, shouting and jumping with every strike and every score, her ear pressed to the radio, her fingers squeezing a handkerchief.

For a time, Tití Angela Luisa lived in the spare room in Grandmother's house, where she made our party dresses, just as she had made Mother's gowns. She worked on my grandmother's old Singer sewing machine, her long foot hard on the pedal, her hands guiding the cloth — silk, crinoline, satin — under the machine's needle, tat-tat-tat, a whir filling the house.

But first Tití, the name we always called her, lay down the crinkling dress patterns that she had bought at a store. She placed them on the floor and laid the fabric she had ironed over each paper pattern. Leaning on her knees, she trimmed and folded the cloth, her lips clamped around straight pins. Later, when the gown was sewn, by her hand and her machine, she selected from plastic bags she kept in her sewing box the sequins and the beads, glassy, slippery pieces. She squinted as she threaded the needle through holes that were invisible to me. She sewed each bead by hand.

When I was three, she dressed me like a ballerina, complete with dancing slippers and a glittery crown on my light brown curls. All through our childhood, she made pinafores and piano recital gowns for Angeles and me, and on our birthdays, she made the dresses and baked the cakes and mixed the icing, squeezing the icing through a cloth funnel, writing our names in pinks and yellows.

Sometimes, like magic, a long white dress would appear, a

grown-up dress with a scooped neck and a big flowing floor-length skirt. That was the dress she made for me for my first debut, when I was seven, at a children's ball at the Caribe Hilton. She pulled my long, wavy hair away from my face and took the sides of my head into her hands. She creamed blush on my cheeks and outlined the rim of my lips with her black makeup pencil, eventually painting my small lips bright red. Just above my upper lip, she painted on a tiny black beauty mark. There I was, in the great lobby of the Caribe Hilton, with a flower in my hair, and a long lavender lily in one hand, leaning over a water fountain, looking ten years older.

Every morning she left for her newspaper job, driving off in her secondhand Volkswagen, pushing the gas pedal as hard as she pushed the pedal on the sewing machine. She was too tall for the car. She was bony, thin, and angular, and, to me, quite glamorous with her loose blondish hair and her headscarves. In her late twenties, she was old for a single woman of that time, but she was different in other ways. She was a woman who traveled abroad alone, who was the hostess or the guest at the interminable lunches, interminably photographed, at the Club Cívico de Damas (she was the one without a hat), a woman whose name was the byline of a weekly column in the newspaper.

It seemed to us that she would never marry, and in her striking solitariness, she was someone who belonged alone.

But she did marry. She married late but quite romantically, to a journalist, a man almost thirty years older than she, who was quite debonair and bohemian. All her friends said he was a charming storyteller and he had written books against the death penalty and against American control of the island. These were books people called important, and he seemed to know everything and everyone.

Jacobo and Tití first lived in an apartment house in another neighborhood. The apartment was tiny — the refrigerator was in the stairwell, the bathroom had no tub, only a shower stall. But it was like a dollhouse to me. When Angeles and I visited, she made us hot chocolate and let us play canasta with them until bedtime. For a long time, for many of the years of my childhood, Tití took Angeles and me everywhere, to the movies, to restaurants, to the drive-in. She took me to my first European movie, *La Strada*, and tried to explain a plot that made little sense to me but seemed very sad. I still see Giulietta Masina in her clown face. The first time I had Chinese food, at a large, bright restaurant on Franklin Delano Roosevelt Avenue, the sort of restaurant where the waiters bowed when she came in and stood at attention near her table (she feigned modesty but clearly expected the beer to be poured just so and the cook to make whatever changes she wished), she taught me to use chopsticks. The first time I saw a newspaper coming off the presses, I was with her. That was at the old building of *El Imparcial*, a blood-and-guts tabloid where she began her career as a society columnist, chronicling births and debuts and weddings.

We were standing in a corridor, at a wall of glass through which we could see the presses churning below. Huge, noisy machines occupied the entire basement. She had to shout so I could hear her.

Mira, mira, she shouted — look, look.

My face was touching the glass. The machines roared and newspapers rolled off cylinders, piling one on top of another. She took me by the hand, and we ran down the stairs to the press room. She shouted to a pressman, and he handed her a newspaper, and she gave it to me. It was warm, like freshly pressed clothes, and it smelled like nothing I had ever known.

Some years later she was on a television quiz show modeled after *What's My Line?* With that and her Sunday column, which she had moved to another newspaper, *El Mundo*, then the island's largest, she became something of a celebrity. She took me to the television studios of Telemundo, where I was seated in a guest room behind the cameras and watched the show.

The studio was air-conditioned, freezing, and the cameras blocked my view of her face. But I could hear her voice, higher-pitched when she was on the air. She was funny, I could tell. When she made a comment, the audience laughed all around me. After the show, people crowded around her, asking for her autograph. I stood beside her, watching her, and watching the people who treated her as if they knew her personally: Angela Luisa, Angela Luisa. I wanted to be her. Craning my neck, I studied how she made her signature, the rounded *A* and the curly *L*, the sharp *T*, and the flourish in the *g*'s. But after years of giving autographs and signing her name to her column, she no longer had to use her last name. Angela Luisa was enough.

The ballet, the theater, the newspaper — her world was mine, and I thought that if I grew up to be like her, I, too, would have front-row seats at the theater and fine dinners at elegant restaurants with movie stars, and newspapers hot off the presses every night.

Every day Grandmother fixed our breakfast, whatever we wanted — soft-boiled eggs, cream of corn, oatmeal — and forced us to drink glasses of warm milk. She didn't eat, but she stayed in the kitchen, keeping up a commentary with no one in particular, her voice rising above the clatter of pans and running water, her hands deep in soapy water.

She had a maid to clean the house and do the daily wash out back, but she liked to do the cooking herself. Sometimes she went out, making her visits to her sisters. But she never went to church, and she seldom went shopping, having been brought up with servants to do the housekeeping and the groceries, having been brought up to make her own clothes or to have a seamstress make them for her.

When she had no maid, she managed somehow by herself. She bought vegetables and fruit off the carts that came down the street, and she made daily lists of groceries she needed and paid the street boys to get them from the supermarket at the corner. Occasionally she had lunch delivered. In those days there were places — bodegas, storefront kitchens — that made entire meals to order and delivered them in fiambreras, aluminum containers that were stacked one on top of another. All over the neighborhood, you saw delivery boys carrying fiambreras, the food steaming, the smells of rice and beans, mofongo, alcapurrias, lingering in the air.

Each day around noon she sat beside her radio and listened to my uncle's comedy show — Now, she would say to me, sit still and listen, José Luis is on the radio. He came to my grandmother's house occasionally, making his entrances with much fanfare (which was mostly my grandmother's, who preened around him, giving up to him her rocking chair, bringing him a cup of coffee, though she knew he would've preferred a shot of rum). His voice carried from the street, full of theater. I recognized it instantly. He sounded just as he did on the radio. He was not a big man, but he had girth, blocky shoulders and a large face, a large nose, a big mustache, and thinning hair. Bluster, he had bluster, and a raucous, hoarse stage voice, and exploded with laughter at his own jokes, which he invented on the spot. Once he went to Spain and he carried on as if he had discovered it — After Spain, there's only heaven, he said over and over, looking up at the sky. Pictures of bloody bulls ran through my head.

When a crowd gathered at his house, as it often did, he entertained in his pajamas and slippers, a handkerchief soaked in bay rum on his forehead. Standing in the middle of the room, he played magic tricks, bringing on laughter each time, and dashed off verses, which he recited with expansive gestures, his arms taking in the whole room, flowery lines that he later wrote down and dedicated to any of us in even more flowery language and signed in a heavy bold hand.

My grandmother rarely went to his house, and months would pass between his visits. She seldom told me stories about him, but she didn't miss his show — those slapstick skits and street jokes she hardly understood but that people loved. The crazy but lovable down-and-out characters he created made him a familiar figure, famous, a picture in the papers, a man known just by his last name.

Late in the afternoon in those days, el panadero came by the house, always at the same time, crying out, Pan, pan, pushing his wheeled cart, which he stacked high with fresh loaves of bread wrapped in plain white paper. My grandmother would go out in her slippers, pick from the cart the warmest loaf she could find, and give the man his five cents. Then she would sit in the dining room and break off a crusty piece and spread it with soft butter. I would climb on a chair and bend over her big steaming cup of coffee, soaking my piece in it, crumbs of soggy bread and melting butter running down my chin.

Just as the sun was setting, after the rainbow that came with the afternoon showers had faded, my mother would arrive from work, walking from the bus stop, a newspaper in her hand, her heels clicking on the pavement. Angeles and I would run to her and hold her around her waist. With a cup of coffee and the newspaper folded beside her, she would sit on the porch with us, holding us to her lap, humming to us, her voice a breeze in my ear, Ese lunar que tienes, cielito lindo, junto a la boca, no se lo des a nadie, cielito lindo, que a mí me toca.

lila downs

🪶 MOTHER JONES

The tender, the warmer — the dealers' father time
I'm lookin' down in limbo and I see Joan of Arc
Surrender to the porno and listen to the cries
My people they ain't votin' see the pepsi man waltz

A victim of her freedom and that is what they say
I'm looking in the mirror but it really isn't me
The diamonds on the monkeys the ladies in the trees
I'm looking to the future I'm dancin' to the beat

Tell me tell me, Mother Jones
Tell me where the spirit goes?
Waiting for the risin' sun
Tuesday comes and Tuesday goes

The flowers in the valley are blowin' in the wind
They come in many colors but she prefers the green
She's running to the north pole with a packet in her seam
She's got to find the money smilin' at the deputy

I want you to find me the day that I'm not there
I'd like you to listen to the things that I've felt
I want you to sit here and hold me when I'm down
I'm lookin' to remember see the pepsi man waltz

Lo tierno y calido — el que manda es padre Tiempo
Estoy mirando al limbo y veo a Juana de Arco

Entrégate al porno y oye los gritos
Mi gente no está votando mira el vals del hombre de la pepsi

Una víctima de su libertad, y so es lo que dicen
Me miro en el espejo pero en realidad no soy yo
Los diamantes sobre los changos y las damas en los arboles
Estoy mirando al futuro, bailando al ritmo

Dime dime, Madre Jones
Dime dime, a dónde va el espíritu?
Esperando al sol que sale
Martes viene y martes va

Las flores en el valle, se mueven con el viento
Vienen en todos colores, pero ella prefiere "el verde"
Va corriendo al polo norte con un paquete escondido
Tiene que hallar el dinero sonriendole al oficial

Yo quiero que me busques, el dia que no yo no esté
Yo quiero que me escuches, las cosas que he sentido
Yo quiero que estés aquí, y que me abrazes cuando ande bajona
Necesito recordar, mirar al vals del hombre de la pepsi

cristina henríquez

◥ ASHES

I'M AT WORK on Saturday when I get the call. Carina, from the front counter, pages me over the intercom, and when I finally get to the phone it's my older brother, Jano, telling me I might want to sit down because he has upsetting news.

"Tell me," I say.

"Do you have a chair?"

"Just tell me." What I have is a hollow feeling in my stomach the size of a coconut.

"Mamá's gone," he says.

"What?" My heart seizes.

"Señora López found her today."

"Found her? Where was Papi?"

"Are you sitting down?" he asks again.

"Stop asking me that. Why can't you just answer my questions?"

"It's a little bit complicated, OK?"

"How?"

But he won't answer that, either. He just suggests we meet when I get off work because we have a lot of things to take care of.

I'm not supposed to use the phone during work hours, but I call Armando as soon as I hang up. I hold the plastic beige contraption trembling next to my ear as I talk. He tells me I should take off early, that my boss will understand because this is an extenuating circumstance. Armando's never had to work anywhere like this, though, and he doesn't get the idea that I'm just a body doing a job, not somebody doing it. Still, I tell him I'll try. He leaves me with "We can go out for dinner if you want. You don't have to cook."

I end up staying at Casa de la Carne for my whole shift. Work helps keep my mind off everything. If I'd left early, I would have been a blubbering thing sitting on the curb in the parking lot — the way I can be only in private, or sometimes, when he's being nice, with Armando. Never in front of my family. I know they think I'm more heartless than them for that, but I know the truth. I know my depths.

The story is that she had a heart attack. She was cooking — like she was always cooking — and she simply fell over on the kitchen floor. Papi was sitting in a wooden chair at the kitchen table, probably smoking a cigarette while she worked, waiting to be served. She fell right at his feet. We think he tried to help her, tried to blow air into her mouth, pumping and puffing. Jano says Papi picked up the phone but couldn't remember the number for emergency, and after trying a jumble of numbers over and over again, he just gave up.

"Why didn't he call one of us?" I say when I see Jano after work.

Jano shrugs. "I don't think he really knew what was happening."

We both know Papi is sick, mentally gone, but we never talk about him in those terms. We like to pretend he's just old.

When Sra. López got there this morning, she found Papi sitting in the wooden chair with the phone still in his hand, buzzing because it was off the hook. She saw Mamá at his feet.

"The oven was on, too," Jano says. "There could have been a fire on top of everything else." He shakes his head.

Sra. López pried the phone from Papi's hands and called Jano. That was earlier today.

"Papi's going to stay with me now," Jano says. "I don't think he can be alone."

"He can stay with me," I say.

Jano shakes his head. "Uh-uh."

"Why not?"

"He'll like it at our house better."

"My place is fine."

"What?" Jano asks. "You have a newfound interest in him?"

"Do you?"

We're at an ice cream shop near my work. The cold air has

turned Jano's lips slightly purple. Besides an employee in a pink apron, we're the only people here. The bright lights bounce off the white counters and smack me in the face. I'm quiet for a minute. Then I start on a reel of questions. How does he know it was a heart attack? What are we going to do now? What's happening to the house? Is his wife, Zenia, OK with Papi being there? What else did Papi say? Why did Sra. López call him instead of me?

He answers every one. He's unusually patient with me. He's waiting to see if I'll break, I know, if this will be the thing that puts me over the edge, brave-faced little Mireya.

The last time I saw her, my mother was sitting with me on her patio. She was in the metal rocking chair she'd had since before I was born, olive-green seat cushions and floral ironwork along the arms. She had her legs stretched out in front of her, knee-high nylons rolled down around her crossed ankles like life preservers, terry house slippers on her feet. She looked relaxed as she lectured me on her favorite subject — politics. She was telling me how fortunate it was that she had named me Mireya, because the president of Panama was Mireya Moscoso. She must have said about ten times, "That could have been you," as if the only prerequisite for becoming the president was having the right name.

She hated that politics held no interest for me. The one thing my mother liked about Armando was his appetite for the political. Just for that, of all the people in my family, she was his only fan.

That day there was an election parade in the neighborhood. Martín Torrijos was riding all over our section of town, shouting from the windows of his van and waving a Panamanian flag in a bid to become the next president. It was the reason we were outside on the patio. My mother was waiting for him. We'd been talking for almost an hour when his big white van, followed by pickup trucks with speakers on the flatbeds blasting music, rumbled up our street. My mother stood and smoothed out the front of her robe. She was old enough that her spine had begun to bow.

Torrijos stopped his van in front of our patio. He asked my mother how she and her sister, meaning me, were doing.

My mother shouted, "What will you do about the hospitals?"

Torrijos smiled and waved.

"And what about the canal?" she yelled into the sunlight.

Torrijos tossed a T-shirt out the window to her. "For you!" he shouted.

My mother let it land at her feet. "Pendejo!" she shouted, and the van continued up the street.

It wasn't everyone who would call a politician an idiot to his face. I smiled until I thought my cheeks would burst. I'd always felt there was something special between my mother and me. Like she was somehow more mine than Jano's. But maybe all children feel that — a sovereignty of ownership over the parent they love best.

When I get home that night, Armando sprints out to see me.

"Pobrecita," he says. He's making a face like I'm a puppy with a broken leg. "I have a poem for you."

"Another one?"

"When was the last one?" he asks, leaning over the kitchen table, reaching for a book. He finds the page he wants and says, "It's by César Vallejo. He's one of the great writers. He wrote for the people."

I sit down as he reads it to me. I don't understand poetry the way he does. Things either sound good to me or they don't. That's it. The poem he reads tonight is short. It's about the poet's brother, who died. My favorite line is "And now a shadow falls on the soul." I feel the tears burn behind my eyes.

"It's nice," I say when he's done. Then I quickly scoot my chair back and head for the shower. Under the spray, the meat juices wash from my fingernails, from my pores. I tilt my head back and let the water stream down my face until I can't tell anymore where the water ends and my tears begin.

Armando comes in after me. He knows this is my place to cry. He peels off his clothes and steps into the stall and tries to hold me. His dark, moppish hair sticks to the sides of his face. His skin slips over mine. He pushes me out of the water and examines my eyes. "Are the tears gone now?"

I shrug.

"Tell me, Mireya," he pleads. It's the split second of something in his voice that, despite everything else, makes me love him.

"I think they're just starting," I say.

He bends down and licks one cheek, then the other, gently, with the tip of his tongue. "I'll get them," he says, and he does.

My father cleaned government buildings at night. He came home in the early morning hours, high on ammonia and bleach, and made my mother prepare dinner for him in the dark. When he worked overtime, she cooked dinner as the sun rose. Many nights, the smell of spicy chicken or ropa vieja woke me and I knew that my father had just arrived. During the day, he should have been sleeping, but more often he was out in bars or with other women or smoking on our front step, ashes fluttering in the air like confetti. My mother was never happy with him. I mean, she must have been at one time, but I'd never witnessed it. I'd hear her, at night, through the thin walls, sobbing in her room.

She knew about everything my father did — I often heard them arguing about his carryings-on — but for all her strength, she was never able to stop him and never able to walk away. There was one time when I thought she came close. My father had taken a job cleaning houses during the day, and at some point he started returning home with hair dryers, mixing bowls, toaster ovens, picture frames. Of course, we knew where these things were coming from. No one said anything, though, until a police officer showed up at our house one afternoon asking questions. It was easy enough to get rid of him — my father offered him a speaker system — but I'd never seen my mother so angry. For a whole week she spoke to him only once, when she told him, "You shamed me."

The only time I even saw a moment of affection between them was much later, after Jano had married and I had moved out on my own. My father had retired, and they were living off his pension and the odd lottery payout. My mother had asked me to get some melons at the stand near my house and bring them over. She was very particular about which melons she deemed acceptable. When I got there, the front door was wide open and inside I saw them, sit-

184 ~ cristina henríquez

ting on our old peach-colored couch, my father at one end and my
mother stretched out at the other, her feet propped on his lap. He
was tickling the soles of her feet with his fingertips and she was
flinching, but laughing. Then he reached over and cupped her hair
behind her ear. She followed the movement of his hand with her
head, like a horse. That was all. But there was real tenderness in it.

Armando is Argentinean, a different breed. We met when I was on
my way out of work one afternoon, heading for the bus. He must
have been standing there for hours, surveying every so-and-so who
walked by. I'm not beautiful. I know that. I'm just this girl with my
mother's squash-shaped body, and dense black hair and a mole on
my right cheek. But I always thought it meant something that he
seized on me. Came right up to me and said, "You look like you
could use a decent meal. Can I take you out?" He had on brown
slacks and a white linen shirt. I brushed him off at first.
   "What's your name?" he asked.
   "Mireya."
   He stopped in his tracks, playing. "That's perfect," he said. "The
reservation is under Mireya."
   It was such a line. But I liked the idea of going someplace where
we would need a reservation, so I said yes.
   We ended up at one of the best steak houses in Panama City,
this spot with gold doors that have an image of a bull carved into
them. It was the first and last time we ever went out to a dinner like
that. He paid for the whole thing, and I ate as much as I could get
in me. At the end of the meal, he asked if he could sleep on my
floor for a few nights. Told me that he'd just arrived in Panama and
didn't know anyone and didn't want to go back to Argentina because of some issue with his parents. I found out later it was
money — his wealthy parents had finally told him he needed to
find a job or get out. The idea of a job was distasteful to a person
like Armando, so he got out. That night, though, he said he would
pay me for a place on the floor, which he never did. And he promised to keep his hands to himself, which he didn't. But he seemed
harmless enough. So there, in the steak house, my belly warm and
full, I said yes.

Carina, at work, says I only fell for him out of habit. The habit of seeing him every day. She says, "Imagine someone put a plate with a nice big pork chop on it in front of you. But you felt like a hamburger, so you said no thanks. And then the next day they brought you a plate with another big pork chop. And the next day and the next day. Eventually, you would start wanting it, even though in the beginning you had no interest. Right?"

"Armando's not a pork chop," I say.

She shrugs. "At least a pork chop would feed you."

Two days pass and I still can't get myself together. It's like a small animal pounces on me every day, clawing at me, tearing me to shreds. I go outside on my break and sit on the concrete step behind Casa de la Carne by myself. The ground is slick with grease and mangy dogs sniff around my feet, but I'm too ruined to care. When my time is over, I mop up my face and reassemble my hair into a ponytail.

I can't stop thinking about the fact that my mother's gone, though. It's bad. I cut my finger twice on the slicer before the day's even rolled around to lunchtime. When I tell them I don't care and that I don't want to wear the steel-mesh gloves while I cut, they send me home.

Armando's on his back on the couch, his socked feet up on the arm, reading. The whole place smells like the sweat from his socks.

"What are you doing here?" he asks, startled, when I come in.

"They sent me home."

"You were fired?" He looks terrified.

For a second, I have this impulse to answer yes, to tell him he's the one who has to find a job now, figure out a way to support us both, just to see what he would do.

I shrug. "They just sent me home."

He purses his lips and looks away, at nothing, like he's weighing what this might mean.

"What? You have someone coming over?" I ask.

"No."

He cheated on me once, when we first started, with this girl who had air conditioning at her place. He told me about it because he would sleep there — no mosquitoes, no night sweats. He claimed it had nothing to do with her, but there were a few nights during a blackout when he went over there just the same. So. He might have left me for her at some point, I don't know, but she moved to the United States, anyway.

"I'm trying to finish this book by tomorrow," he says, holding up what's in his hand. "You won't bother me, right?"

"I'm going to make lunch." I raise my hand to show him the bandages, but he's already back to his book.

"Meatballs and patacones for me?" he asks hopefully. "Oh, and your papi called. I think it was him. He said it was him at first, and then he kept saying he had the wrong number. The man is messed up, Mireya. You guys should put him in a hospital, you know?"

I glare at him as he reads. I unwrap the tape and gauze — pink with my blood — from my fingers, balancing them in my hand, and consider throwing them at him. But I don't. I just leave them at his feet to see if he'll even notice.

I call my father back that night. Zenia answers. She's never liked me. I think when she and Jano started together, years ago, he told her not to trust me. My brother has always suffered from the belief that I came into the world to steal my parents' attention from him. When I was younger, he claimed that for the entire ride to the hospital while my mother was in labor with me, she had shouted, "I don't want it!" "You see?" he said. "Even then she knew you were a bad idea." My mother heard him and swatted him on the arm so hard that a patch of red bloomed on his skin.

"Is my father there?" I ask.

"He's having a good time here, you know."

"Please, Zenia. I want to talk to him."

She sighs. "Momentito."

"Aló?" he says when he gets on the phone. "Who is this?"

"It's Mireya."

"La Presidenta?"

"No. It's me. Your daughter."

It sounds like he's chewing on something.

"How are you doing?" I ask.

"Fine. There's a fan in my bedroom," he says.

"What are you eating?"

"I'm drinking."

"You're chewing your drink?"

He's quiet.

"Are you OK over there? Are you happy?"

"I miss you," he says, unexpectedly. I wonder if he even knows who he's talking to.

"Me?"

"That fan makes a lot of noise, though."

"I'll tell Jano to fix it for you."

"I used to live in my own house. Is that right?"

"Yes."

He's silent again.

"Do you want me to come visit you?" I ask.

My father was drunk almost every day while I was growing up. He was hardly around, a shadow of a father. It's no secret that Jano and I hardened ourselves to him. But still, it's amazing how much I want him to say yes.

"Our dinner is ready," he says instead.

"OK, Papi."

"We're having arroz con pollo."

"I'm going to get off now. I'll see you in a few days."

"Yes. It would be very nice to see the president."

"Goodbye, Papi."

When I show up at Casa de la Carne the next day, Carina pulls me aside and asks what I'm doing there. "I thought you got fired," she says. I assure her I was just sent home early because of personal problems. She shakes her head at me, her gold hoop earrings swaying against her jaw. "No," she says, drawing it out as if the word were a rubber band. "I think you should talk to Tino." But as soon as she says it I understand. I didn't wear the gloves, which is a safety violation, which is a big deal. I was an idiot to think that they were just giving me some time off to pull myself together. Tino confirms it.

I don't go home right away, though. I get on the bus to my parents' house. They lived on a sloping street where the houses press against one another, side by side, like children in a line holding hands. Theirs looks like all the others: a big cement patio out front, bars over the windows, wire trash bins held up on poles by the curb. I open the gate and step onto the patio. For some reason I'm feeling nervous, like I'm trespassing, like someone else has already taken over this house. Even so, I'm doing OK until I notice the chair where I last saw my mother. The seat cushion is still flattened from her weight, the imprint of her bottom depressed into the foam. It splits my heart in two. I take a few deep breaths and make my way to the chair. Slowly, I lower myself into the impression she formed. The air is steaming hot, the sun piercing. I sit for as long as I can take it, and then I have to leave.

Memories are thin, watery and fragile, like gas rising off the pavement on the hottest days. But there are times I can see clearly.

I was eight. We had driven to my Tía Cre's house for a party. The boys abandoned us, locking themselves in a room doing who knows what, but no one asked because they were boys and anything was permissible. My cousin Juanita and I went down to the spiny shores of the bay, rooting around in the small pools between the rocks for snails and crabs. This was my mother's favorite place. She was forever reminiscing about growing up in a house on the bay, about the days when she and Tía Cre basically lived among the rocks and on the crescent of sand at their base.

My cousin and I were barefoot, and the ocean rolled in far enough at times to lick the rocks until they glistened. I was stepping down from one rock to another when I slipped. My feet shot out in front of me and I fell backward. My spine landed flat on a rock and my head snapped back against a rough crest of stone. I must have blacked out for a few seconds. When I was conscious again, I reached back and felt the blood, sticky in my hair. I had a gash like a long slug, just behind my ear. My cousin ran screaming back to the house. I don't remember much between then and when my mother arrived.

I saw her bending over me. I saw the sunlight filtering through her black hair, curled at the tips. There was a look of consternation on her face; she looked like she wanted to slap me but couldn't bring herself to do it. She had a white apron around her waist — she must have been helping Tía Cre in the kitchen — and I remember it fluttering over me as she leaned down and scooped me up in her arms.

The blood stopped soon enough. Tía Cre cleaned and bandaged me. The adults were worried and then not worried. My father looked at me blandly — he was drunk — and declared that I would be fine. Jano came out of the bedroom carrying a joystick, the cord stretching all the way across the floor. He peered at me, and then walked away shrugging. I think he thought I was just creating a show to get attention. To prove him wrong, I bit my lip to keep from crying. I haven't cried in front of my family since.

In my cousin's dark bedroom, the windows wide open, the curtains blowing, my mother stayed with me while the party went on. She climbed into bed with me and held me from behind.

"I'm not happy," she said.

"I didn't mean to do it," I told her.

"You aren't allowed to leave me, you know."

I could smell the vegetable oil and cooking gas that had crept into the fabric of her clothes and her hair.

"Everyone else can leave, but not you."

My head stung, pain pulsing around me like a halo. I could hear the muffled sounds of the party through the door — ice clinking in glasses, spontaneous riots of laughter, a faint thread of music.

"I'm sorry," I said.

She sighed and then pinched a bit of skin on my arm and twisted it. I knew then that she really had wanted to hit me back on the rocks. The pinch was a compromise.

"Be more careful," she said. "From now on, you do that for me."

The day before the funeral, I'm cruising around town on the bus. There's not much else to do. Everyone still thinks I have a job, so I have to leave the house during the day.

The bus is maybe a kilometer out when, through the window, I see Armando. From the back, but I can tell it's him. He's walking with his arm around a woman's shoulder, her arm around his waist. Her wrist drips with jewelry, expensive-looking stuff, the kind you could get only at a place like Mercurio. I get off at the next stop and walk back toward them.

I'm about ten meters away when Armando sees me. He drops his arm from the woman's shoulder. "You're not at work," he says when I'm close enough.

"I don't work there anymore."

The woman next to him is wearing big round sunglasses that are probably designer.

"What do you mean?"

"I just don't." I stare unblinkingly at the woman as I say it. I can't see her eyes, but I can see her eyebrows above the sunglasses.

"Hey," he says. It's that soft "hey" he gives me sometimes in the middle of the night when he wants to wake me, because, he says, he misses me. Then he takes me by the arm and drags me a few steps away.

"Is that the same girl from before?" I ask. As soon as I say it, though, I realize I don't want the answer. Either way, it's bad.

He shakes his head.

"Who is she, then?"

"Mireya, please."

"How long have you been with her?" I say.

He shakes his head again.

"Tell me how long!"

"A few weeks, OK?"

"She's rich?"

"She gives me what I need." He looks defiant suddenly. He's over his shame, or he's pretending to be over it.

"I don't? I go to work so you can eat!"

"Armando," the woman calls.

That's when I lay into him. Just sock him one in his chest. He stumbles backward, and the next thing I know I'm lunging at him, tearing into his pockets, grabbing hold of what I can. He clutches my wrists, trying to pry my hands away. But I want it — whatever he has, I want it. With both of us pulling, the seam of his pocket rips and he starts yelling at me to stop, but I won't. He rams the top of his head against my shoulder, trying to create some distance between us. And somehow we end up on the ground, tiny pebbles pressing into my skin, the sidewalk baking underneath us. Faintly, I hear the woman saying "Ay, Dios," again and again, and I catch glimpses of her towering over us as we fight. Finally Armando manages to pull free of me and stand. I get up, too, and brush myself off.

The woman says, "Armando, this girl is crazy."

I'm a firestorm inside — everything exploding and burning — and I'm trying so hard not to talk, because I know if I do I'll cry.

Armando tells the woman to wait at the corner. You can tell she's not used to being instructed to do anything, especially by him. But she does it.

It doesn't help that eventually I would have left him anyway, or that anyone could have seen this coming, or that I always knew we were bound to fall apart.

We stare at each other, squinting in the sun. His face is light — he's always been too pale for this country — and shiny with sweat. I can't help thinking that there were moments when he was good to me. I wait for him to say something, but he doesn't. I feel weightless standing there, like I'm not sure if the soles of my shoes are connected to the sidewalk anymore.

"My mother was the only one in my family who liked you," I finally say. It's a petty impulse — wanting to hurt him because he hurt me — but I don't care.

He looks like I just slapped him. "Your mother?"

I grab my bag from the ground and start walking away.

I hear his shoes shuffle behind me for a second and then stop.

"What about you?" he yells. "Didn't you like me?"

It's such a heartbreaker. Because here's the answer: "Yes, I did. Who knows why, but I did." But right then I can't do it. I just walk away.

The funeral is what it is. I kiss a hundred cheeks and listen to a hundred stories about what a wonderful person my mother was. Everyone's asking where Armando is, but I say again and again that

I don't want to get into it. Jano ran an obituary in the newspaper. He looks terrible, his nose red, his eyes swollen like little ravioli. Zenia, in a long-sleeved white dress, never leaves his side, her arm hooked through his. My father is seated in the front pew and I wave to him because I'm not sure what he would think if I hugged him.

At one point, Jano comes over and asks if I'm OK.

"I'm fine," I tell him.

"Are you sure?"

"I'm sure." But I'm not.

When the time comes, I go up to say goodbye to her. I remember, when my grandmother died, walking up the church aisle, gripping my mother's hand. I was five. In my memory, the other people in the church are blurry, only watercolors. When my mother and I got to the casket, I could see my grandmother's face — powdery and calm. I wanted so badly to touch her; I stood there forever thinking about doing it, but I didn't know if I was allowed to. I didn't want to do it and make a scene, one that Jano would chide me for later. That afternoon, I asked my mother if I could have done it. She told me of course. For all these years, I've hated the fact that I didn't.

Now there's no casket, just a gold urn on a small table. What can I do? Reach my hand in? A photograph of my mother sits on an easel next to the urn. It's black-and-white, all soft edges and haze. She is too young for me to recognize her. I wonder, if I hadn't been her daughter, if I had just met this woman in the photograph at any time on the street, would I have liked her? But it's a stupid thing to wonder, because of course I would have. I would have loved her anytime.

When I'm done, I take a seat beside Papi. He smiles. His long, thin fingers are folded in his lap, and he looks as light and unbothered as a cloud.

"How are you?" I ask. I feel none of the anger I usually do around him.

"I tried to save her," he whispers, leaning sideways.

"I know, Papi," I say.

"Human beings can't save each other from anything, though."

"I'm sorry," I tell him, because I don't know what else there is to offer.

He nods. "Nothing to be sorry about."

"OK," I say, and he pats my knee.

Afterward, I take the urn with me. Jano has already said, without any discussion, that he will keep it at his house, but in my mind it's inconceivable that it could belong to anyone but me.

Holding the urn in my lap, I take a taxi straight to the bay, passing billboards and wire fences, fields of overgrown grass freckled with tiny flowers and small fires, ramshackle houses and brittle palm trees.

When we get to the bay, I pay the driver. He has a stern face and he simply nods before shooting off into the gathering darkness. I carry the urn over to the rocks and sit down, balancing it beside me. I take off the lid and reach my hand in, letting my fingertips graze the dust. Then I cover it again. I sit there for hours, my bottom growing damp from the glaze of water clinging to the rocks, and look out for anything I can see.

manuel muñoz

❧ GOOD AS YESTERDAY

T HE DETENTION FACILITY is six miles from town, bordered by cornfields and peach orchards and on the northern end by an old airstrip where crop dusters rise up to cloud the fields with fine mists. Today is the first day that Vero has driven Nicky out here, her younger brother, a sixteen-year-old who cannot get around on his own, because in these parts a car means everything about being able to leave home. Vero drives their father's old Chevy Impala, and she is cautious with it even though her father does not care for it as much as he used to. At their town's grocery store, he has returned many times to find long key scratches etched deep in the paint; other times, dents in the chrome from someone's jealous, hard-kicking boots. He does not wash and wax the car as before, does not scour local dealers for repairs and parts, does not spend the time honing the engine. Not to see his car treated that way. So he lets Vero use it to drive around town and here she is, easing slowly into the parking lot of the detention facility because the lot is only a large square of gravel and railroad ties to bump tires against. The low fields are all around them, and a duster lazily drones off from the airstrip as Vero stops the car. She wonders if the air ever blows the pesticides into the parking lot, into the dirt courtyard of the detention facility where these Sunday visits are held.

Her younger brother Nicky is ready to get out of the car before she quits the ignition. He has his fingers on the door handle and holds a Macy's shopping bag between his legs. He has made Vero drive him to the mall in Fresno so that he could ask for a paper

194

shopping bag, the kind with the small loops at the top, even though he did not buy anything. Macy's is the nicest store around, and for this visit, her little brother wants to enter the detention facility with a measure of attention, even though the Macy's bag holds nothing but a bucket of fried chicken and store-bought rolls and little packets of butter, the knives and forks that come in separate plastic packages. He has bought a six-pack of Cokes and a stack of paper plates, though they will only use three.

Sunday afternoons are lunch visitations in the courtyard, sitting on picnic benches that look like they belong in a playground or a school, not a detention facility. There are full, shady trees in the courtyard, but no green grass, and the facility officers hose down the dust before the family arrivals. Already there is a line of people with ice chests and grocery bags waiting patiently in the heat. Near the entrance, a blue tarp is strung taut over the door for shade, and beyond that Vero can see the green-gray uniforms of the detainees as they peer from the windows, patient in the long barracks across the courtyard.

To say there is a line of people is inexact: there is a line of women, mostly young ones, Vero's age. Vero is twenty years old, four years older than her little brother, but she feels the saddled burdens that must (she thinks) be the lives of the young women just like her standing in line. They are young women with babies in tow, mothers once if not twice, but she does not recognize any of them from her own town. The detention facility is for the northern part of the county, a holding place for people of the most minor offenses — vandalism and bar brawls, excessive speeding violations, drunken driving, child-support evasion — all bad things to Vero, but common in her town and in the towns where these women are from. Ivanhoe and Tulare, Yettem and Cutler, Exeter and Lindsay. She is grateful that she is twenty but not completely like them.

She is in no rush to get inside the facility, but Nicky hurries. He is walking quickly with the Macy's shopping bag in his left hand, the other hand extended out. She hates to see his hand extended out like that, his exaggerations, his boldness at sixteen. Inside the bag, Nicky has brought more than food. He has brought cookies

and magazines, though Vero has warned him that the detention facility will probably prohibit gifts. Nicky has walked every day after
school to buy greeting cards from the drugstore in the center of
their downtown, and he has spent long hours writing his messages
and sealing them away. He has gone into the small crafts store that
sells nectarine-wood frames and expensive glassware and has purchased bright orange ribbon, taking scissors to it and curling the
edges, bundling up the greeting cards. The cards with the ribbon
are in the bag.

Nicky is standing in line already, still a few minutes from the in-
spection point but impatient. She hears his voice echo, "Come on!"
and the other people in line turn around to look at him. He has
cards to give; the chicken is already cold. He is sixteen years old and
cannot wait any longer.

Vero walks forward. The voices of her friends keep chiding her.
You do too much for that brother of yours, Vero. Let him be his own. She
stands and waits with him. Her feet hurt. She has a job at the auto
parts store in downtown, a family-owned business losing out to the
new strip mall, a job where she stands all day at a counter. She is
twenty and unmarried in a place where most have either left or
married by that age, and she knows so many of the men in town
from the store. They look for parts to repair a wife's car, a cousin's
work truck, stepping into the shop with its cement floor and the
loud rotary fans hung high in the ceiling, the cool chemical smells
of lubricant and oil and new rubber. They buy spark plugs and fan
belts, handing them over to her with hands just as smooth and
young as hers, the wedding bands glimmering. She could have it
worse, she knows. She could lose the job if the strip mall takes
away too much business. She would have to move to another town
for work, she knows, and then what? How long can the Impala run
without her father fixing it as he used to? What would happen to
her little brother if she were not around?

They inch closer and closer to the guard, and when they arrive,
the guard turns to Vero as if he recognizes that she is the older sib-
ling and asks, "Who are you here to see?"

"Julián Orosco," she says. Nicky is holding the bag to himself, as
if he does not want the guard to see, but the guard waves him to

open it and peeks inside, reaching in to move things around. The guard is an old man and takes his time. He opens the bucket of chicken and closes it. He shifts between the store-bought rolls and the butter and the plastic. When he sees the bundle of cards, he says, "Those out, please," and Nicky takes them out. "Unwrap them, please," he orders, and Nicky looks down at the orange ribbon, snug so tight around the envelopes that it has made little bends in the paper, and then he does his best to push one of the loops off the edge to keep the ribbon intact.

The guard takes the bundle from Nicky, and Vero sees his old hands run through each one, thumb and forefinger, feeling for anything suspiciously thick. She can read Nicky's pretty writing: JULIÁN and MI AMOR and SIEMPRE NICOLÁS and the intricate hearts he has sketched on the back flaps, brooding and pulsing fleshy hearts with blood dripping like sweat.

"You can't bring in anything sealed," the guard says finally. "You'll have to open these." Behind them, Vero can hear the shifting of someone impatient with both the old man's adherence to rules and Nicky's foolishness in bringing the cards in the first place. Nicky looks pained and when he turns to Vero to begin his protest, she gives him a look that says, *Do it*. It is not the way he wanted it to be: these cards are for Julián Orosco, the man he thinks he loves, and he hesitates.

So Vero takes the cards and begins unsealing them, handing them over to the old guard, who looks inside each one attentively. She is careful not to rip the envelopes completely, and it pains her that she is doing this for her little brother. There are fifteen cards in all, and she does the math in her head, the money he has spent for this visit: the cards and the chicken, the cookies and the magazines. She has given him spending money. She has made too much of this possible.

Satisfied, the old guard hands the cards back, and Vero cannot look at Nicky as he struggles to put the ribbon back in place. Behind them is the rustle of irritation. Nicky cannot get the ribbon to fit again, but she waits patiently for him to finish because she knows that when he sees Julián, he wants everything to be in order.

~ ~ ~

Their mother never liked Julián. She never liked him because he wore the cheap, tight muscle shirts that came out of the package, the cotton fabric thin enough to see his dark nipples underneath. He wore his pants low to show his boxers, and their mother frowned at what it all suggested. Vero had brought him to the house, not to introduce him but to show her parents that she was twenty and could do what she wanted — she was a grown woman and here was a guy her age who had his own job and apartment. She had not told their mother that she had met Julián at a party and that he had invited her to the backyard where there was no light and she had let him come on the inside of her leg while they were pushed up against the fence. Their mother is not a churchgoer or a bitter divorced woman like so many in their neighborhood. Their mother is pretty — a heavy woman and tall and imposing, but pretty — a conservative force in the house. She had looked at Julián without offering to bring him a drink and left the living room. Their father had already left the room: he stayed out of the way of visitors. Their father had not been like Julián; their father had been the churchgoer, though their mother had made him stop going.

If Vero had had any hesitations about bringing Julián to the house, it had to do with Nicky. Nicky had changed lately. He had been giving their parents a lot of lip, though their father never was one to push things. It was their mother who demanded better manners and punished him with curfews, but Nicky defied her every chance he had. He stayed out late with his new group of friends. He spent the money he had from his own part-time job as a stock boy on clothes and movies and then demanded money for lunch, and it was their father who gave it to him because their father never liked yelling in the house.

Nothing could have happened between Julián and Nicky on that first day, but Vero always imagined that something had. She had never left the room. Nothing had happened except hello. But she knew Nicky had stared too long at Julián, that he had shaken Julián's hand in the many-fisted way that Julián shook hands. And he had shaken hands that way because Vero knew that Nicky had wanted to touch him. He had wanted to touch his broad shoulders and the tight chest peeking through his white muscle shirt. It would be later in life that she would admit that their mother had wanted to do the same thing, that the gold chain and the brown skin and the hairless chest had reminded their mother of her girl days when she did not pay her own parents mind. Nicky had wanted to do these things; their mother had; Vero had. Later, angry at Nicky, she had wanted to believe that Julián stood in their living room and looked Nicky up and down, thirsting for the easiness of a sixteen-year-old, not caring that she was in the room.

To not anger their mother, Vero lies about their visit to the detention center and tells her that they will be going to the mall to buy Nicky clothes, but their mother is angry anyway. "Why does that boy need more clothes?" she asks, not looking at Vero, not looking at Nicky, who is in the room. She is flipping through the television stations because Sunday on Spanish television is bad movies or *fútbol* soccer and she doesn't like either. "*¿Con qué dinero?*" she asks the television, and Nicky says he has money and goes back to his room so that he can tuck the cards with orange ribbon under his shirt.

Vero's friends resent what Nicky gets away with. They warn her that Nicky is looking to get another beating, the way he walks around in school, haughty in his new clothes. Vero ignores her friends when they complain because she cannot tell them simply that she loves her younger brother. Because she sometimes thinks that she doesn't. She doesn't love him when he tells her that she is like their mother — heavy and tall and imposing, but pretty. She doesn't love him when he complains about their parents and how much they don't love him. She wants to tell him that they do, but the simplicity of love is too difficult: she wants to tell him, sometimes he is loved and sometimes he is not. He is loved and then not loved because he can be petulant and arrogant.

She has always wanted to tell him that she loves him because of how he came home on his sixteenth birthday. He had come home running. He had come home bleeding. In one of the alleys in their neighborhood, six boys had dragged and beaten him. All six of them had taken turns, boys he went to school with, boys from another neighborhood, boys he grew up with, boys he had secretly fooled with on back porches. Gaudio, Peter, Alex, Fidel, Israel, and Andy. They had said they were tired of him. And when their mother had tried to calm him down, saying, "Who did this to you? Why did they do this to you? Why?" Vero had known that their mother did not know anything about Nicky and how the cuts and deep bruises spelled out who he really was. Her friends had warned her: *Tell your little brother to stop acting like that. Tell him to stop looking at the guys like that. They don't think it's funny.* Nicky had been sobbing, and he had spat out a thin mixture of blood and saliva into the bathroom sink, and Vero had tried to clean him up. She had wanted to tell him that it was OK and that she loved him, but he had his head bent down and cried the way the mothers and grandmothers do at funerals. He had his head down, and she had felt like their mother, looking at his beautiful black hair, the cuts on his ears, the scratches on his neck. She wondered why on earth he believed he could act like this with the boys at the high school and not expect this outcome. She could see dark spots on the cloth of his shirt, and she made him take it off — more cuts, more blood, bruises as purple-deep as orchard plums, yellowing in some places. "Nicky," she had said, but that was all she said. She motioned for him to get in the shower, and he rose slowly to close the door so that he could take off the rest of his clothes and clean himself.

Vero does not want to sit at the picnic tables and eat. She watches Julián and he watches her back, though he is no longer ashamed like he used to be. There are other families around, the girls her age from other towns with kids running circles around their tables, kicking up the watered-down dust in the courtyard. Everywhere there is food and two-liter soda bottles, foil and aluminum cans, and men in gray-green shirts like Julián. None of them looks dangerous. Vero turns away from Julián and Nicky, who is taking out the food from the Macy's bag, and she studies the men in gray-green shirts. Like Julián, they are here for something stupid and small. They are here making the girls her age sadder than they already are for having their kids. There is one who is skinny, with a goatee and his hair slicked back, looking uncomfortable and sunken in the gray-green shirt, and the family around him seems to kid and pity him at the same time.

"Vero, come eat," she hears Nicky say to her, and she turns back to Julián and her younger brother. She can see the greeting cards on the table.

Nicky serves them, gives Julián three pieces of chicken, piles his paper plate with the store-bought rolls. He is enjoying this display, feeding his man, imitating the aunts in their family who linger in the kitchen and bring out hot plates to the uncles. She knows the people around them subscribe to this way of thinking, too, and she wonders if they are looking over at Nicky and wondering why he is doing the work and not her. Julián eats before them and Vero finally speaks to him directly, because she still finds him difficult and Julián was never much of a talker in the first place. "They're not feeding you anything good, huh?"

"Umum," Julián says, and keeps eating.

"What do they make you do?" Nicky asks.

"Nothing. I don't do anything all day. Just sit around. Play poker."

He will be here for two months because of unpaid traffic tickets. That was all. They had caught him speeding late one night south of Fresno, and Vero remembers the phone call to their house, their mother peeking from the bedroom door to make sure it wasn't a dead relative in Mexico, and Julián saying, "I gotta talk to Nicky. Put him on, Vero." And Nicky cried over the few tickets like it was the end of the world. "You're where? For how long?"

"It's just the food that's a bitch," Julián says, taking another piece of chicken, another roll.

Around them, the families are tossing trash and clearing the picnic tables. They are sipping soda. The children at every table look bored, the courtyard nothing but dirt and shade. The families are talking quietly. Not many of them are laughing.

Nicky begins. He pushes the bundle of letters over to Julián and says, "These are for you, Julián. The guard made me open them." Vero wants to leave, but around them is nothing but the other families, all the tables occupied. In the parking lot, there would be nothing but the old airfield.

"I want you to open one up in the morning and then another one at night before you go to sleep," Nicky says. "Promise."

Vero turns away. She hears Julián say, "Nicky . . ." in that hesitant voice, the kind that anyone in love cannot recognize as frustration. She hopes Nicky will be quiet for his own sake.

"I love you, Julián," Nicky says, and she can tell Julián is trying his best to pull away from the table as Nicky leans forward. Vero herself looks around to see if people are listening but doesn't wait. She is embarrassed by this as much as Julián. "That's enough, Nicky," she says softly, and Nicky says no more.

When they leave, Nicky is in tears because Julián did not hug him, only patted him on the shoulders like a brother and then tucked the bundle of cards under his armpit and made his way back to the barracks.

"Nicky," she begins, "you better calm down before we get home." She wants to tell him to shape up, that Julián only has a matter of a few weeks, but it is his first real love and so she lets him. She tells herself that she is doing the right thing, that she can ignore her own humiliation at having her younger brother carry on like this with someone she has known intimately. She tells herself that she is stronger, that ultimately she has more options than someone like Nicky will ever have in a place like this, and that she is twenty and she could be like the girls from Cutler and Ivanhoe.

Because he is still crying, Vero drives the car toward Fresno. They will go to the mall and walk around in the air conditioning until he calms down. When they reach Highway 99 and can go faster, Nicky leans back as if he knows where they are going.

"No stealing," she tells him, because Nicky has done it before, every now and then. A shirt he's stuffed into his pants. A CD or two after he put electrical tape over the bar code. Even the greeting cards, she knows, were not all honest purchases. Vero has not shared this with their parents. It is one of the ways that Nicky changed after he was jumped by the boys he grew up with. He's

become more brazen with everything but has yet to face conse-
quences. He had to walk around school with deep red rings around
his eyes as the bruises healed there, his lips swollen. Then one
morning he went to school without trying to blend Vero's makeup
around his wounds. He left it thick and noticeable and walked out
of the house sullenly. He came back home at the end of the day just
fine.

"I won't steal a thing," Nicky promises.

Her friends (always her friends) told her what Nicky had done.
They had seen Julián's car at the old drive-in. His car had pulled in
about ten-thirty, and he had to park in front because the back of the
lot was full. They told Vero they were sure it was Julián's car. They
saw Nicky go to the concession stand and come back out with big
Styrofoam cups of Coke and a bucket of popcorn. They saw Julián
leave the car later to go the bathroom: *Vero,* they told her, *both of
them were there together.*

"What movie?" she had asked them, because it had been a long
time since she had gone to the drive-in, even though it still did
business.

Why does that matter? they told her back. *Who cares?* They wanted
to know what she was going to tell Julián.

"You can't prove anything," she had told them, and all of them
huffed because they had been at the drive-in, open only on Sunday
nights after the flea market, and they knew why people went there.

At the mall, Vero leads Nicky to a bookstore because Nicky takes
too long to look at clothes and she wants to avoid that. Vero sifts
through the magazines and they stand there flipping through all
the pages. Nicky picks up the teen-girl magazines with the pictures
of blond boys on the cover. "Put that down, Nicky," she tells him,
and he does, wandering off.

When she finds him later, he is in front of a display of movie
books, the big thick expensive books with glossy black-and-white
pictures. "Do you know who this is?" Nicky asks and holds up a picture of Bette Davis.

"Bette Davis," Vero tells him, because her name is scrolled underneath.

"How about her?" he asks, flipping pages and stopping on a studio shot of *A Streetcar Named Desire*.

"Vivien Leigh," says Vero, because she recognizes her from watching the afternoon movies on channel 26, and then she points at the woman standing next to Blanche DuBois.

"Do you know who Kim Hunter is?" Vero asks.

"Not really," Nicky says. He has done this before: he rented an old Joan Crawford movie once because he thought he was supposed to like her. But he turned it off after twenty minutes and said, "This is so fucking boring."

At home their mother does not ask them where they have been but complains that they have been gone all day. Their father sits in the living room watching *fútbol* soccer, and he closes his eyes as soon as the talking starts. "Hi, Papá," Vero tells him.

Nicky shuts himself in his room and does not come out when dinner is ready. Their mother pounds on his door, but he will not listen. A few hours later, he comes out dressed in ironed clothes, and their mother asks him where he is going on a Sunday night. He says, "To the drive-in," and outside, as if by magic, a whole carload of his friends from other towns rolls up to the front of the house. They honk once and he is gone.

When Vero and Nicky were much younger, their parents took them on Sunday drives. They went to mass in the morning because their father insisted, over to the old one-room church on Whittaker Street in the bad part of town. She remembers the church well, the long aisle and the faint outlines where old walls had been, separating the rooms of the old house the church used to be. It was either too hot or too cold, and after the service, their father would linger at the front door with other members, his shiny Chevy Impala at the curb with their mother inside, impatient. Vero and Nicky ran in the church's yard with the other children, panting with the effort and then waiting in line to drink from the outdoor fountain, an old por-

celain basin with a small globe in the center where the water bur-
bled up. The pipes ran along the outside walls, green with moss,
rusty in other places, and always leaking — the church placed ply-
wood over the soggy ground where the line to get a drink would
form. And Vero would take her time, lowering her head like the old
black woman had done in the afternoon movie on TV, an old black
woman quivering in her step as a crowd gathered to watch her take
a sip of water. Vero would take her sip like that, like everyone was
watching her on Sunday, as if water never tasted so good.

Afterward, they went home to change clothes. They put on softer
shoes, and she and Nicky brought playing cards and marbles and
dolls for the back seat. Their father drove the perfectly conditioned
Chevy Impala with its whole bench seat in the front and controls
on the side that moved the whole thing forward and only he was allowed to touch them. Their father wore clean white T-shirts, and
Vero remembers how massive and strong he looked and how their
mother stretched her arm across the wide bench seat to hold his
right shoulder while they drove. Their parents spoke to each other
in soft Spanish as Vero and Nicky played in the back seat, the orchards rolling by. They always headed east to the Sierra Nevada,
where the orange groves started to slant on the foothill slopes, and
their mother would say, "Look, kids," to stop them from their playing. The Valley would give way in front of them, the flat ground
surrendering to the big, sudden hills with tight rocks jutting out of
the grass, the roads winding and curving. Vero and Nicky were the
ones to say, "Look, look," because they could see out the back window, at the Valley floor beginning to broaden, so wide. Their father
drove carefully, the road twisting and their mother holding their father's thick shoulder, but their parents kept talking about whatever
things they had been talking about. They climbed up, up, up, until
their ears popped and then finally stopped at Kings Canyon National Park, where there were wooden tables, and they got out and
ate everything their mother had quietly stored in the trunk of the
car while they had been changing out of their church clothes — the
homemade burritos, the chips and salad, the cookies and Coke.
They ate together at the tables beneath the giant mountain trees,

their father smiling, their mother's gold hoop earrings swaying a bit when she leaned to kiss him.

Vero has forgiven her younger brother for stealing Julián, though she does not think that Julián was worth fighting for anyway, was not worth any humiliation. He had taken her into the backyard at the party and, against the fence, had put one, then two fingers in her, and she had let him. But so had another girl, one in Porterville, who her friends said did more than two fingers and ended up pregnant with his baby. She does not want Julián's baby. Nicky does not have to worry about having any babies — catching something, maybe. There are plenty of men, Vero knows, even in a small town like this, and the possibility of having a man with a wedding band no longer seems sinful to her. She notices how all the men, band or no band, look at her in the auto parts store, at the car she drives, at her own unadorned hands. She has grown accepting of all the possible ways of getting what she needs, daydreaming at the counter of the store, the cool chemical smell sometimes making her woozy.

Vero remembers how Julián came on the inside of her thigh: he pushed at her so he could rub himself clean on her skin. She forgives her younger brother because the whole experience with Julián was nothing to remember really, and she pities him for believing that someone like Julián is worth loving, that her little brother mistakes actions for affection. Vero wonders what goes through his mind when he steals the greeting cards, when he thinks of what to write in them. Sometimes she can't help thinking about what Julián and her younger brother did at the drive-in. She is ashamed to think of Julián coming on the inside of her younger brother's thigh. She is embarrassed to think of one, then two fingers.

Though Vero is not the one who is waiting for Sunday, the rest of the week is interminable. Nicky slouches. He slinks through the days, doesn't eat. Their parents grow more restless with each other, their father turning the volume up on the television, sometimes giving up altogether and going outside to the front lawn to stare at nothing. Though their father does not want to hear bickering, silence bothers him, too.

Their mother senses something amiss, and Vero knows, after a matter of days, that their mother has figured out what has happened. She does not know that Julián is locked up in the detention facility, but she has finally noticed his absence. She stops pestering Vero on Thursday morning.

On Sunday, everyone is silent. Their mother has made fried potatoes and eggs and fresh tortillas. They all eat separately, except Vero and Nicky. Nicky eats standing up, and he is ready to go by eleven. Under his shirt, Vero can see where he has tucked another little stack of cards in the waist of his pants.

She drives Nicky to buy a bucket of chicken, to the market to buy rolls and soda. The Macy's bag waits in his lap. About to suggest that they buy something different for the week, Vero realizes that perhaps Julián has asked for his favorite foods. It is not something Julián ever shared with her.

The sky is clear and blue, and the crop dusters on the old airfield are running at an oddly vigorous pace. When Vero pulls into the parking lot, she cannot hear the tires of the car rumble against the gravel underneath them. They stop the car in the middle of all the noise in the air, and Nicky does not hear her when she asks if he has everything.

The guard recognizes them but dutifully searches the Macy's shopping bag. She wants to tell Nicky to stop looking impatient and petty, because the older man takes more time on the letters, his thumb and forefingers along the envelopes. When he is done feeling them, he orders the cards opened, strict in his protocol. Vero thinks that he is an old man on a county work program, eager to follow rules, the paycheck important if not essential to his living. He reports everything, and he looks at Nicky much longer than he did last week.

From the bag, with Nicky surprised that he pulled it out, the older man fishes forth a little blue velvet box. He opens it as Vero watches, wondering what it is. She can see a gold cross and a chain, the older man's fingers fumbling through the padding, searching.

"Nicky," she says under her breath as they make their way to the picnic tables. "What is that? Where did you get that?"

"I bought it," Nicky answers, his voice as low as hers.

Julián is there to greet them, seated at a picnic table in a corner of the courtyard, and he does not get up when they approach. Nicky is awkward with his shopping bag and his half-stretched arms trying to encourage a hug, but Vero takes the bag from him to bring out the food. "Let's eat," she says.

When all the food is out, Julián moves to fold the bag but cannot because Vero has not removed the cards or the gift. He peeks into the bag and then, under his breath, says, "Nicky, no more cards. OK?"

Nicky's face stiffens. "Why? Why no more cards?"

"Just don't bring them anymore," Julián answers, busying himself with the food. "I can't have them around."

"Are they not letting you keep them?" Nicky asks. "Where are the ones I gave you?"

"Jesus," says Julián. "Vero . . . ," he says, without any hesitation. Without any shame, Vero thinks, in asking to stop the beginnings of a quarrel.

Around them, Vero notices that the men in gray-green shirts are keeping an eye on them. The talk around the families jumps and starts, it seems to Vero, because mothers and girlfriends stop their week's stories to find out if the men are actually paying attention to them. She thinks she sees the men in gray-green shirts looking over the shoulders of their families.

She wants the visitation time to pass quickly. If they are watching Nicky, they are seeing him eat the fried chicken and separating the skin and bones. They are seeing him cast eyes at Julián, his mouth moving quickly because he is telling him something. They are seeing Julián pay too much attention to Nicky and not her. They are seeing that Nicky is not Julián's little brother. They are not seeing that she is the woman at the table. They are not seeing her mother — imposing but pretty. They are not suspecting that she and Julián were the first ones to be involved with each other. She thinks the men are looking with disbelief at Nicky: that this must be the one who has written the letters, that the cards got away from Julián's possession in some way.

"Nicky," she says. "Please," she tells him, though he is saying nothing wrong.

"What?" he asks her. There is that petulance in his voice that their parents hate, and though no one is turning around just yet, Vero knows that a commotion is the last thing any of them wants. She wants to tell Nicky to tone everything down, that these men are capable of repeating what was done to him in the alley when he turned sixteen. But then she wonders if it is Nicky she wants to save from sadness, if she cares or not about Julián once he goes back inside. She wants to tell Nicky that this kind of anguish is for when you're married, when you are older and it means much more to lose someone. She thinks she is too young to know any of this but she does, because of the young girls all around them, because their mother and their father don't talk anymore and she does not want to be like them.

"Let's just finish up," Vero says, and Julián goes right on eating. He eats in big bites and hurriedly, but she can tell it isn't out of hunger.

They do not speak for the rest of the visitation, drain every last drop of the lukewarm soda, eat all the food, clear the table together. A little girl from one of the other families stumbles over to their table, her tiny shorts plump around the bottom from her diaper, and one of the young mothers runs to get her. She looks at Nicky.

When they rise to leave, Vero says, "I'll wait for you in the car," because she knows Nicky has been itching for an appropriate close. She wants to tell him not to do it, but she moves on to the exit. It is not her choice, not her life. She hurries quickly to the parking lot, nodding at the old guard, who nods back as if he sympathizes.

Nicky is crying on the way back, the Macy's bag folded and tucked under his arm. As he is approaching the car, she knows he is on the verge of believing he will fall apart and not piece himself together. He wants the turmoil. It is not the time to tell him she knows that he stole the necklace. It is not the time to tell him that this is not love, that he should not have tried to put the necklace on

Julián in front of all of those people. He will learn on his own and maybe Julián will, too.

"Ready?" she says when he gets in. "We can go to the mall again. I'll pay for dinner later," she says, pulling out of the parking lot. Nicky looks out the window as they leave the facility, cries some more, and then leans back into his seat.

She holds hope for Nicky: she wants Nicky to be his own man. She wonders what got beat out of him; they kicked something out of him in the alley and something else has replaced it. He's become a thief so he can wear nice shirts with a group of boys like him in Fresno. After a long time at the mall, she dropped him off for the evening at a coffee shop where many of them hang out smoking cigarettes and holding their right elbows as they blow smoke into the hot night air. They stand around and look pretty, and all of them are sixteen like her younger brother, teasing each other, acting like girls. The confident ones act like girls. They smooth their shirts and pants and take another drag from their cigarettes, their sculpted hair glimmering in the coffee shop light.

Tonight she has circled Shaw Avenue and Blackstone to clear her head and is now driving by to pick up Nicky and he waves her on — he'll catch up to her in a few minutes — and she goes to park the car. She's been in the coffee shop before, going in to get him because he has taken too long. The shop is comfortable chairs and ashtrays, skinny girls behind the counter, even skinnier boys. On the walls are the angry hairdos of Joan Crawford and Bette Davis. Their names are fake-signed in the corners of these posters. On a bulletin board is a flurry of old movie stars and someone has scrawled, "You're only as good as yesterday."

Once again Vero has to park and go inside to get him. On the bulletin board, she can see a crumpled and folded picture that she knows is from the bookshop because of Nicky's pretty writing. "I wish I was Kim Hunter tonight!" he has written, on a picture of a bare-chested Marlon Brando. She wonders if any of them give a damn about these old stars or if they just think they should. In the group of boys, Nicky is laughing and joking, his arms loose and fingers splayed as if he is showing them rings. He is beautiful to look at, and Vero can see what Julián must be drawn by to behave the way he does in a town like theirs — her little brother holds so much promise in his fine bones, his beautiful hands, the way his face widens in a grin as he speaks in a place where he can feel like his true self, to boys his age who marvel at the picture he has shown them of his jailed boyfriend, the romance of so much trouble and muscle rolled up in one man who doesn't look like any of them. But Vero is not listening to what he is saying. She says, "Nicky, let's go," and he is so reluctant to pull away, and she wants to tell the rest of the boys in the shop — little mice, teeth, pretty clothes — to let him be his own man. Let him figure it all out for himself.

Nicky is going to cry again on the phone, Vero knows, because Julián has just called. Julián is telling Vero, "Find some way to tell him." He is telling her that they cannot come to visit on Sunday. She cannot listen to him: her own humiliation is not serving her well. This is the man who came on her leg and has done the same to her younger brother. This is the man who has done more than that and is not ashamed to speak with her. "Vero," he says, and his voice is shaking, "they cut my throat. They cut me and I have a scar all the way round my neck, Vero. Tell Nicky he can't come."

"God," she says to Julián and nothing else, because he is scared and what can she do.

Nicky comes into the living room when he hears her talking too softly. "Who's on the phone?"

"I have to go," she says, and hangs up quickly.

"Who was that?"

"None of your business," she says, but Nicky presses. He follows her into the kitchen.

"Was that Julián?"

She checks to make sure their mother is not around. "Sit down, Nicky."

"What for?"

"Because you need to sit down," Vero says, but she is worried that their mother will walk in, or their father, and there is no time to soften him. "We're not visiting Julián on Sunday."

"I knew it!" Nicky begins, but she stops him.

"Nicky, listen to me," she says. "Trust me . . . ," she tries.

He keeps at it. "Vero . . ."

"Your cards, Nicky . . . You just can't do that kind of thing, don't you see?" she says, looking as hard as she can into her younger brother's eyes, because he is rushing into life too quickly and the tears that are forming are not of real hurt. Not yet. Nicky is not their mother. She looks as hard as she can into Nicky's eyes before he closes them to shed his tears and begin the whole storm of anger. He puts his head on the table, as if a few weeks is too much to bear, and she waits to tell him the details. He does not need the added drama of a gang of men with secret knives. He does not need to lie awake imagining Julián with his eyes peeled in the dark — she knows he will come out safe. She suspects that the cut throat is not as serious as it sounds, that it is a scare and nothing more, that the young men in the gray-green uniforms already resent being in a low-security barracks and know that life at a real prison is not worth the deepening of whatever sharp object they held to Julián's neck. She remembers the old guard thumbing the envelopes and his strict vision, and she reasons that the cut on the throat is made with something sharp but ultimately benign. A scrap of aluminum can, a filed rusty screw extracted from a bedpost, a thin razor tucked under the tongue of one of those Ivanhoe girls rocking a two-month-old baby.

"Vero," their mother asks her one night in the living room. "Is Nicky taking drugs?"

Their father tells them to be quiet and turns up the volume on the television.

"He's sleeping all the time, he doesn't come out of his room, he's not eating."

"I don't think there's anything to worry about," Vero says, and in the light of the television set, she tries her best not to look back at her mother, who must be feeling foolish. Her mother must know that something more than drugs would keep away sleep and hunger. Vero thinks they both remember how their mother behaved years and years ago, when their father changed from being the man with the big shoulders and the shiny car. There was anger between them. He left, and their aunt had to care for them because their mother slept all through those days and did not eat. After their father returned, he had insisted on quiet. Since then it has been so, all of these years.

"I'm just so worried," their mother says, but her voice doesn't convince Vero. She thinks their mother only wants to sound worried, because they both know that soon enough Nicky will be leaving the house again, gone until the beginning of the next day.

Several weeks later she drives Nicky to the detention facility, and she expects to see Julián standing in the parking lot with a plastic bag of clothes, but no. They park the car and go to the main office, where Julián waits for thin yellow papers. He is issued a little sack containing his wallet and his car keys and even the old tissues that had been in his pockets, and he is asked to confirm that everything is in order. He is wearing the brown khakis and the white muscle shirt that he came in with, his dark hair thick and in need of a cut. Vero sees his neck: just as he told her, he has a thin purple line looped around his neck, a permanent deep mark. Nicky is looking at him, too, and she tries to see if he is looking at the purple scar or at the gold cross and chain that doubles over it. The chain hides the scar and draws attention to it at the same time.

Maybe because Nicky knows better, there are no words between them in the lobby, only Julián putting down the pen and receiving his thin yellow papers. He says to them, "Ready?" with a small smile on his face. He is sporting a goatee, thick and unruly, and he has lost weight from the bad food.

They exit, passing a young woman with a child in tow; she rushes in anticipation. It is her day to see whoever is inside get out. Her black hair is done up. Nicky looks at her and his face holds a slight grin, and Vero cannot say if he is making fun of her or not.

In the car, Nicky turns his whole body around to speak to Julián, beaming the entire time. A crop duster flies directly over the road as they are leaving, descending onto the old airfield, Vero slowing down as if the plane were about to clip the top of their car.

"It's nothing," Nicky says, turning to look, but keeping his body turned backward, Julián finally out. "It's nothing."

"So how's it feel?" Vero offers.

"Good," Julián says, matter-of-factly.

"You wore my necklace," Nicky says, and Vero looks at Julián in the rearview mirror. He is staring at her younger brother with a sad smile, and she can see the beginnings of the scar descending into him, into the space where the mirror can no longer show him. There is so much she wants to say to both of them now — that this will be the last time she will do this much for her little brother; that Nicky will finally see what kind of man Julián really is; that this happiness her little brother feels should be reserved for someone who wants more than just his pretty looks. She wants to tell Nicky that he is as pitiful as the young woman with the baby in tow that they just saw. There will be better than this, she wants to say to Nicky, *someone to treat you right*, but they are driving through the empty fields six miles from their small town and that kind of love might not be here for him.

She looks long at the deep mark on Julián's neck and sees herself running her finger across it, the way she knows Nicky will do later. Vero stares at him too long, drifting, and the car dips briefly into the slant of the shoulder, but she corrects quickly. "Sorry," she apologizes as the car jostles a bit.

"Doesn't scare me," says Nicky.

After their meal under the trees of the national park, their mother and their father had gotten them back in the car and they started the descent into the Valley. The vehicles on the way up came so slowly, and their father zipped along the curves, hugging the car so tight against the walls of the mountains looming above them. Their mother clutched his shoulder and told him to slow down, but her voice was playful and enjoyed the thrill. On the one side, the proximity of the mountain wall. On the other, Vero and Nicky could see the steep drops on the sides of the road, a tumble of river canyon and thick trees. The car went faster and faster, their stomachs heavy with lunch, and their father laughed, lightly pressing the brakes, and told them that when they learned to drive, they should not wear out their brakes. They should coast. They should let things handle themselves and just stay in the lane and there would be nothing to be scared of. Their mother clutched his shoulder because she was afraid and because she loved him. Vero watched them. On her side of the car, the mountain wall was so close she thought she could roll down the window and scrape her knuckles; she flinched away from the window as if in pain. On the other side, at the drop into the canyons, Nicky hung close to the window to see into the deep and Vero reached over to lock the door because she did not want her little brother to fall out. They went faster, their father laughing, their mother loving him, Nicky peering out of the window, out at the edge.

ana menéndez

❧ LOVING CHE

L OVING CHE was like palest sea foam, like wind through the stars.

Savior, murderer, brutal love of my own creation. In the dark, his necklace of bones in my mouth. Entire afternoons passing in the time it took to close a fist or open the slits of our eyes.

I am at the window, looking down over the courtyard. Across the way, a woman sits ironing white shirts at her kitchen table. One by one she takes the shirts out of the starch and lays them out in front of her. Her hand smoothing the fabric is almost a caress. She is speaking something to herself or maybe singing. I lean closer, but her lips are soundless. She moves the iron slowly, now and then stopping to poke the coals with a small stick.

When I turn back to my work, I find Ernesto standing against the wall. He has entered so quietly and now he stands watching me, arms folded across his chest like wings. Take off the necklace, he says, not harshly but without smiling. I hesitate. Why? Because I ask you to. I stand for a moment. Is the door locked? He nods. I take the necklace off. And the blouse, he says. I lift my chin to him. It has never been like this. Always he has taken off my clothes himself, slowly, teasingly, so that I have barely been aware of my own nakedness. Please.

I do as I'm told. I unbutton the blouse. I look back at him but he doesn't speak. I slip the blouse off my shoulders. The skirt, he says. It's a pin-striped skirt I bought a long time ago at El Encanto. I unzip it. And the slip, he says. I let it drop with the skirt. I'm in my underclothes. It is hot, but the sweat on my skin makes me shiver. He has not moved. He is watching. He nods. I shake my head no. He points to me. Do it.

I reach back to undo my brassiere, the lace one that I wear in the daytime for him. And then, not wanting to show embarrassment, I bend to lower my panties. I roll them down as I go, and the movement of this last layer over my skin introduces me to a new anticipation. I stand bare-breasted and open to this foreigner, like some fetish of a woman, some stone carving from the mountains of his travels.

But he does nothing, only looks. For a long time, he looks. And then he walks slowly to me. Without touching me, he bends and picks up my brassiere, helps me with it. He lifts my leg, one and then the other, and pulls my panties up. He pats my skin, lingers at my waist. And then the blouse — hole by hole, he buttons it. He slides on my slip. He holds my skirt open so I can step into it, my hand at his shoulder for balance.

For hours after he leaves, scarcely aware of my hands, I work, charcoal staining my fingers like smoke.

I trace his face, lightly at first, the way memory returns, indistinct, held together by the barest outlines. And then I dig deeper into the paper, darken shadows, rub light into the places where his forehead protrudes. When I was younger, truth was a flat plane, dimensionless, weightless; and the white paper was more honest than all the false green pastures of paint, a single blade of grass more real for its ignorance of space, its vegetable disregard for eternity.

But now I know that this is also true: that I can conjure his features from dust, blacken the paper with fire-ash, and have him speak to me again, if only in this language of deaf-mutes. I can form his soundless lips to my memory and only I will understand why I have given him half a face, dissipated half his features over the wide world. This much remains of my own possession: this curl in the hair, this eye that turns down in sleep and sadness, this eye that narrows in private joy.

~ ~ ~

I sit back, a little tired, but also filled with longing, my heart beating fast, in the old way. I am still for a while, only the movement of my chest rising and falling. And then I take the stick of charcoal to my hand, pressing into the flesh of my palm. When I've darkened my hand, I move around my wrists and up the inside of my arm, casting myself in pale shadow. It's like the old days when I could trace a pen to paper for hours. I move the charcoal into my armpits, and my skin shivers beneath its tracks. I close my eyes, nothing but the soft dusting of coal, wandering gray. The hand of God painting my skin, tracing riverbeds in some ancient map. And now I am far away from myself, and the only thing connecting me to my body is this dusty string, this story forming beneath my fingertips.

Daughter of my heart: You must remember that all our walking is a stepping into the other. We enter rooms and canvases, we look into one another's eyes, we open packages, we travel into other lands. We laugh and taste with wide-open mouths and our hands seek to touch and hold.

So it was with Ernesto and me when we opened the door to the small room at the top of the stairs so we might enter different lives. My going again and again to him, wanting to be lost in his body, thinking that this next time it would finally happen. To feel him in my hands as one might touch one's own self in a lost afternoon. To explore, to conquer. To take hold of a lover, to live inside another's silence.

Oh my child, these secrets locked tight so long. Soon I will lie at the end of a long hallway where you will no longer be able to reach me. And I think now that you might be a child again and suckle my breasts, hold them in your tiny hands. That you might fold time and reenter me, light the dark corners of your memory, back to the place where you began.

Trimming my roses one morning, I recoil at the sound of the stem breaking. I sit with my head in my hands. A bullfrog calls to me across the grass and in the old ceiba a bird wakes. The tiptoeing of a beetle echoes with a giant's step. Beneath my feet, the ants churn up the ground and the sound of earth tumbling on earth blots out every other sound in the world.

At the studio, the portrait of the man and the woman sits where it has for many months. I know that I will never finish it. And for a brief moment, as if illuminated by a flash, I see the future waiting for me. I know that I will give birth to a girl and that I will send her away. I know that I will wait in vain for my lover to return, will wait even after he is dead. That my whole life will be this waiting, pure and hopeful, and the days and years will stretch no longer than the moment it takes a cloud to cross the night.

I'm in my studio the day El Encanto burns. I hear the explosion and run down into the street. Already the crowds are gathering, running past me, bumping me. The sound of fire engines. Screaming. I walk quickly. On Galiano, I stop. Ahead of me, El Encanto is burning, ugly, smoke-ash, smell of plastic. And the sound of glass breaking and breaking, up and down the front of the building, pop, pop, pop as the fire engulfs everything: the dresses from Paris, the gold jewelry, the transistor radios, the glass display cases, the white columns, the front windows. The front windows, with their pale mannequins. I come close enough so that I can feel the heat on my face. The flames take the mannequins, crawling up their stiff limbs like a caress, setting their hair aflame, and they stand, unfeeling, in the same old pose until they start to melt, the smile still on their painted lips . . . The building is destroyed, and the only casualty is a worker named Faith, who had gone back inside to retrieve some paperwork.

I'm not going to lie to you, sweet Teresa, he says. My vocation is to roam the highways and waterways of the world forever, always curious, investigating everything, sniffing into nooks and crannies, but always detached, not putting down roots anywhere, not staying long enough to discover what lies beneath.

CONTRIBUTORS

Lalo Lopez Alcaraz is the creator of the nationally syndicated and politically charged Latino comic strip *La Cucaracha,* featured daily in the *Los Angeles Times, Denver Post, Arizona Republic, Houston Chronicle, Chicago Sun-Times, San Diego Tribune,* and sixty other major newspapers. He began his illustrious career drawing editorial cartoons at his college paper, the *Daily Aztec,* at San Diego State University. His latest books are *Latino USA: A Cartoon History* (with text by Ilan Stavans) and *Migra Mouse.* Alcarez coedits the satirical magazine *Pocho.*

Rane Arroyo is a poet and playwright who was born in Chicago. He received a Ph.D. from the University of Pittsburgh, where he wrote his dissertation, *Babel USA: A Writer of Color Rethinks the Chicago Renaissance.* Among his books are *Home Movies of Narcissus* and *The Singing Shark.* He teaches creative writing as an associate professor at the University of Toledo.

Richard Blanco was born in 1968. His book *City of a Hundred Fires* received the 1997 Starrett Prize from the University of Pittsburgh Press and was published the following year. His work on the Cuban American experience has appeared in numerous literary journals and anthologies.

Giannina Braschi was born in San Juan and lived in Madrid, Rome, Paris, and London before settling in New York in the late 1970s. Her Spanish titles include *El Imperio de los Sueños,* translated into

English by Tess O'Dwyer as *Empire of Dreams; Asalto al Tiempo;* and *La Comedia Profana.* In Spanglish, she is the author of *Yo-Yo Boing!*

Oscar Casares was born in Brownsville, Texas, in 1964. His book of short stories, *Brownsville,* was published in 2003. His stories have also appeared in *The Threepenny Review, Northwest Review, Colorado Review,* and *The Iowa Review.* He received an M.F.A. from the University of Iowa in 2001, and in May 2002 the Texas Institute of Letters awarded him a Dobie Paisano fellowship and the Copernicus Society of America presented him with the James Michener Award.

Daniel Chacón received his master's degree in creative writing in 1992 from Fresno State. He is a professor in the Master of Fine Arts program at the University of Oregon. Among his published works are the novel *And the Shadows Took Him* and a collection of short stories, *Chicano Chicanery.*

Susana Chávez-Silverman grew up between Los Angeles, Madrid, and Guadalajara, Mexico, the daughter of a Jewish Hispanist and a Chicana teacher. She is the author of *Killer Crónicas: Bilingual Memories* and the coeditor of *Tropicalizations* and *Reading and Writing the Ambiente.* She is a professor of Latino and Latin American studies at Pomona College.

Culture Clash (Richard Montoya, Ricardo Salinas, and Herbert Siguenza) was formed in 1984 with the goal of "show[ing] cultures in opposition . . . and bringing them closer together." The threesome has performed at South Coast Repertory, the Mark Taper Forum, Los Angeles Theatre Center, La Jolla Playhouse, the Japan American Theatre, Off-Broadway Lincoln Center, and the Kennedy Center and at many universities and colleges throughout the country. In 1992, *A Bowl of Beings* premiered on PBS's *Great Performances* series, and Fox Broadcasting has aired thirty episodes of Culture Clash. Culture Clash has also appeared in the films *Encino Man* and *Hero,* and its members were individually seen in *Falling Down, Mi Vida Loca,* and *Star Maps.* The group coproduced, cowrote, and starred in an award-winning 1992 short film entitled *Columbus on Trial*, directed by Lourdes del Portillo.

Lila Downs grew up in the Sierra Madre of southern Mexico as well as in Minnesota. She has performed her music internationally. Some of her songs are in Spanish, English, Mixtec, Zapotec, Maya, Nahuatl, and other Mesoamerican languages. Her records include *La Sandunga, Tree of Life, La Linea,* and *La Cantina*.

Dagoberto Gilb is the author of the short story collection *The Magic of Blood*, which won the PEN/Hemingway Award; *The Last Known Residence of Mickey Acuña*, a New York Times Notable Book of the Year; and *Gritos*, a collection of essays. In 1992 he won a National Endowment for the Arts creative writing fellowship, in 1993 he received the Whiting Writer's Award, and in 1995 he was awarded a Guggenheim fellowship.

Stephanie Elizondo Griest was born in Corpus Christi, Texas, and has published more than two hundred articles in the *New York Times*, the *Washington Post, Latina Magazine,* and other journals. Her first book was *Around the Bloc: My Life in Moscow, Beijing and Havana.* She speaks Russian, Mandarin, and Spanish as well as English. She lives in New York City.

Cristina Henríquez has roots in Panama and lives in Dallas. She is the author of the novella and stories *Come Together, Fall Apart.* Her stories have appeared in *Agni, The New Yorker, TriQuarterly,* and *Glimmer Train*.

Jaime, Gilbert, and **Mario Hernandez**'s *Love & Rockets* is the alternative comics success story of the 1980s and 1990s, and the publication of *Love & Rockets #1* in 1982 could be said to officially mark the beginning of the eighties comics renaissance clumsily called alternative comics. Both Gilbert and Jaime credit the punk rock explosion of the late 1970s with broadening their horizons and leading them to reflect their personal experience in their comics. Fantagraphics began publishing the Hernandez Bros. in 1982.

Juan Felipe Herrera is the author of sixteen books of poetry and prose, including *Akrilica, Giraffe on Fire,* and *Notes of a Chile Verde Smuggler.* He is an associate professor of Chicano and Latin American studies at California State University, Fresno.

Hip Hop Hoodios is a Latino-Jewish urban music collective led by Josué Noriega and Abraham Veléz and includes participation by such notable Latin and Jewish acts as Santana, Jaguares, the Klezmatics, Orixa, Los Mocosos, Midnight Minyan, and Los Abandoned. The group's repertoire ranges from Latin funk to klezmer to cumbia to straight-up hip-hop. *Agua Pa' La Gente* is their first full-length CD.

Michael Jaime-Becerra (a.k.a. Michael Jayme) is a native of El Monte, California, and a graduate of the University of California, Riverside's creative writing department. His early work was collected in 1996 as *Look Back and Laugh* for the Chicano Chapbook Series, edited by Gary Soto. The following year he began publishing under the surname Jaime-Becerra, and shortly thereafter, a limited edition collection of prose poems, *The Estrellistas Off Peck Road,* was released by Temporary Vandalism. *Every Night Is Ladies' Night* is his first full-length collection.

Luisita López Torregrosa is an editor at the *New York Times.* Her articles have appeared in the *Times, Vanity Fair, Condé Nast Traveler,* and *Vogue.* She lives in New York City.

Felicia Luna Lemus was born in Boston in 1975, grew up in southern California, and received an M.F.A. in writing from the California Institute of the Arts. *Trace Elements of Random Tea Parties* is her first novel. She lives in New York City.

Ana Menéndez is the daughter of Cuban exiles who fled to Los Angeles in the 1960s before settling in Miami. She worked as a journalist for six years, first at the *Miami Herald,* where she covered Little Havana, and later with the *Orange County Register* in California. Menéndez is a graduate of NYU's creative writing program, where she was a *New York Times* Fellow. She has published two books, *In Cuba I Was a German Shepherd* and *Loving Che.*

Manuel Muñoz is the author of *Zigzagger*, a short story collection. His work has appeared in *Colorado Review, Boston Review, Epoch, Swink, Glimmer Train,* and other journals and is forthcoming in *Rush Hour.* His second collection of short stories will be published in 2007. Born and raised in Dinuba, California, Muñoz graduated from Harvard University and received his M.F.A. in creative writing from Cornell University. He lives in New York City.

Salvador Plascencia was born in Guadalajara, Mexico, in 1976. He received a B.A. from Whittier College and an M.F.A. from Syracuse University. He received a National Foundation for Advancement of the Arts Award in 1996 and the Peter Nagoe Prize in 2000. In 2001 he was awarded the Paul and Daisy Soros Fellowship for New Americans, becoming its first fellow in fiction. *The People of Paper,* his debut novel, appeared in 2005.

Aleida Rodríguez was born in Cuba and is the author of *Garden of Exile.* Her prose and poetry have been published in many literary magazines and anthologies nationwide, including most recently *In Short: A Collection of Brief Creative Nonfiction, The Spoon River Poetry Review, Southern Review,* and *Ploughshares.* Her essays have appeared in ZYZZYVA and in *Sleeping with One Eye Open: Women Writers and the Art of Survival,* edited by Marilyn Kallet and Judith Ortiz Cofer.

Nelly Rosario was born in the Dominican Republic and raised in Brooklyn, where she now lives. She received a B.A. from the Massachusetts Institute of Technology and an M.F.A. from Columbia University. She was named a "Writer on the Verge" by the *Village Voice Literary Supplement* in 2001. Her novel *Song of the Water Saints* won the Pen Open Book Award.

Luis Alberto Urrea was born in Tijuana, Mexico, and is the author of *Across the Wire,* winner of the Christopher Award, and *By the*

Lake of Sleeping Children: The Secret Life of the American Border,
The Devil's Highway, The Hummingbird's Daughter, and seven other
works of poetry and prose. He is the recipient of an American Book
Award, a Western States Book Award, and a Colorado Book Award,
and he has been inducted into the Latino Literary Hall of Fame. His
poetry has been included in *The Best American Poetry,* and his book
Six Kinds of Sky won the 2003 *ForeWord* magazine award for best
book of the year. He and his family live outside Chicago.

ABOUT THE EDITORS

Harold Augenbraum is the executive director of the National Book Foundation, the presenter of the National Book Awards. He edited *Latinos in English* and coedited *The Latino Reader* and *U.S. Latino Literature: A Critical Guide for Students and Teachers* with Margarite Fernández Olmos, and *Growing Up Latino* with Ilan Stavans. He has also translated Alvar Núñez Cabeza de Vaca's *Chronicle of the Narváez Expedition* and José Rizal's *Noli Me Tangere*. In 2002 he codirected the National Steinbeck Centennial with Susan Shillinglaw.

Ilan Stavans is Lewis-Sebring Professor in Latin American and Latino Culture and Five College 40th Anniversary Professor at Amherst College. His books include *The Hispanic Condition, The Oxford Book of Latin American Essays, Latino USA: A Cartoon History, On Borrowed Words, Spanglish, Dictionary Days,* and *The Disappearance.* He edited *The Poetry of Pablo Neruda;* the three-volume *Isaac Bashevis Singer: Collected Stories; Rubén Darío: Selected Writings;* and the four-volume *Encyclopedia Latina.* His work has been translated into a dozen languages. *The Essential Ilan Stavans* was published in 2000, and *Ilan Stavans: Eight Conversations,* by Neal Sokol, was published in 2004. The recipient of numerous awards and honors, including a Guggenheim fellowship, Chile's Presidential Medal, the National Jewish Book Award, and the Latino Hall of Fame Award, Stavans is the host of the PBS show *Conversations with Ilan Stavans.*

GROWING UP LATINO

Edited by Harold Augenbraum and Ilan Stavans

From the mean streets of the barrio to the house on Mango Street, the stories and memoirs collected here transport us across geographies and through cultures to articulate the joys, struggles, defeats, and triumphs of Latinos coming of age in the United States.

ISBN-13: 978-0-395-66124-6 / ISBN-10: 0-395-66124-2

THE LATINO READER

Edited by Harold Augenbraum and Margarite Fernández Olmos

A rich overview comprising nearly five centuries of an important American literary tradition, this anthology presents a broad and intriguing range of Latino voices and perspectives, from Cabeza de Vaca's mid-sixteenth century writings to recent works from authors such as Cristina Garcia and Sandra Cisneros.

ISBN-13: 978-0-395-76528-9 / ISBN-10: 0-395-76528-5

LENGUA FRESCA

Edited by Harold Augenbraum and Ilan Stavans

A fresh, provocative, and sometimes irreverent collection, *Lengua Fresca* offers an unconventional window on a vibrant culture. Featuring an eclectic mix of Latino writing — including fiction, journalism, essays, comics, and even cultural ephemera — this unique anthology showcases literature found in unexpected places. ISBN-13: 978-0-618-65670-7 / ISBN-10: 0-618-65670-7